# Murderous Requiem

### Jamie Fessenden

## DSP PUBLICATIONS

Published by
# DSP Publications

5032 Capital Circle SW, Suite 2, PMB# 279, Tallahassee, FL 32305-7886  USA
www.dsppublications.com

This is a work of fiction. Names, characters, places, and incidents either are the product of author imagination or are used fictitiously, and any resemblance to actual persons, living or dead, business establishments, events, or locales is entirely coincidental.

ISBN: 978-1-63476-550-3
Digital ISBN: 978-1-63476-551-0
Library of Congress Control Number: 2015953074
Published March 2016
v. 2.0
First Edition published by Dreamspinner Press, 2013.

Printed in the United States of America
∞
This paper meets the requirements of
ANSI/NISO Z39.48-1992 (Permanence of Paper).

Dedicated to the Brethren.

# Author's Note

THE ANCIENT Greek text used for the libretto, which we first see translated in chapter twenty, was taken from a fragment of text attributed to Euripides. Although I'd seen the fragment (officially designated "Euripides fragment 912") referenced in several books on ancient Greek magic and knew it would be perfect for this novel, I was unable to track down an English translation. Fortunately, my husband is a student of several ancient languages and was able to translate it for me. The following is the translated text, with some notes he wrote concerning it:

Euripides fragment 912, translated by Erich Rickheit

"For you who rules all things, this libation and broth I bring, Zeus or Hades, as you are content to be called. From me accept the sacrifice, the unburnt offering of all fruits that complete has been poured forth for you, out of the gods and the sons of Ouranos, take in hand the scepter of Zeus, and with Hades share the rule of earthly things, send to the light the souls of those below, those willing for a contest to know beforehand from where will sprout the root of evils, what must be offered up for the blessed to find rest from toil."

Notes:

The sons of Ouranos: the Titans.

Willing for a contest: everything is a contest to the Greeks; maybe this means "send up those souls prepared to bargain their prophecies against a chance of rest."

The blessed: the blessed dead.

Rest from toil: this is the usual translation, but *mokhthon* can mean general suffering, not just hard labor.

# Murderous Requiem

Jamie Fessenden

# Prologue

I KNEW his voice. Even after eight years, it was familiar and ordinary, as if he were just calling to see if I wanted him to pick up something on the way home. I knew it was Bowyn, though he'd said nothing more than "Hey, it's me."

That's how he always began a phone conversation. At least, with me.

"Who is this?"

"Come on, Jeremy. Don't play games."

I sighed and dropped the pretense. "All right, Bowyn. What can I do for you?"

"I need to see you. It's important."

Embarrassed that I'd become instantly erect at the thought of seeing him again, I thanked God he wasn't there to see the tent in my bathrobe. It had been almost a decade, but the mere sound of that soft, smooth voice was enough to make me horny as hell. I wanted him. I wanted him as badly as I had every day we'd been together.

"I don't know—"

"Seth has acquired a document," he rushed ahead, trying to stop me from hanging up. "One you need to see."

The mention of that name quenched my desire as though someone had tossed a bucket of ice water on my crotch. It wasn't that I hated Seth. Once I'd loved him—almost as much as I'd loved Bowyn. But things had been… awkward… when I left. And it still hurt to think about. "I'm sorry. I really don't have the time."

"An original manuscript by Ficino," Bowyn went on as if I hadn't spoken. "And it includes a mass written in four-part harmony."

Marsilio Ficino was a fifteenth-century philosopher and doctor. He'd been responsible for translating the complete works of Plato from Greek into Latin and was well-known for his own writings on philosophy and magic, including works on the healing properties of music. I'd done my master's thesis on Ficino. Bowyn had helped me organize my notes and critiqued several of my drafts.

"It's a fake, Bowyn. Ficino wrote about music, and he composed some pieces for the lyre, but he never wrote anything as complex as a polyphonic mass."

"We can't know for certain it was written by him—not yet—but it does date to the late fifteenth century," Bowyn explained patiently. "Seth has someone in Greece working on a translation of the libretto, but he needs someone with your expertise to transcribe the Renaissance musical notation into modern notation."

"Greece?" I asked.

"The libretto is in ancient Greek."

It wasn't impossible. Ficino had known ancient Greek, of course. But most of his work had been written in an archaic Italian dialect, and the text of a mass—the libretto—would generally be in Latin.

"Maureen?" Our friend Maureen had helped us with ancient Greek translations when we were in college.

"No. We couldn't track her down. But we found a professor at the University of Crete who was willing to do it."

I grabbed a mug from the kitchen cupboard, filled it with water, and set it in the microwave. It was more for something to do, to stop my hands from shaking, than a desperate need for tea.

"Ficino was a skilled musician and singer," I protested. "But a polyphonic mass…?"

"That's why we need you, Jeremy. You're the only one Seth trusts for this."

"Why me?"

"Because you're one of the Brethren."

I slammed the box of tea I'd taken from the cupboard down on the counter, my temper flaring. "I am *not* one of the goddamned Brethren!"

Bowyn laughed gently. The bastard had always found it cute when I lost my temper.

"Damn it, Bowyn! How many years do I have to put between me and that place before Seth will acknowledge that I'm gone?"

"You know how he is," he responded soothingly. "He considers you family, no matter what."

I bit back an angry response. He was right. Seth was incapable of processing the idea that anyone could ever leave him. At a fundamental level, he was convinced everyone adored him. Once I *had* adored him....

That I was capable of doing the transcription, I had no doubt. Earlier in the week, I'd been in London, where I'd been transcribing Renaissance musical pieces at the British Museum for a planned article on performance variations. It was a demanding task. The notation was very different from modern musical notation, and damage to a manuscript often rendered sections difficult or impossible to read. Educated guesses had to be made to fill in the gaps. But I had years of experience, and I was good at it.

It's impossible to describe to someone who isn't as fanatical about Renaissance music as I am just how my pulse started racing at the idea of working with an untranslated, untouched original document by Marsilio Ficino. Perhaps not as mind-blowing as it would be for a Christian scholar to get his hands on something written by one of the apostles... but pretty close. Bowyn knew me and knew I would never be able to resist bait like that.

But I'd closed the door on my life at the Temple, and I had no desire to reopen it. I made one last attempt to at least keep myself safely rooted in Durham, rather than make the trip up north. "Look, Bowyn, if Seth really wants me to work on this, have him e-mail me high-resolution photos—"

"You're taking the semester off to work on a paper," Bowyn chided. "The receptionist in the music department told me."

"Vivian needs to stop giving information to strangers on the phone."

"We only need you for a week, Jeremy. Maybe two. You'll know better than me once you've had a look at it. I'll be at your place tomorrow afternoon to pick you up."

Then he hung up while I was still trying to think of a response. The bastard knew he'd won. I'd never been able to deny him anything.

Except once.

# *Chapter One*

THE NEXT morning I tried to work on the paper I'd been researching, but it was a lost cause. The thought of Bowyn showing up on my doorstep in a few hours had my stomach in knots. All the hell we'd gone through eight years earlier—all the arguments, all the failed attempts to get him to understand why I couldn't go on the way things were—kept flooding back to me.

That and an odd dread that once we saw each other, I'd see how much he'd changed. Perhaps he'd let himself go, cut off that beautiful long blond hair I'd loved running my fingers through, or lost it to a receding hairline. What if I just didn't find him attractive anymore? I hadn't realized until this moment that part of me had been harboring a faint hope we could someday reconcile, even after all this time. What if seeing Bowyn proved it was finally and absolutely over?

It was mid-October, which could get pretty cold in southern New Hampshire, but today was warm. I took one of the best books I had on musical settings of the Catholic mass in the early Italian Renaissance out to the front porch and sat there nursing a cup of strong Irish tea while I read. The fresh air and the vivid oranges, reds, and yellows of maples and oaks along Riverside Drive calmed me.

The car that came down the street shortly after two o'clock must have belonged to Seth, unless Bowyn had changed completely from the man I'd known. It was some kind of sports car—I couldn't tell one from another—sleek and low to the ground, with the convertible top down. Not red, like the clichéd midlife crisis vehicle, but gunmetal gray.

Bowyn was behind the wheel, and I could tell, even before he'd pulled into the driveway and eased his lanky body out of the car, that he hadn't changed at all. Not physically, anyway.

Even at thirty-five, he was still naturally athletic, dressed in torn jeans and a plain T-shirt that was stretched taut by well-defined stomach and chest muscles I knew had never seen a gym. His beautiful, sensuous face was framed by long, straight blond hair that hung nearly to his waist and didn't have a trace of gray that I could see. He was running around barefoot, as though he were still a rebellious college student.

"You're supposed to wear shoes when you're driving," I said, standing as he pulled off his shades to reveal amazing, clear blue eyes.

Bowyn laughed, sauntering up the walkway. "Are you going to give me a detention, Professor?"

"We don't give detentions in college."

"Then how about a spanking?"

I groaned. How I was going to survive a week or more in his company, I couldn't imagine. The mere sight of him made me want to ravish him, right there on the porch, in front of all my neighbors. There had been a time when I might have done it. But Seth had come between us, and he was still there.

It wasn't exactly that Bowyn had left me for Seth. We'd both been Seth's lovers at one point, in a passionate and intensely sexy triad. But I'd thought Bowyn and I belonged to each other, regardless of who might share our bed. After all, we'd been a couple long before Seth came into our lives. When I left, I'd expected Bowyn to come with me. But he chose to stay with the Temple—and with Seth.

"You look good," Bowyn said more seriously, climbing the few wooden steps that separated us and reaching out to trace his fingers lightly along my upper arm. Against my will, I shivered at his touch.

I'd never had the body he had, but apart from a little graying at the temples, I supposed he was right about me not having changed much either. Still thin. Still the same short, dark brown hair and argyle sweaters. Bowyn used to tease me about looking like a professor long before I'd actually become one.

I stepped back from him—just a bit, but enough for him to get the message. What that message was, exactly, even I wasn't sure. It certainly wasn't "not interested." Perhaps it was "slow down." I still needed to wrap my head around what was happening.

He dropped his hand.

"I guess we can go now." I'd packed a bag, so I stepped inside to get it, leaving Bowyn waiting on the porch.

I knew full well I'd be staying at the Temple. There was no way Seth would let me stay at a local hotel. I wasn't his slave, of course, but there were some things it just wasn't worth fighting over. Besides, the

Temple was far enough off the beaten path that staying in a hotel would be impractical.

"Did you make arrangements for someone to feed your cats?" Bowyn asked as we climbed into the convertible.

"What on earth makes you think I have cats?"

"A dog?"

"No. No pets."

Bowyn shifted the car into reverse and backed out of the driveway. "Your boyfriend's allergic to animals?"

I rolled my head in his direction to give him a sour look. "Subtle."

"You like that?" he asked, flashing me the cheeky grin I'd always found so adorable. "I thought it up on the ride down."

"No, I don't have a boyfriend."

Bowyn laughed. "Well, that's good. Because you'll be rooming with me while you're at the Temple."

That figured. But even though it wasn't exactly a surprise, it still ticked me off. "And fucking you, I presume?"

"I certainly hope so."

While I was mulling over a response to that one, Bowyn threw the car in first gear. We shot out of the comfortable suburban cul-de-sac I lived in, heading north toward the White Mountains… and the Temple.

The Temple was a large plot of land Seth had purchased about twenty years ago, just northwest of Berlin, New Hampshire. The grounds contained a large old Victorian… well, it might as well be called a manor house. A wealthy mill owner had built it sometime in the eighteen hundreds, and it reflected the opulence of the period. The place was enormous. In addition to housing Seth and his "family"—something that was a bit difficult to define—it now served as living quarters for most of the Order. There was also a chapel on the grounds, along with a stable converted to a garage and a number of other outbuildings.

"Are you still with Seth?" I asked as we flew up Route 16 to Conway and then continued north toward Berlin. It was a bit blunt, but if he was planning on me sharing his room—and his bed—for the next several days, we needed to get a few things clear.

Obviously, Bowyn still *lived* with Seth. But he knew what I meant. He laughed and shook his head. "Not much. He has a new boy toy now. Rafe. Seth picked him up in Munich last year."

"Munich… Germany?"

"He's what a less kind person might call 'Eurotrash,'" Bowyn replied good-naturedly. "Bumming around Europe, burning through what's left of his inheritance—his parents have both passed away. Seth was there for the manuscript auction where he bought the Ficino, and somehow they hooked up. You'll meet him. You can probably fuck him, if you play your cards right."

But I was still mulling over "not much." That was a long way from "not at all." Likewise, the fact Bowyn wanted to have sex with me probably meant very little, other than he still found me attractive. That was good to know, but I'd left because I couldn't handle how attached he'd gotten to Seth. I wasn't sure I was emotionally ready to deal with the two of them, if they were still involved.

I didn't actually disapprove of the casual sex that went on at the Temple. I'd participated in it when I was there and I'd enjoyed it. It was just that I'd wanted more—some kind of... stability... permanence. Not so much sexually as emotionally. I'd needed to know I was the center of Bowyn's world, as he'd been the center of mine. Bowyn hadn't been able to give me that. And that was what had finally hurt enough to drive me away.

Bowyn glanced at me briefly and gave me a gentle, sympathetic smile before returning his attention to the road. "Hey, if you really don't want to stay with me, you don't have to."

"No, it's fine."

"We don't *have* to have sex. Of course. I just figured we were both adult enough to share a bed without too much drama. And there really aren't any spare rooms available at the moment. But I'm sure Marianne would be happy to share her room, if you don't mind sleeping on a cot."

I ignored that last suggestion. "You know perfectly well that we *will* end up having sex."

"Well," he replied, a grin lighting up his handsome face, "I was hoping. Is that so bad?"

Was it? A lot of people might think so. But we were on our way back to the Temple, where casually jumping into bed with whoever happened to be willing was the norm. In that context, Bowyn wasn't being unreasonable.

Additionally, I found I had no desire to ask for another room or share one with Marianne. I wasn't sure exactly what I was feeling—a longing for what we once had, perhaps, combined with the most intense feeling of desire I'd experienced since my exodus eight years ago. I wanted Bowyn, *badly*.

Just a scant hour or two earlier, I'd been dreading seeing him. Now that we were sitting mere inches away from each other, with him looking exactly as he had when I'd left him, I realized my desire for Bowyn hadn't dissipated. Not at all. Nor had my feelings for him. For eight years I'd managed to convince myself it was over and done with. Choices had been made—by both of us—and there was no going back. But the moment I'd laid eyes on him, all those years had melted away, and all my convictions crumbled. I'd thought I could keep him at arm's length during my stay, but I'd been foolish to think so.

So, yes, I would sleep in his room. And I would have wonderful, heartbreaking sex with the man I'd never stopped loving. Then I would leave, miserable and broken. It seemed inevitable. I just prayed the Ficino manuscript would be worth the hell I was going to go through for it.

# Chapter Two

THE SUN had set by the time we found ourselves on the winding road to the Temple off Route 110, not really that far from the city of Berlin but still seeming remote. It was a beautiful drive, but almost four hours. I was dead tired. And Bowyn had been tormenting me. The little sports car he was driving was a standard, and he kept deliberately brushing my leg with his fingers whenever he shifted.

It was a relief when the lights of the Temple came into view. Even in the dark, it was beautiful. Seth had a fondness for the Victorian era, so he'd put a considerable amount of money into restoring the original manor house. He'd even had the lampposts along the winding drive replaced with Victorian reproductions. They were electric, but they flickered like gaslights. The effect was eerily like stepping back in time about a hundred and thirty years.

Bowyn parked the car in the renovated stable alongside three others, and we went in through the kitchen entrance. He didn't have to lead the way—I knew the house as well as anybody. I'd lived there for four years in the early nineties, during the original restoration, and as far as I could see, not much had changed.

"Jeremy!" a female voice cried out as soon as I stepped into the warm kitchen. "Oh my God! I haven't seen you in ages!"

A woman with an abundance of loose blonde curls enveloped me in a hug, almost before I realized who it was. But a heady mix of herbal teas dominated by jasmine wafted to my nostrils, bringing with it fond memories of brewing magickal teas, making herbal tinctures, and staying up late chatting in the kitchen.

"Alex," I replied, as Seth's wife released me and stepped back. "It's great to see you."

And it was. In her late forties now, Alexandra was still a strikingly beautiful woman, still healthy and vibrant in a loose-fitting sundress decorated with some kind of elaborate East Indian print—

the type of dress made popular by hippies in the seventies. And she was barefoot, as always. Apart from some faint creases in the corners of her eyes, Alex hadn't changed any more than Bowyn had, or the Temple itself. I was beginning to feel as though I'd stepped through some kind of time warp.

Alex took my hand, her large hoop bracelets jangling as she pulled me to a seat at the massive oak table.

"Seth mentioned he was trying to bring you up for some project he was working on," she said, smiling at me fondly. It was typical of her to be unconcerned with the details of Seth's "projects." To the best of my knowledge, the two were still married, but they'd lost interest in each other in a romantic/sexual sense long ago. Seth had his occult studies and his pretty young things—both male and female—and Alex had her herb gardens and tinctures and kitchen magick. It had been that way since I'd first met them, and it seemed to suit them.

"Seth will want to see him right away," Bowyn reminded her, not very subtly, but Alex dismissed the idea with a wave of her hand.

"The Grand High Inquisitor can wait. Last I saw, he was heading upstairs with Rafe to 'meditate,' anyway." Her tone made it clear she had a low opinion of Seth's current plaything. He had to be pretty obnoxious for Alex to even notice his existence. "Would you like some tea, Jeremy?"

So we had tea. Alex might not have been Seth's lover anymore, but she was still a power to be obeyed at the Temple. When I'd lived there, she'd never had much interest in participating in the occult workings of the Order, and I got the distinct impression she still didn't. But this was her home. She'd lived there for twenty years. And she was not to be trifled with.

After about an hour of catching up, Bowyn and I were finally able to extricate ourselves from the kitchen. It wasn't all that late—perhaps ten. But I was tired from the trip and not at all disappointed when Bowyn said he wanted to turn in for the night. Though I knew what he had in mind before I'd be allowed to sleep, and I wasn't sure if I was ready for that.

As we slipped through the back hall into the large foyer in the front of the house, with its massive curved staircase, we passed people in the downstairs rooms. Most were dressed in the somber, plain brown robes of Order initiates, though there were a number of neophytes in off-white robes. A few were simply naked. The Temple was still clothing-optional, as it had been when I'd lived there. A few smiled at Bowyn and waved, but I didn't recognize any faces.

After climbing two flights of stairs, Bowyn said, "Let's say hi to Seth before we turn in."

I suppressed a groan. I'd known I'd have to deal with Seth sooner or later if I was going to be working on the manuscript for him, but I'd hoped it could wait until morning.

Several of the initiates and all the neophytes were housed in rooms on the second floor, which gave that floor a college dorm atmosphere—people running back and forth, conversations in the hall, occasional roughhousing. Anyone with any rank generally preferred to be on the third floor, away from the noise. Seth's room was the first one at the top of the front stairs on that floor, so as soon as I'd climbed the stairs, Bowyn was knocking on the door.

"What is it?" came a voice from within.

Bowyn glanced at me with a wicked smile and moved his face close to the door. "Your prodigal son has returned."

I rolled my eyes at him. Then a second later, the door flew open and Seth was standing there, stark naked.

He had to be over fifty by now. But apart from a distinguished silver sheen to his close-cropped hair, Seth still had the body of a man twenty years younger—broad shoulders, sharply defined abs and pecs, and the legs of a runner. Apart from the fact that he was naked, reminding me of how often I'd made love to that body, I would have described him as looking like a father from a fifties sitcom. He had that classically handsome face with a strong jaw, strong nose, and a killer smile with the most perfect teeth I'd ever seen. A bit like the father on *The Donna Reed Show*, except Seth oozed sex out of every pore, in or out of his clothes. It didn't hurt that he was extremely well-endowed and partially erect at the moment.

His eyes fixed on me with a look of pure delight, and then he immediately pulled me close in a bear hug. Almost against my will, I hugged him back, unable to stop myself from liking the feel of his smooth skin and taut muscles under my hands and the thin layer of sweat on his skin that told me he'd been… exerting himself just before he opened the door. I knew his body and whether I liked it or not, part of me still craved it. It didn't matter that this was the man who'd introduced Bowyn to the idea of open relationships, which ultimately led to my jealousy tearing our relationship apart. It didn't matter that I'd once felt smothered by Seth's idea of "love." I could feel my resolve to keep him at a distance crumbling at the familiarity of his touch, just as it had with Bowyn.

I turned my head and allowed him to kiss me in a most unfatherly fashion.

# Chapter Three

IT'S HARD to explain the conflicting emotions I was experiencing at that moment, with Seth pressing his naked body up against my front, his erection mirroring my own while Bowyn stood close behind me, one hand resting possessively on my shoulder. I'd been determined to give Seth a wide berth for the duration of my stay. It was going to be difficult enough just dealing with Bowyn. The last thing I needed was Seth slipping into bed with the two of us.

Part of me desperately wanted them—*both* of them. I had issues with Seth beyond mere jealousy, but at that moment the temptation to pull him down onto the Victorian carpet in the hall and fuck him right there was strong. And I had been wanting Bowyn since he called the night before.

But the two of them together? That really wasn't something I thought I could handle. It would be too much like old times; too much why I'd been forced to leave.

Fortunately, a smooth, deep voice behind Seth interrupted us. "Are you going to introduce me to your friend?"

This must have been Rafe. When Seth broke the kiss to turn to the young man, I saw Rafe was strikingly handsome, with jet-black hair and a smooth olive complexion. He was naked too, and the smile he gave me was nothing if not flirtatious. I'm not all that bad to look at, I suppose, but this wasn't the kind of guy I could picture going after thirty-five-year-old music professors in argyle sweaters. I suppose I might have been judging him unfairly, based upon the fact that he looked like a fashion model, but I doubted he'd give me the time of day under normal circumstances. Still, he'd just seen his lover—the frater superior of the Order—giving me a long, passionate kiss, and that might have made me intriguing.

"Rafe," Seth said pleasantly, "this is Jeremy—one of the Brethren."

The Order had begun with just me and Bowyn when we were in college together, fellow students of the occult. The name had been deliberately ironic, since there weren't enough of us to really make up an "order." But then we met Seth and Alex at an open house put on by the Masons in Portsmouth. None of us ended up joining the Masons, but Bowyn and I had been enthralled by this older couple who had more accumulated experience with the occult than anyone we'd ever met, including having been members of the Ordo Templi Orientis—the occult order Aleister Crowley had taken control of in 1925. We invited them to participate in some of the ceremonial magick rituals we'd been fumbling through. Soon our Order had four members, and then six when we initiated our friends, Marianne and Jack.

We'd called ourselves "the Brethren" as a sort of in-joke, puffing ourselves up with an important-sounding title. We also used it as a singular title, such as "Brethren Jeremy," even though it's really just the archaic plural of "brother." The deliberate misuse of the word was another lighthearted poke at our own pretentiousness.

Thirteen years later, according to what Bowyn had told me in the car, our original six had expanded to a mind-boggling three hundred. There were multiple generations of initiates included in that. I now had some kind of status as one of the founding members, and I found that to be fucking creepy.

Rafe placed one hand over his heart and lightly touched his genitals with the other as he bowed low. "Brethren. It's an honor."

I didn't quite know what to say in reply, so I merely repeated the bow. When I looked up, Rafe was once again giving me a look that said he'd love to take the old man out for a spin and see how much mileage he had left in him.

"If you don't mind," Bowyn said, taking my elbow in an attempt to steer me away, "Jeremy and I have some catching up of our own to do."

I hadn't had any action in over a year, and now I had three gorgeous men looking as if they'd like to draw straws for who'd get to have me first. *Christ.*

"I'm sure you do," Seth said, taking my other elbow, "but not before I show Jeremy something."

"I'm really pretty tired," I protested.

But Seth just smiled and replied, "You'll want to see this."

So, still stark naked, he practically dragged me through the upstairs hallway, Bowyn and a naked Rafe at our heels. How quickly it was starting to feel like old times again.

We passed by a few people, both men and women, either wandering the halls of the house or in their bedrooms with their doors open. Some of them were doing things that would have warranted closing their doors in any other house. But not at the Temple. One of our basic tenets, from the beginning, had always been "People have penises and vaginas. Cope." It had largely been due to the influence of Seth and Alex, who'd been part of a naturist commune in Vermont in the eighties, but the rest of us had been randy college students at the time, so we didn't object.

Seth led us up to the attic, where there were more bedrooms, smaller rooms converted from the old Victorian servants' quarters. There was also a room that was locked—an oddity in the Temple. Seth, of course, had no keys on him, but Bowyn had a key of his own. At a nod from the older man, Bowyn unlocked the door.

Then we stepped into an airlock. I'd never seen one in real life, but I'd seen them in movies. It was a small triangular space, a bit cramped for four people, with another metal door on the largest wall. This wall also had climate controls with displays for the temperature and humidity of the room beyond. Bowyn produced an electronic key card from his pocket and swept it in front of a card reader. The inner door unlatched and he pushed it open.

Inside, we found a beautiful old Victorian library with floor-to-ceiling bookshelves on every wall and ladders on runners to provide access. The furniture in the room consisted of antique stuffed chairs and mahogany tables with Tiffany lamps casting a soft light to read by. In one corner there was a large antique globe. There was even a fireplace, though it was electric and probably put out no heat in the climate-controlled environment.

"Didn't this used to be a spare bedroom?" I asked as I wandered out into the space.

Bowyn answered, "It used to be *three* spare bedrooms."

"Now," Seth said, "it's the Order's occult library." He began circling the room, gesturing as he spoke. "All first editions, collected from all over the world—Crowley.... Fortune.... Levi.... Dee.... Mathers.... Regardie.... Waite.... The original works, in their first incarnations. You won't find any reprints here. No cheap mass-produced paperbacks." He said the word "paperbacks" as if it were a revolting concept to him.

"All under lock and key?"

"Every fifth- and sixth-level initiate has a key," Seth replied. There were only seven levels in the Order, the Brethren being the seventh and highest. "All the others can access the entire library on an internal database, but only high-level initiates can come up here and actually *touch* the books, read them first-hand."

Knowing Seth's fascination with antiques and history, I wasn't surprised it was so important to him to hold a first edition of *The Book of Lies* in his hands. It seemed a bit extravagant, especially if it was being paid for out of Temple funds—which I suspected it was, at least in part. But as long as it was approved by the others in the Order, I supposed I had no quarrel with it. I had to remind myself it wasn't really my concern, in any case. I'd left the Order.

Seth moved to the far wall, where there were a number of wide, recessed drawers. "This, however, is the pride of our collection."

I moved closer as he slid one of the drawers out. It contained several pages of what might have been a single document—quite an old document, judging by the yellowing of the parchment and the faded ink—secured in position under a large plate of Plexiglas. "We've collected some of the oldest occult texts still in existence. Fragments of medieval grimoires; pages from works by Agrippa, Fludd, Paracelsus, Weyer, Borrichius…."

He flipped a switch on the side of the drawer and long black lights on the inner sides of the drawer came on, causing the faded ink on the manuscripts to luminesce. "And here, my prodigal son, is what you've come home for."

I ignored the annoying reference, my full attention caught by the beautifully shimmering staves of music now visible on the pages. I stepped closer, dismayed to see the poor condition of many of the pages. The edges were frayed and crumbling, and fingerprints—perhaps not noticeable when they were made, but now etched into the parchment—obscured some of the writing. A small stain of some unknown liquid smeared the ink in the upper corner of one page. In many places, I would have to make an educated guess as to which notes were meant.

But it was beautiful. The frontispiece was an elaborate etching in the incredibly detailed style of the time period—a man standing with his arms crossed over his chest in the sign of Osiris slain while lions and dragons and angels sported about him, amidst geometric symbols representing the four elements and other alchemical objects and processes. The entire image was enclosed in a giant snake biting its own tail—*Ouroborus*, the World-Serpent—and even the serpent had planetary symbols etched on it in the bottom half of the illustration. It was amazingly complex.

"Judging by the date on the manuscript," Seth was saying, "it was written toward the end of Ficino's life."

"Please tell me you aren't relying on that for authentication," I said with a grimace. "Any forger can write a date and sign a famous name. It was common practice throughout the Middle Ages and Renaissance."

"Of course," Seth replied. "We've consulted a handwriting expert, who compared it to other manuscripts by Ficino. We've also had the frontispiece and other etchings in the document analyzed. We're as certain as we can be that it dates to Ficino's lifetime and the handwriting appears to match."

"Why has nobody heard of this work?" I asked. "He wasn't exactly secretive."

"It was never finished, and no part of it was ever published. Cavalcanti held on to the manuscript, until he died ten years later."

Marsilio Ficino, one of the greatest thinkers of the Italian Renaissance, had been gay. And rather unapologetic about it, for his time period. Perhaps that had been what attracted him to Plato. Due to his reputation, and the fact that Ficino became a priest in later years, he was lucky enough to have his proclivities largely ignored during his lifetime. But the Catholic Church diligently suppressed that little tidbit of information for a considerable time after his death.

Giovanni Cavalcanti was a poet in Florence whom Ficino was rumored to be involved with, and the recipient of the passionate love letters that were later published in Ficino's *Epistulae*.

"How did you get a hold of it?"

"Cavalcanti's family kept it," Seth explained. "And it was passed down through the generations as a private family heirloom."

"Five hundred years is a long time for a family heirloom to be passed along."

"It's not unheard of. I acquired it at an auction in Germany. It was being sold by a man whose grandfather had bought it at an auction in Italy, over sixty years ago, just after World War II. By that time, the original owners had lost their wealth in the war, and most of the remaining descendants' land and property was being sold off to pay debts."

I wasn't sure I believed the story, but it was at least feasible. I also wasn't sure it was legal for Seth to own a document that might be considered a national treasure by the government of Italy. But all that could wait. I needed to have a close look at it for myself.

"We'll need to photograph these pages to avoid any further damage to the parchment while I study them."

Seth nodded. "Already done, my love. Digital copies have been sent overseas to our Greek translator and copies have been loaded onto a laptop reserved for your use."

"This illustration," I observed, indicating the frontispiece, "contains an amazing amount of alchemical symbolism. Have you deciphered it?"

"Some, though certainly not all. Apart from the music, there's very little information about its purpose in the manuscript, but I'm convinced that this is the key to the entire operation—the timing of it, the order… everything we need to know to perform the mass and the accompanying ritual."

It had been quite common for the details of alchemical and magickal operations to be encoded in symbols throughout the Renaissance, in order to avoid discovery by the authorities and the uninitiated.

"What makes you think there *is* a ritual?"

"Because I can feel it," Seth replied. "If nothing else, these planetary symbols"—he pointed at the glyphs written on the body of the Ouroboros—"indicate a specific alignment. And that means a specific time."

"A time to perform the mass?"

"What else?"

I raised my eyebrows, not quite sure what to make of his theory. "If that's true, then when?"

Seth tapped on the Plexiglas above the frontispiece with his index finger. "What do you see?"

I looked at the planetary symbols closely. There were four of them etched on the lower half of the body of the Ouroboros—the symbols for the sun, the moon, Mercury, and Saturn. The alchemical symbol of the sun is merely a circle with a dot in its center. The moon is *usually* a crescent. In this instance, though, it was represented by a circle filled in with black, the symbol of the new moon.

The Ouroboros itself was shaded darker on its upper half than its lower half, with little tadpole-like symbols written at the very top and bottom. As I recalled, those symbols simply represented night and day, reinforcing the light and dark shading.

"The night half is ascendant," I said, "which might indicate the operation should take place during the night. And the fact that the darker shading takes up more than half the circle suggests it would be after the equinox, when the night is longer than the day."

Seth was delighted. "Excellent! I see the past eight years haven't dulled your wits." He pointed to the planetary symbols on the lower half of the Ouroboros. "And what do you make of these?"

"Saturn is in the light part, on the left, as if it's just set in the west, and Mercury and the new moon are about to rise on the right."

"I would agree with that assessment." Smiling, Seth leaned in closer. "Now... just when do you think this particular planetary alignment is likely to occur next?"

"Tonight?" I was being facetious, since I had absolutely no idea. But I suspected that it had to be soon, or Seth wouldn't be so excited.

"No," he corrected. "Next week. In seven days, to be exact, at approximately 11:00 p.m."

I laughed out loud. "You don't seriously expect me to have this finished in seven days?"

"I have faith in you, Jeremy."

I was back to being annoyed with him. "Seth, you have no idea what the performance of the mass is for, assuming that it has a purpose—"

"It has to have a purpose, Jeremy! You don't specify a planetary alignment for something that doesn't have some kind of magickal purpose."

"Perhaps. But if you needed me to transcribe the music in time, you should have called me in weeks ago—better yet, *months* ago."

"You were in London when I tried to find you three weeks ago," Bowyn said, spreading his hands apologetically.

"Jeremy," Seth said, "I realize conditions aren't ideal. But we're presenting you with an unprecedented opportunity—the chance to be the first scholar to transcribe what is most likely the only complete polyphonic mass ever put to parchment by Ficino. How can you pass that up?"

I couldn't and he knew it. I looked again at the pages of the manuscript, already feeling a powerful urge welling up within me to begin deciphering them. The notation was breathtaking, meticulously written out by hand at a time when music wasn't yet printed, the notes closely spaced, rising and falling like waves across the page. The accompanying libretto was carefully inked on a separate page, as opposed to underneath the staves as we do today, and had a tendency to slant to the right. Nearly illegible annotations were scribbled here and there in a script that certainly *looked* like the samples I'd seen of Ficino's handwriting, with its tidy, almost constricted lettering offset by dramatic sweeps in the upper and middle zones. The frontispiece itself was gorgeous, its myriad symbols calling to me across the centuries.

On a more base level, I knew if I could prove this document had been written by Ficino and present the first—the *definitive*—transcription of it, my reputation in academic circles would increase a hundredfold.

"All right," I said. "I'll do it."

# Chapter Four

AFTER WE'D locked the library, and I'd politely but firmly refused Seth's invitation to join him and Rafe in whatever game they'd been playing before my arrival, Bowyn and I were finally able to go to our room at the end of the third floor hallway. When I say "our room," I'm not merely referring to the room we'd be sharing for the week. I mean that it was "our room"—the room Bowyn and I had shared eight years ago, in the rear of the house, overlooking the chapel.

I supposed it made sense for Bowyn to continue living in that room. But I hadn't really been prepared for that. I guess I'd thought of the room as belonging to the two of us, and some irrational part of my mind had assumed it had dissolved into nothingness along with our relationship. But of course it hadn't.

Things weren't exactly as I'd left them. Bowyn had replaced the ratty old yellow bedspread we'd picked up at the Salvation Army with a plush, wine-colored spread, and the posters on the walls reflected a new interest in *The Lord of the Rings* films. But my poster of the zodiac was still on the wall, a bit faded now, and I recognized some of my books in the bookcase. There was no creepy shrine dedicated to my old underwear or anything like that, but it was still disconcerting.

"Amazing," I said, looking around while Bowyn closed the door behind me. "Nothing seems to have really changed around here."

"Well, you saw the library."

"True."

"And Jack…."

That brought me back to reality a bit. I turned to give Bowyn a sad smile. "Yes. There's Jack." I'd heard about it through an e-mail from Marianne, shortly after it happened. She and Jack had been engaged before the cancer took him. I hadn't been able to make it to the funeral. "How is Marianne these days?"

The expression on Bowyn's face was oddly reserved, as if he were bothered by something, but all he said was, "She's fine. You'll see her tomorrow, I'm sure."

And just like that, we ran out of things to say.

He stood in front of me, looking just as strangely shy as he had the first night he'd proposed we become more than just college roommates. I'd had no qualms about leaping into his bed then, but now things were different. I wasn't really sure what I wanted.

"So, what happens now?" I asked, glancing at the wide four-poster.

"Well," Bowyn began slowly, "unless you have some objection to it, I was planning on tossing you on the bed and having my way with you."

I laughed, but I couldn't think of a response. I still loved Bowyn, and I still wanted him. There were good reasons to avoid having sex, but I was having a hard time remembering what they were at the moment.

When fate had dropped us into the same dorm room all those years ago, Bowyn and I had quickly discovered that one of the things we had in common was our respect for Aleister Crowley. I realize, of course, that many people consider Crowley to have been evil, but to us he'd seemed more a brilliant occult scholar who just happened to get a kick out of frightening the locals.

One of the most fundamental principles of Crowley's magickal philosophy was "Do what thou wilt shall be the whole of the law." It was frequently misinterpreted to mean "act like a selfish jackass," but what he'd basically meant was you should determine what your higher purpose is and always act in accordance with that. It could also be interpreted as not being fearful of doing what you *know*, deep down, your heart and conscience are leading you to do.

This was part of what went through my head at that moment as I stepped toward Bowyn and pulled him into my arms. He was startled, but when my mouth found his, he closed his eyes and returned the kiss hungrily. His arms came up behind my back and pressed me against his muscular chest, and I was unable to stifle a groan. His lips were soft and warm and, even after eight years, so familiar I could hardly believe I'd gone so long without tasting them. I realized with dismay that I would never truly be free of Bowyn. I was as much his now as I'd been the night he first took me on that uncomfortable, too-small vinyl mattress in our dorm room.

Bowyn gently guided me backward until my legs bumped up against the side of the bed. I allowed myself to be lowered onto the dark red bedspread and groaned again as he climbed on top of me. He ground his erection against mine through frustrating layers of denim and cotton while his tongue probed deeply into my mouth.

After a few minutes of this, I could no longer stand the clothing that kept our bodies apart, and I gasped, "I want you naked!"

Bowyn chuckled and kissed me tenderly on the tip of my nose before pushing himself up off me. He stood and slipped his T-shirt off, revealing that perfectly formed chest and the tight, rippling muscles of his stomach. The sight of his body literally made me salivate. I wanted to lick every inch of that smooth, golden skin; *taste* it. I'd once selfishly thought of that body as mine—until Seth laid claim to it. Now, although I knew it was childish, I desperately wanted it to be mine again.

I sat up on the bed and reached out for him. Bowyn came to me without hesitation. I wrapped my arms around his waist and ran my hands up the hard muscles of his lower back, feeling the heat pouring off his skin as I kissed his abdomen. Following the light trail of sandy hair from his navel downward, I encountered the waistband of his battered jeans.

"Take them off," I growled.

Bowyn laughed at my sudden aggressiveness and did as I asked, popping the button at the waistband and unzipping his fly. He wasn't wearing underwear. He never did. I inhaled his musky scent, clean but very, very masculine, and it was like a drug, driving me insane. I gripped the back of his jeans and yanked them down.

Freed from the confines of his pants, his hardened shaft brushed against my cheek, warm and satiny smooth, and I quickly took it into my mouth. It fit perfectly there, as if Bowyn's cock had been created for my mouth and my mouth alone. I sucked it in deeply, my own cock rock hard in my pants as I strove to take him in as far as I could.

Bowyn moaned and ran his fingers through my hair, helping me take him in, until at last he said, his voice ragged, "I want to be inside you."

Technically he already was. But I knew what he meant, and I wanted that too. More than I'd ever wanted anything in my life.

I stood and pulled my sweater off, then let Bowyn slowly unbutton my shirt, watching his face for any hint he would no longer find me pleasing. But all I saw in his eyes was desire and rising excitement.

"My God," he said in a whisper, "I've missed being able to touch you."

He undid my belt and slid my pants and underwear down to my knees in one motion, then knelt and took me into his mouth. I reveled in what he was doing to me. He knew what gave me pleasure more than anybody else, and a blow job from him was worth a week of sex with any other man. But still I wanted more. And so did he.

Reluctantly I pushed him off my cock. "That's wonderful. But I need you to take me before I go out of my fucking mind."

Bowyn laughed again, giving the head of my dick a quick, teasing lick. He stood and walked over to the nightstand, where he took out a small bottle of lube and a condom while I sat on the bed to remove my shoes and pants.

When he saw me watching him put the condom on, he said, "This isn't because I don't think you're safe. It's just that, with all the free love going on around here, I've learned to be cautious…."

I wasn't offended. Truthfully I was relieved to learn he hadn't been having unprotected sex with God knows how many people all these years. "No problem."

I finished undressing and lay on the bed, spreading my legs shamelessly for him, like a dog in heat. I was already dripping precome, and when Bowyn crawled on top of me and slipped his hand down between my legs so his finger could seek out my sphincter, I thought I would explode right there.

"Oh yes," I sighed, impatient for him to go deeper.

He leaned down to kiss me, and his tongue penetrated my mouth while his finger found my prostate. I willed myself not to come, determined to have Bowyn thrusting deep when I reached orgasm. It wouldn't be easy. As he slipped another finger inside, I spasmed and leaked a little more precome.

"Put yourself in me," I said breathlessly. "Now!"

"Okay, baby. Here it comes."

I was still tight when he penetrated, but there was no pain. Only the ecstatic pleasure of taking the man I loved deep inside. He might not love me—at least, not as much as he loved the Order and the Temple—but he wanted me. And for now, that was enough. I clung tightly to him, sweat pooling between our overheated bodies as he thrust again and again, and wished it would never end.

Neither of us could last long after the frustration that had been building up in us throughout the day. Bowyn grunted into my mouth and gave one final, hard thrust. I felt his cock pulsing in my depths, and it sent me over the top. I erupted thick ropes of come between our stomachs.

Bowyn lay on top for a long time, kissing me tenderly while we caught our breath.

"I've missed you, Jeremy," he whispered, his voice catching, as if he were on the edge of tears. "You have no idea how much."

I brought my hand up to caress the nape of his neck under that golden hair, which cascaded over his shoulders, as soft as corn silk. "I think I know."

More needed to be said, but neither of us wanted to disturb the connection we felt at this moment. There would be time to rehash the old arguments later; time to remember why what we felt for each other hadn't been enough to keep us together. But for now we could allow ourselves to revel in the discovery that those feelings were still there, even after all this time.

Eventually, he slipped out of me and said with a boyish smile, "Sorry, but I have to go pee."

Yes, he said "pee," as if he were five. I'd always found that kind of cute.

"Fine. But I'm still horny. So if you're gone more than two minutes, I may have to go find Rafe."

Bowyn groaned and shook his head. "Like I said, if you want him, I'm sure you can have him. The guy gives new meaning to the word 'slut.'"

"Jealous?"

"Of you fucking him? No. I've already fooled around with him, and, trust me, his appeal wanes pretty quickly. But I could probably arrange a threesome, if you want. Or we could make it a foursome if you want to bring Seth in."

I was beginning to regret teasing him. The thought of being able to have my pick of cute men in a variety of combinations was appealing, but I really wasn't in the mood to think about Bowyn and Seth together right now. "No, thanks. Just go take a leak and get your ass back here."

"Yes, ma'am!"

He ran out into the hallway without bothering to put anything on. After a minute I grew bored with lying on the bed by myself, so I wiped myself off with my discarded shirt and then got up to drift around the room. I suppose I was curious about whether he'd kept any reminders of me. I was pleased to find there were some photos of the two of us, usually with Seth or Marianne, or some other combination of our old gang. But there was one that was just the two of us—a small photograph, taken by Marianne when we were napping together on the couch in the living room downstairs. I was lying with my back to Bowyn, his arm draped protectively around my middle.

I was suddenly struck with an overwhelming sadness, looking at this proof I'd once had something wonderful… and lost it. I put the picture frame back down on the fireplace mantel.

There was a small doorway set in the wall, not far from the fireplace. To anyone not familiar with the house or Victorian houses in general, it might have looked like a closet. But I knew it wasn't. I opened the door, noting there still wasn't any means of locking it, and peered into the tiny dark hallway on the other side. It was part of a maze of hallways and staircases that connected all the rooms of the house. In Victorian times, servants used these passages to move quietly from room to room without disturbing their masters. Bowyn and I had explored them to some extent when we first moved in and made use of them for a short time before the novelty wore off. Judging by the thick cobwebs that blocked most of the doorway, Bowyn hadn't used it in a very long time.

I shut the door and gave up my exploration for now. Bright moonlight was shining into the room, though I recalled it would only be half-full tonight and waning. Even living away from the Temple for all these years hadn't cured me of the obsessive monitoring of lunar phases students of the occult often fall into. Besides, Seth had said the astrological correspondences for the ritual—one of which would be the new moon—would be in alignment just seven nights from now.

I went to stand by the tall multipaned window to look out on the Temple grounds. From somewhere outside, a low, soft church bell rang out—just a single note in the middle of the night. It seemed odd, since there had been no bell the last time I'd been there, but I didn't waste much time thinking about it.

I remembered the view being lovely in daylight, since the window overlooked the chapel behind the house and the mountains beyond. At night the chapel entrance was illuminated by more of the fake gas lanterns, presenting a beautiful, if somewhat eerie, gothic image.

There was somebody out there—a man standing on the cobblestone path near the chapel entrance. And he was naked.

That might not have been so odd for the Temple if it weren't October. By this time of night, it had to be pretty cold to be standing around like that outside. The man seemed very young, perhaps a teenager, though

I certainly hoped he wasn't under eighteen. The Temple had never admitted anyone underage in the past, and I would be dismayed to find that policy had been disposed of.

When I heard Bowyn enter the room again, I said, "There's someone out there."

"So?" He crawled back onto the bed, not terribly interested.

"He's naked."

Bowyn laughed. "Streaking or masturbating?"

"Neither."

What *was* he doing? It was hard to see from here. But he was facing north and appeared to be making the Sign of Water—the thumbs and index fingers of each hand placed together to form a downward-pointing triangle, in front of the stomach. I glanced at the old-fashioned clock on the mantel. It was midnight. "I think he's performing Resh."

Resh was a ritual meditation we'd borrowed from Crowley's Thelemic rituals, though we'd replaced the references to Egyptian deities with calls to Greek deities. It was performed at sunrise, noon, sunset, and midnight. For each time of day, you faced a particular direction, corresponding to the sun's position in the sky. For midnight it would be north. Then you took on certain postures and performed the ritual chant for that time of day. It was largely, in my opinion, for instilling discipline. As it wasn't very conducive to my current work schedule, I'd long ago slacked off. Apparently so had Bowyn.

"Does he look like a blond, beautiful cherub?"

"He's blond, but he's too far away for me to really see his face. He has a bit too much pubic hair for a cherub, I think."

"Wait 'til you see him up close. His name is Christopher. And just about everybody here wants a piece of him."

Bowyn often found things humorous that I didn't. And that phrasing sounded a bit too predatory for my tastes. "He's legal?"

"Barely," Bowyn said. "He was sending us e-mail for over a year, begging us to take him in. But Seth wouldn't allow it until he turned eighteen. That was just about nine months ago."

Christopher finished the ritual, retrieved a robe from the ground, and pulled it over his head. Then he disappeared into the shadows.

I went over to sit on the bed beside Bowyn, but I wasn't sure I was still feeling very horny.

"Does Seth still seduce every new neophyte who walks through the door?" I didn't bother to disguise the contempt in my voice. Seth had done that more times than I could remember, and it had always disgusted me. It wasn't illegal, and he didn't force himself on anyone, but it was still unethical. And it was the type of behavior religious cult leaders were famous for.

Bowyn shrugged. He'd never gotten as bent out of shape about Seth's rutting as I had. "He hasn't gotten anywhere with this one. Christopher is straight, I think. But more than that, he was pretty badly sexually abused by his father. He freaks out if anyone tries to touch him."

Bowyn caressed my thighs as I stretched out beside him on the bed. My body began to respond, despite the unpleasant thoughts swirling in my head. "Just as long as Seth isn't forcing the kid into anything."

"Seth isn't *that* bad. He's oversexed, but he's not a rapist. The kid is fine. I mean, he's kind of weird, but he seems happy here."

He nudged me to roll over onto my back so he could go down on me, and I let him. But I couldn't help but wonder if a place like the Temple was really the best place for a young man with sexual abuse issues. If he was as beautiful as Bowyn claimed, I had no doubt Seth was hitting on him, even if he wasn't forcing anything. And that just sounded like a disaster waiting to happen.

# Chapter Five

I WOKE early the next morning to find Bowyn standing in front of his window, performing Resh to the rising sun. Apparently, he wasn't totally slacking off, after all. I felt a little guilty for not joining him, but it had been so long, I was no longer certain I remembered all the words. I just lay there watching until he was finished.

He turned to me and smiled, the sunlight backlighting his naked body and giving it the illusion of glowing. "Morning, handsome. I was planning on letting you sleep in."

I stretched, loving the feel of the plush mattress under my body. "I'll get up if you are."

"Breakfast should be in about a half hour. I was going to head down to the showers."

"The showers" turned out to be a new addition. When I'd lived there, everyone in the house had to fight over two full bathrooms, one half bath, and an old porta-potty behind the stable. This had led to a complicated shower schedule that everyone hated and a vile weekly porta-potty emptying duty for the neophytes. We lost at least two neophytes because of that, but Seth kept insisting it was part of their discipline training. Personally, I thought the guy had watched too many episodes of *Kung Fu* as a kid.

We'd always talked about installing some kind of locker-room-style shower facility in the basement, and that had finally been implemented while I was away. The water pressure wasn't wonderful, but there were eight stalls, curtained off for a modicum of privacy. Not that everybody bothered to close the curtains. It was unisex, so when Bowyn and I walked in, we found both men and women standing naked in the center of the steam-filled room, talking and horsing around with each other as they waited for an available stall. A separate section in the back contained toilet stalls and periodically someone would call out "Flushing!" so everyone could leap out of the shower spray before the water temperature turned to scalding. It felt as if I were in summer camp. Well, a Paul Verhoeven version of summer camp, anyway.

To my annoyance, as soon as Bowyn and I entered the room some of the neophytes gave up their place in line for us. The same sort of thing happened when I took karate—the lower ranks always deferred to the higher ranks. I just wasn't suited to the idea of outranking someone. Bowyn, on the other hand, seemed to accept it as perfectly normal. Which it pretty much was for him.

We showered and dressed in the brown cotton robes initiates at the Temple wore when they weren't bopping around in the altogether. I didn't object to the robes. They were amazingly comfortable. If I'd had my choice, I would have worn one all the time—even back at the university.

We went up to the dining hall, which had *not* changed in the past eight years and was still forced to operate in shifts. The dining room table could seat about twenty, and there were a lot more people living in the Temple than there had been in my day. People ate quickly to allow others to take their spot, or they simply gave up on the idea of sitting and ate while standing. Others took their plates into the living room and perched on couches or chairs there. There had been some discussion, Bowyn informed me, of adding an extension to the house to include new sleeping barracks and a larger dining room. But some of Seth's acquisitions for the library—including the Ficino manuscript, which had cost a few hundred thousand—superseded these plans for the moment.

But of course, there was no convincing the man the library wasn't essential to the Order. Bowyn appeared to tolerate Seth's eccentricities with good humor, but I was rapidly remembering why I had escaped from this place. Yes, there were elements of the Temple I missed and people I missed—especially Bowyn—but Seth.... Well, I didn't hate him. I actually missed him a bit too. But the guy managed to push all my buttons.

The food, as always, was excellent. Alex presided over all food preparation, cracking the whip over a handful of kitchen staff, and she was truly a magician in the kitchen. Since she'd grown up at the tail end of the hippie generation, this meant the Temple was on a strict vegetarian diet. But it was terrific, so there were seldom any complaints. At least, there hadn't been in my day. If the new initiates dared to defy Alex on the matter… well, they had more balls than I did.

We popped into the kitchen briefly to say hi, but all she had time to do was blow a kiss at us before tearing off after an unfortunate neophyte who'd dropped a tray of textured vegetable protein sausages on the tile floor.

*Requiem in pace, neophyte.*

As far as the ranking system went, neophytes were newcomers to the Order, before they were considered knowledgeable enough about the basic operations and tenets to be promoted to first-level initiate. And while they weren't treated with the same contempt and disregard as, say, a first-year cadet in a military academy, they were still at the bottom of the totem pole. While they were training for their first degree, they were also expected to do most of the menial labor around the Temple. Not all of it, of course. There weren't nearly enough new people coming in to keep up with *all* the chores involved in the day-to-day upkeep of the house and grounds. But they got the crap jobs. Seth's opinion on the treatment of the neophytes was, if they couldn't handle a year of doing dishes and cleaning toilets, we didn't need them in the Order. I wasn't thrilled with that attitude, but at least nobody ever died from hazing as a neophyte at the Temple. Fortunately for this new batch, the porta-potty had been dispensed with years ago.

It generally took about a year of slavery, memorizing postures and chants and studying the occult foundations of the Order, before the neophyte would be initiated into First Degree. Everyone from First Degree to Sixth Degree was called an "initiate." And above Sixth Degree, of course, was the Brethren—the seventh rank and the only rank that was unattainable to anyone who wasn't already Brethren to begin with. Which meant either we'd all die off one day, or Seth would have to change the criteria.

After breakfast, I followed Bowyn to the chapel for morning services. The Order wasn't religious, in the sense of believing in a specific deity or deities. We believed there were forces underlying the structure of the universe—forces constantly shaping and reshaping the order of things—and that the human will was capable of affecting these forces and thereby affecting the world around us. Some might call that religious, and I wouldn't argue, but our services were less worship services than philosophical lessons, accompanied by exercises to increase our ability to focus our will. At my insistence, the Order also had a choir that performed at the end of each service.

One thing I had to give Seth credit for was that he knew how to put on a great show. He could stand in the center of the chapel floor in his full regalia—robes of silver and burgundy with jewelry that would have made Cleopatra jealous—and recite from Plato or Aristotle and somehow make it the most riveting thing you'd ever heard in your life.

That morning he was speaking about Orpheus, no doubt inspired by the Ficino manuscript.

"Orpheus was born of a human father—King Oeagrus—but his mother was the muse Calliope," Seth began, "and it was from her that Orpheus learned to sing. The god Apollo, who was courting one of Calliope's sisters, came to know the boy on his visits to her home. He took a liking to young Orpheus and gave him a golden lyre, which he taught the boy to play.

"Orpheus excelled at music and made some modifications to the lyre Apollo had given him, until he was able to play and sing so beautifully that it was said he could charm wild beasts and even coax the trees and rocks to dance!"

Seth executed a little dance step that caused a ripple of laughter to go through the congregation.

"But the most famous story to come down to us involves his wife, Eurydice. One morning, she was killed by a viper bite while walking in the fields, and Orpheus was so struck with grief that he journeyed to the underworld, determined to bring her back. There, his music so softened the hearts of Hades and Persephone that they allowed Eurydice to journey back to the upper world with him.

"However," Seth said with a dramatic pause, "there was one stipulation. He was to walk in front of Eurydice and never look back until they were both safely in the upper world. Orpheus obeyed their command until he stepped into the upper world. Then anxiety overtook him and he glanced back to make certain his wife was still behind him. But Eurydice hadn't yet stepped into the light of day. As Orpheus watched in horror, she faded away and returned to the underworld… forever."

The sermon, if you could call it that, ended with a performance of a choir piece I myself had written at least a decade ago. It was a setting of one of the so-called Orphic hymns—poems that were traditionally attributed to Orpheus himself, though that was highly improbable. It was unlikely Orpheus had ever truly existed. Even Aristotle doubted it at a time when his historicity was generally accepted. Still, it was a nice poem.

I was amazed by the beauty of the choral piece. Not so much because it was a work of genius on my part—it wasn't bad, considering I'd written it in my twenties—but the mesmerizing, ethereal voice of the lead tenor lifted it out of mediocrity. Sung by that voice, my rather plain melody brought tears to my eyes. And it didn't hurt that the singer had an otherworldly beauty of his own.

That this was Christopher, I had no doubt. His blond, almost pure white hair framed a soft, boyish face that *did* look like a cherub. Or at least like an angel. But though he may have been eighteen, he looked so young and vulnerable his beauty didn't engender desire in me. It simply instilled a powerful urge to comfort and protect him. His enormous blue eyes seemed on the verge of crying as he sang, as if the lyrics of the song were so sublime it hurt to sing them. If anyone could coax the rocks and trees to move with his songs, this young man could do it.

# Chapter Six

"JEREMY!" MARIANNE'S voice called my name the moment I stepped out of the chapel.

I hadn't even had time to turn my head before her arms wrapped around my neck and her high-pitched squeal caused permanent hearing loss in my right ear.

"I can't believe it's you! I thought you'd gone away for good, you brat." The latter was accompanied by a playful cuff to the shoulder as she let me go and stepped back.

She was a pretty woman, with a warm, friendly face and flaming red curls, but she'd always been a bit on the pudgy side. I used to tell her it made her look cute and I meant it. But of course she hated that. She didn't want "apple-cheeked cute girl next door." She wanted "hot babe who has to beat the men off with a stick."

Apparently life at the Temple agreed with her. Or perhaps more specifically Alex's healthy cooking agreed with her. Marianne wasn't exactly built like a supermodel now—she still had a bit of a belly—but she'd slimmed down quite a lot.

"You look fantastic!" It was delightful to see her. She really did look great.

Marianne giggled and did a little rotation. "Does it show?" she asked, knowing of course it did.

"You look gorgeous."

"Thanks. 'How do I look so young? Quite simple. A complete vegetable diet, twelve hours sleep a night—'"

"'And *lots* and *lots* of makeup.'" I completed the quote from Neil Simon's comedy, *Murder by Death*.

We both broke into giggles.

Bowyn had come up behind me and now he rolled his eyes at us. "Here we go again with the movie quotes. You two are going to be impossible."

"Come, darling," Marianne told me, ignoring him as she linked her arm through mine. "Have you had the grand tour yet?"

"It doesn't look to me like much has changed since I left," I replied truthfully.

"Probably not. But this will give us an excuse to catch up."

At some point, I needed to get to work on the Ficino manuscript. But for now, the three of us headed out across the grounds, jabbering away about all that had happened in the past eight years. Ultimately the answer was "not much." True, Jack had passed away—something we acknowledged with sadness, but tacitly agreed not to dwell on right now. And I'd become a professor at the university. There had been some renovations at the Temple, but I'd pretty much seen them all.

I'd feared that Seth and Bowyn would have become an inseparable couple by now, but I should have known better. Seth hopped from Cute Young Thing to Cute Young Thing like a bee gathering pollen. That would never change. Bowyn was still hot as hell, so he could spend a night with Seth whenever he felt like it, and he still sometimes did. But I got the impression those were rare occurrences these days.

"You aren't seriously expecting me to believe you haven't found someone else?" I asked, being far more obvious than I'd wanted to be.

Bowyn smiled shyly and shook his head. "Believe what you want, babe. I've fooled around a lot over the years. Of course. But there hasn't been anybody serious."

I would have been happy to hear that if it hadn't been for the odd expression on Marianne's face. She was pretending to be interested in something across the yard, but for just a moment, a look of—what? Jealousy?—flickered across her features. Was it possible she'd developed a crush on Bowyn? That could be bad.

Another thought occurred to me then, and I suddenly felt a bit nauseated. Marianne hadn't been one of the people Bowyn had fooled around with, had she? I can't fully explain why that bothered me more than the thought of him whoring around with legions of other initiates. (Well, maybe the correct term would be "slutting around." Whores charge.) But it did. Maybe because we'd known Marianne for so long. She wasn't just some casual fuck on a lonely night that Bowyn would barely remember. She was a friend. Was it possible she was more than a friend now? Could they be a couple?

I knew, even as I thought it, that I was falling back into a familiar pattern—feeling jealous whenever Bowyn slept with anybody more than a couple of times. It had been the reason I'd finally decided I couldn't stay with him at the Temple anymore. I could handle him just having fun with people at random. I'd done the same. But I'd been bothered by him spending entire nights with Seth, sometimes for several nights in a row. Oh, it had always been open and I'd always known I could join them if I chose. But that fear Bowyn might come to love Seth more than he loved me had tormented me, until at last I gave him an ultimatum—either stay here with Seth or come back to Durham with me.

He'd chosen to stay.

The idea that Bowyn might be bisexual was a little strange, but I didn't worry about that. In and of itself, it wouldn't change much as far as I was concerned. But what if he'd fallen in love with Marianne? Bowyn and I were no longer a couple, I had to remind myself, our sexual acrobatics in the bedroom notwithstanding. His relationship with Marianne—or anybody else—really wasn't my concern.

Suddenly, Marianne's eyes appeared to focus on something specific near the edge of the forest above the backyard, and her mouth quirked up at one corner. "Oh look! There's Saint Francis."

I followed her gaze and saw Christopher standing near the trees. He had a bag of something—breadcrumbs?—and he was tossing handfuls to a huge flock of large black birds that had gathered around him. They could have been crows, but they seemed too large. Ravens, perhaps. They'd been rare in New Hampshire when I was a boy, but I'd read they'd become more common in recent years, especially this far north.

"Be nice," Bowyn warned.

"I'm just teasing." Marianne rolled her eyes at me, as if she thought Bowyn was the squarest square in Squaresville. "He feeds them every day," she told me, obviously referring to Christopher. "He spends more time with the birds than he does with people."

"Bowyn told me a little about him last night," I said. "It really sounds to me as if he might have issues the Temple can't help him with. I know I'm not an expert, but if he really can't deal with people touching him because he's been abused… doesn't that seem like something he should see a therapist about?"

She appeared to consider this but shrugged it off. "You might be right. But what can we do about it? We don't have any legal authority over him, so we can't force him into counseling. And if we ask him to leave, who knows what would happen to him? He was pretty badly hooked on heroin when he got here. At least he's drug-free now."

*Christ.* The more I learned about the kid, the more he was starting to get under my skin. Regardless of what Marianne said, I made up my mind to talk to Seth about him. Not that I could really do anything to help. I wasn't a psychologist. And maybe Bowyn and Marianne were right in thinking a safe place to retreat from the world that had been so cruel to him was what Christopher needed right now.

Still, I needed to reassure myself that Seth had the young man's best interests at heart.

I GOT my chance to talk to Seth just before lunch. As much as I loved reminiscing, I'd been getting antsy to get to work on the manuscript. So as soon as I could politely excuse myself, I left to find Seth. I'd half expected Bowyn to come along, but to my surprise—accompanied by a slight twinge of suspicion and jealousy—he chose to remain with Marianne.

I forced myself to stop being paranoid and focus on the business at hand.

It took a bit of searching and asking around, but I finally found Seth in the showers. With Rafe. And they weren't just washing each other. In fact, quite an audience had gathered to watch, something Seth had always gotten off on. I won't say it was exactly dull to watch him plow Rafe's perfect ass under the spray, but it was a bit like getting an hour into a porn film and realizing all the sex scenes with a particular star were basically the same. Seth always had to be on top; he always liked to bite the neck a bit—especially when he came—and he never really cared whether you got off or not. He didn't even bother to give Rafe a reach-around while they were fucking. Rafe had to jerk himself off.

I knew Seth was going to make a play for me before the week was out. It was inevitable. I also knew Bowyn wouldn't mind if I went for it. And if I were being honest with myself, I knew I wanted it. At least, part of me did. But watching Seth in the throes of an orgasm, with poor Rafe still furiously stroking himself to catch up, I made up my mind.

I was going to be the top this time. That or nothing.

When the show was over and the crowd had dispersed, I waited for Seth and Rafe to finish showering, responding with a good-natured "Not right now, thanks," when Rafe gave me a lascivious look and informed me he'd be good for another round in just a few minutes. I had work to do.

Seth sent Rafe off to find something else to occupy his time, much like a parent ordering a child to go out and play, and then escorted me up to the library. His hand somehow kept managing to find my ass as we climbed the stairs, but I ignored it. It wasn't going to be that easy for him. Not this time.

To Seth's credit, he rarely got upset when his advances were ignored. To him it was all a game, and I think he enjoyed the chase more than the sex at the end. Not immediately giving in just ramped up the excitement level for him. Once you understood that, he could be managed.

It was the neophytes who had trouble. Too often they felt inordinately flattered by Seth's attention, not realizing it was merely the fact that they were *new* that made them interesting to him. They then gave in too soon, only to find he'd grown bored after the first fuck. Sometimes, if a young man or woman was attractive enough, Seth might be able to sustain an interest in them for a few weeks or months. But it never lasted long.

Bowyn and I had managed to sustain his interest for years, but I think that was largely because we were his first men. His relationship with Alex had already deteriorated to a nonsexual level by the time the four of us met at that Masonic open house. When we all went out to dinner afterward, Bowyn and I gradually became aware Seth was hitting on us. I think he'd just begun to come to terms with his interest in men, and here were two twenty-one-year-olds who were both enthralled by him *and* gay. We played hard to get over the next few weeks, not really knowing how Alex would feel about it and not knowing if we wanted to expand our sex life to include a third person. But that just made Seth all the more determined to have us. And eventually he did, once Alex told us privately she was fine with it.

"I'VE TOLD Bowyn to get you a key," Seth said as he unlocked the library. "Your own key card as well. As one of the Brethren, you should have them anyway."

I frowned at the back of his head as I followed him in. "I'm not one of the Brethren, Seth. I dropped out eight years ago."

"You can't just stop being one of the Brethren. The Brethren were the founders of the Order. How can you stop being a founder? It's a *fait accompli*."

I knew it was hopeless to argue with him, so I let it drop. I'd need a key for the duration of the week at any rate, and I'd need to keep on his good side if I wanted to get anything lasting out of this arrangement. I still had plans to write an article about my transcription if I could get him to agree to it.

In daylight the library's stained glass windows—UV shielded, Seth informed me—were illuminated from outside, casting colored patterns of light onto the carpet. The windows were positioned so as to keep sunlight from hitting the old books in the stacks while still admitting a small amount of outside light. It truly was a magnificent room.

Seth didn't go to the drawers where the Ficino manuscript was being stored. Instead he directed me to a mahogany desk near the fake fireplace, where someone had set up a laptop.

"Your workstation," he announced proudly.

It was brand new and fairly powerful. I booted the thing up and stifled a groan at the artfully rendered and highly overblown insignia of the Order on the desktop, a silhouette of a raised sword piercing a crescent moon, carved into blue-gray marble with yellow-red flame shining through from the inner core of the stone. There was a folder on the desktop called *Missa Spiritus*—the Mass of the Spirit—which contained several high-resolution image files, and when I opened the first image, I could see that this was indeed what the composer had called it.

The name sounded vaguely alchemical. Like many alchemical scholars, Ficino believed in a World Soul—the *anima mundi*—which was the soul of *everything*, of all living things. It is from the *anima mundi* that our individual souls arise. In a sense a man's soul is conceived within the *anima mundi* as a thought is conceived in the mind. And that soul, that individual *anima*, is the perfect image of the man, realized in all his potentialities. The human body, on the other hand, is inert and lifeless without the soul. But there is an ethereal substance called the *spiritus*—spirit or breath—which links the soul to the body, allowing the soul to "animate" the body and experience the physical world through the senses of the body. It was Ficino's belief that the human spirit would respond to the proper musical harmonies, causing the link to the soul to be strengthened. And as the link is strengthened, the body is drawn closer to the perfect image of itself that is the soul, and in doing so leaves behind illness and imbalance and is restored to full health.

In addition to the image files, there was a simple music notation program installed on the laptop that I'd used before. That would make my life easier. The laptop also had the basic Musical Instrument Digital Interface—MIDI—playback capability all computers have these days, so I could listen to the transcription as I worked on it. The MIDI instruments on the computer wouldn't sound anything like real human voices singing the mass, but it would be invaluable in cases where the manuscript was difficult to read.

"Am I allowed to take the laptop out of the library?" I asked.

Seth looked genuinely shocked. "Allowed? There are no rules here for you, my love. You can do whatever you like."

"Really?" I retorted, not pleased that he kept calling me "my love." "In that case, I think I'll take a piss on the Ficino manuscript pages. Or maybe I'll just burn them."

Seth laughed and flopped down in one of the antique stuffed chairs on the other side of the fake fire. "Touché. That would annoy me. Let's say you can do anything you like, within reason. And taking the laptop to your room or outside to work in the fresh air is perfectly reasonable."

"What if I want to take it back to the university?"

"I'd rather you didn't."

I'd remained standing while checking the laptop out. Now I took a seat in the leather-upholstered wooden chair drawn up before the desk. It was comfortable, though more for reading than leaning forward over a computer. A proper computer desk chair would have been preferable, but this would do. "Since I'm not being paid for this—"

"Oh, Jeremy! I thought you'd be delighted at being the first to transcribe such a rare piece of music."

"—I'd like to write an article about my transcription and submit it to an academic press." Getting something like this into a peer-reviewed publication would be enormous. At least, in the academic circles I traveled in.

Seth stopped his protests and gave me a shrewd look. He'd never told me what he'd done in the corporate world before retiring early, but the man was certainly no stranger to wheeling and dealing. "The manuscript belongs to the Order and the Temple."

"And I am a high-ranking member of both," I persisted. "Or so you keep saying."

"So you are."

Perhaps I should have kept my mouth shut on that point. I seemed to have just conceded him a minor victory and taken another step back into the world I'd been trying to stay on the fringe of.

Seth's fingers drummed out a haphazard rhythm on the arm of his chair. "How long do you think this article will take?"

"A few months," I replied. I would try to have the transcription done by Seth's deadline, but then I'd want to check and recheck my work and do some research to compare it to similar musical works from the time period. There was no sense in rushing it, since as far as I knew nobody else was even aware that the manuscript existed. "Perhaps half a year."

That seemed to satisfy him. He nodded and stood. But if I thought he was going to leave me to my work, I was mistaken. I watched him as he wandered into the stacks for a moment and then returned with a copy of Carl Jung's *Alchemy*.

Falling back into the chair, he glanced at me questioningly. "You don't mind, do you? If I do some research of my own while you work?" Jung's book was an in-depth analysis of the symbolism of alchemy from a psychological standpoint, and it was as good a reference as any for sorting out what the frontispiece of the manuscript might have encoded into it.

"No, I guess not."

I left Seth to that task while I turned to the computer and opened one of the image files. The first thing I needed to do was enhance it to make it more legible, and once again I found Seth had considered that. The software I needed was already installed.

I bent over the laptop and got to work.


ANYONE WHO'D seen the film *Amadeus* might imagine that as I transcribed the Renaissance notation, I could hear the melodies and harmonies taking form in my mind, and I was overwhelmed by its magnificence. Sadly, that was never my experience. I could sight-read well enough, picking my way through a written melody without the aid of a musical instrument. But transcribing fifteenth-century notation from a poorly preserved document was a slow, finicky process. It would be a day or so before I had anything coherent.

A couple of hours later, Seth broke into my concentration to say, "That's enough for this morning. Lunch is going to be served in about five minutes."

I looked up from the screen, blinking at him like a groundhog poking its head up into daylight. "Already?"

"Come along. You can get back to it after you've eaten."

I stretched and realized my body was extremely unhappy with the position I'd been sitting in for so long. Perhaps taking the laptop down to Bowyn's room wasn't a bad idea.

I packed it up into the laptop case I found tucked under the desk and then followed Seth downstairs.

While we were on the landing between the third and second floors, the church bell sounded over the grounds again.

"Noon," Seth explained, and it took me a moment to realize he meant it was time to perform Resh.

The large arched window on the landing looked out upon the front of the house, which meant we were looking south. By a happy coincidence, this is the direction one should face when performing Resh at noon, since the sun is in the south at that time of day. At least, if you're in the northern hemisphere.

"Resh" is the letter of the Hebrew alphabet that corresponds to *R* in the Latin alphabet, and its name translates to "head." Performing Resh is about maintaining spiritual discipline, but not only that. It's also about honoring the head, represented by the sun—intellect and conscious thought—and reaffirming your dedication to what Crowley called the "Great Work." That is, the work of achieving higher consciousness and spirituality, of establishing communication with your higher being.

Seth fell naturally into position, making the sign of fire—an upright triangle, made by pressing the thumbs and index fingers of both hands together—a couple of inches in front of his forehead and chanting, "Khaire o Helie! We greet Thee, Helios triumphing, Helios the beautiful, who travelest over the heavens in Thy chariot at midday. Thy fire-darting steeds, Pyois, Aeos, Aethon, and Phlegon draw Thee across the heavens. Khaire su ek thronon eou! We greet Thee from the Throne of Morning!"

Anyone familiar with Crowley's version of this adoration would immediately recognize that we'd changed it. In the infant days of the

Order, a friend of ours—Maureen Katt, a student of ancient Greek religion—had assisted us in coming up with ancient Greek versions of the adorations that were more in sync with what we were doing.

I set the laptop down in the corner and followed along as best I could, feeling self-conscious because I could only remember *most* of the chant.

No doubt all our chanting and postures would have seemed bizarre and silly to someone who hadn't studied ceremonial magick. It certainly had seemed that way to *me* when Bowyn and I first became interested in it all those years ago. But Bowyn had been raised Catholic, and he assured me Catholics had their own rituals that weren't all that different, from his perspective. I took his word for it. I was raised Baptist, and we were all taught that Catholics were idol worshippers and misguided tools of Satan.

I shuddered to think what Reverend Thompson would say about me now.

Outside, on the front lawn, several initiates and neophytes had stopped what they were doing to perform Resh as well. Seen from this perspective, it was an eerie sight, reminiscent of the old *Star Trek* episode in which everybody in town suddenly stops in unison at a certain time of day and goes temporarily insane. Except the people on the lawn were standing still, chanting, rather than running around tearing their clothes.

Then, just like that, they all started moving again, going about their business.

One person in particular caught my eye. It was Christopher again. The young man had not only stopped to perform Resh like the others, he'd stripped his robe off to do it. And we didn't wear anything under our robes.

Seth followed my gaze and smiled. "I don't know where that boy got it into his head that he has to be naked to perform Resh—or pretty much any other ritual. But I can't say I mind. He's lovely, isn't he?"

His tone, like a man showing off a new piece of art he'd just purchased, irritated me. I turned on him and said curtly, "And from what I've heard, off-limits."

"He's eighteen."

"What I mean is, I've heard he doesn't like to be touched, due to a history of abuse."

"Are you annoyed you can't have him?"

That pissed me off even more. "No. I'm concerned about him. The Temple is the last place I'd send a young man with those kinds of issues."

"He's perfectly safe here," Seth said with a dismissive wave of his hand.

"I've already heard the spiel about how he's happy here, and he'll end up a junkie living on the streets if we turn him away." I hadn't meant to say "we," but it had slipped out.

Seth continued to watch Christopher through the window, and his expression did at least seem more compassionate than lascivious. "Did Bowyn tell you Christopher's father not only molested him, but also rented him out whenever he needed cash or heroin?"

I felt nauseated. Apparently I'd been leading a very sheltered life, because I couldn't conceive of a parent being that evil. "No."

"Do you really think that the Temple—that *I*—am worse for the boy than that?"

His tone seemed less angry than hurt, giving me a strong desire to reach out to him, to say something conciliatory. But there was one thing still bothering me. "Bowyn told me Christopher was corresponding with you for an entire year before he came here."

"He was underage. Nobody under eighteen is allowed to come to the Temple. You were there when we instituted that policy."

"Yes. But why didn't you do anything to help him during that year? Why didn't you call the police? Or Child Services?"

Seth shook his head and sighed. "I swear to you, Jeremy, I would have if I'd known what was happening. But I didn't. Honestly. All he ever talked about in his e-mails was how much the philosophies of the Temple were in sync with his own beliefs—largely based upon what he'd read on our website—and how desperate he was to come join the Order. The only thing he said about his home life was that he was miserable living with his father and needed to get out of there. It sounded like typical teenage melodrama to me. I'm no psychologist."

He took me by the shoulders and looked me directly in the eye. "I was so happy when you came back, but you seem bound and determined to hate me."

"Don't be melodramatic," I replied, but I added more gently, "I don't hate you."

"What is it, then?"

We'd been over all this when I left. And a lot of what I'd been feeling eight years ago no longer seemed to matter. But some things still did. "I love you, Seth." He started to smile, so I quickly added, "But I don't trust you."

"Why?"

"You manipulate people. You always have."

"To do what?"

"To love you."

Seth looked stunned for a moment, releasing my shoulders and taking a step back. But he was never one to remain off balance for long. "I don't have to manipulate anyone into loving me, Jeremy." He smiled and waved his arm in a flourish. "They just can't help themselves."

I couldn't help but laugh. In a way, he was right. He was pure ego, but he manifested it with such a childlike joy, most of us found it endearing. Even Alex, who'd known him longer than anyone, tolerated his antics with wry amusement.

"If you hadn't made Bowyn choose," he pointed out, "we could have stayed together—the three of us. We could have worked out our differences, and we would all have been happier for it."

I wasn't sure I could argue that. Certainly *my* solution hadn't made any of us happy. "You might be right."

He leaned down to kiss me gently on the mouth, and I let him. "Let's get to lunch, my love. You're welcome to talk to Christopher directly about the correspondence he and I had before he arrived. If he gives his permission, I'll be happy to let you read the e-mails. I'm sure they'll put your mind at ease."


LUNCH WAS just as frenzied as breakfast had been. I was disappointed Bowyn and Marianne were nowhere to be found, but when I wandered into the living room with my sandwich of marinated tofu dipped in spiced nutritional yeast and fried, I found Christopher perched on one arm of the sofa. I couldn't escape from this kid. Of course, we were all living in one house, even if it was an enormous one.

I decided this was a good time to get to know him a little. The room was full of people, so I wasn't going to start prying into his personal life, but I could at least introduce myself.

I sat down on the sofa next to him, which put him in an odd position, looking down at me.

"Hi, Christopher. My name is Jeremy."

I extended my hand but he ignored it. He simply nodded and said, "Hey."

"I heard you singing this morning," I persisted. "You have a wonderful voice."

Instead of saying "thanks" or something equivalent, his eyes narrowed suspiciously and he said, "Look, I'm sure you've heard all kinds of shit about me, but I don't let guys fuck me anymore. Okay?"

Well, then. So much for my evil plans. The kid was making me feel like a letch just for talking to him. "I wasn't trying to come on to you, Christopher."

"You've been watching me."

I wasn't sure how to respond to that, particularly since it was true. One of the young women walking by laughed and told him, "Everyone watches you, beautiful."

She disappeared and Christopher continued to look at me accusingly.

"It's true," I confessed. "I have been watching you. For a number of reasons. But not because I'm trying to have sex with you."

"Why, then?"

"Well, to start with, I'm a music professor, and I've been conducting choir for five years. I wasn't lying when I said you had a beautiful voice. I would love to have the opportunity to conduct you in a choir someday."

"I just sing for the gods," the young man said.

"Any gods in particular? Or all gods?"

"Odin."

*The ultimate father figure*, I thought. And a somewhat dark one. A god of warriors, Odin was inclined to "reward" his followers by arranging for them to die in battle so they could sooner join him in Valhalla. As a god of war, Odin's pets were animals that scavenged battlefields for corpses to eat—wolves and ravens.

"Is that why you feed the ravens?" I asked.

But I'd said the wrong thing. Christopher looked very uncomfortable and stood up to leave. "I'd really like it if you didn't keep watching everything I do."

Then he walked away, and those people who'd been sitting near us made a concerted effort to pretend they hadn't been listening.

Christopher was making me feel like some kind of stalker just for taking an interest in his welfare. But I supposed he was right. He was eighteen and legally an adult. Just because he looked like a wounded angel was no reason to assume he couldn't take care of himself.

At any rate, he'd specifically asked me to butt out, so I didn't have much choice.

# Chapter Seven

I RETREATED to Bowyn's room after lunch. As nice as the library was, I really didn't need Seth hovering over me while I worked. And part of me was starting to fret about not seeing Bowyn. He hadn't come in to get lunch, and neither had Marianne.

I knew I had no right to be jealous if they were involved with one another. I'd left him—not the other way around. Sure, I'd expected him to follow, and he'd made his decision. But, as Seth had pointed out, if I'd never forced him to make that decision, we might still be together. He had the right to be with Marianne or anyone else now. He'd slept with me last night, but that didn't necessarily mean anything in Bowyn's world. He'd always had a casual attitude toward sex, even in college.

Anyway, this was all speculation. I could be completely wrong in my suspicions.

I did my best to focus on the Ficino manuscript, far too conscious of the time crawling by as I secretly hoped for Bowyn to walk into the room.

The garage was toward the back of the house, which meant I could see part of it from the bedroom window. That was how I saw the same car Bowyn had picked me up in pulling in sometime around eight. A moment later, Bowyn and Marianne walked out—both in street clothes—and headed into the house. Along the way, Bowyn glanced up at the window where I sat, and I instinctively pulled back, hoping he hadn't seen me spying on him.

He opened the door to the room a couple of minutes later.

"Hey," he said, attempting to sound casual. But there was an odd tightness to his body, unlike the fluid way he normally moved. He was tense about something. "Have you gotten much done?"

"A little," I replied. Then, without really thinking, I added, "You've been gone a long time."

Bowyn hesitated and then slowly closed the door behind him before responding. "Yeah. Marianne had a doctor's appointment in Berlin, so I drove her. I didn't realize how long it would take. Then we went out to dinner. Did you need me for something?"

"No," I answered truthfully. "It's none of my business. I was just curious."

"It's cool. Here," he added, tossing a key ring to me. "Seth had me stop to get this made up for you."

The ring had both a key and a magnetic key card attached to it. They were obviously for access to the library. "Thanks."

There was an awkward pause, during which neither of us knew what to say next. I couldn't recall that ever happening when we were together. But I was stuck, wanting to pry into what was going on with him and Marianne but knowing I had no right to. And apparently he wasn't going to volunteer anything.

At last, Bowyn walked over to the desk and peered over my shoulder at the music notation I'd been entering into the MIDI program. "Can I hear it?"

"Not yet," I said, shaking my head. "It's a complete mess right now. I just entered my best guess for all four parts, but when I try to put them together, they don't harmonize well and they end in different places. Whoever wrote this used some unconventional notation," I added. "Though the conventions in this time period did fluctuate a lot."

In modern musical notation, at least for piano and choir, we're used to seeing all the parts laid out on what's called a grand stave—the soprano, alto, tenor, and bass parts on two or four staves, one above the other, so the harmonies are obvious to anyone who can read music. But in the fifteenth century, each part was written out by itself, often on entirely different pages of the manuscript. And a part with many notes might fill up an entire page, whereas a part with fewer notes of longer duration—equaling the same amount of time, musically—might only be a couple of lines long to save space. It was up to the performers and the conductor to put them together into a coherent whole when the piece was performed. To further complicate matters, the duration of notes was somewhat vague in the notation. Long notes were often represented by long marks on the staff, and short notes were represented by short marks. If several notes were meant to be strung together melodically, thin lines might connect them. In other cases they were blurred together like a line written in thick magic marker. Rests were often even more vague. And forget bar lines, time signatures, and ties. Those were for wussies. If the performers sang their parts correctly, they would line up and everybody would finish at the same time.

*Good luck. May God go with you.*

"You still aren't convinced it's Ficino, then?" Bowyn asked, no doubt because I'd said "whoever wrote this."

I shrugged. "It's possible," I admitted. "What little handwriting there is in the margins looks like his, though I'm hardly a handwriting expert." I would probably be forced to accept the conclusions of the experts Seth had hired. But I was hesitant. If I published a paper making the outrageous claim that Ficino had written a full polyphonic mass, and it turned out to be a fake, nobody would ever take me seriously in this field again.

"Can you read any of it?"

"Some. But most of the Italian notes are directions to the choir about how to perform certain passages. Nothing that would clearly point to Ficino as the composer. I really wish I knew what was in the libretto."

Bowyn nodded and went over to the closet. I was acutely aware that he'd neglected to kiss me or even touch my shoulder. Something was clearly bothering him.

I watched him undress, loving the smooth, golden skin and well-defined muscles I was presented with as each item of clothing came off. He slipped into one of his brown robes and tossed his street clothes into the basket in the bottom of the closet. He must have changed into his street clothes while I'd been up in the library earlier.

As Seth had done in the library, Bowyn proceeded to grab a book to read. He flopped down on the bed and glanced quickly at me before asking, "Do you mind if I stay while you work?"

"No, of course not."

He opened the book and began reading, so I turned back to the laptop.

In addition to the technical issues I was having with the music, there were other elements of the mass that were bothering me. Initially it had a fairly typical structure for a mass, beginning with the Kyrie and Gloria. The libretto for the Kyrie was in Greek, but it's the same for every mass, so there was no difficulty translating it:

*Kyrie eleison;*
*Christe eleison;*
*Kyrie eleison*
"Lord, have mercy;

Christ, have mercy;

Lord, have mercy."

The Gloria was in Latin, which I do read, but again it's the same for every mass, so hardly a challenge. But the next section in a traditional mass would generally be the Credo. Yet that was missing. In its place was something else entirely—a very slow-moving choral piece that gradually built and intensified, with an increasing amount of sustained notes and suspensions toward the end.

In Samuel Barber's *Adagio for Strings*, there is a sustained note at the climax that seems to go on forever—nine beats, in some performances. Far longer than we expect it to. I was once in a room full of people engaged in conversation while that piece played on the stereo. Suddenly everybody noticed at the same moment they'd stopped talking, because that note was forcing them to hold their breath. It finished, and in the long moment of silence that followed, everyone collectively gasped. There were passages in this section of the Ficino manuscript that put me in mind of that, with notes that threatened to exhaust the performers as the music built in intensity.

In practice, of course, a choir could sustain very long notes simply by staggering breathing. If a performer ran out of breath, he or she could quietly take a breath and then fade back in, as long as nobody else took a breath at the same time. It wasn't uncommon for breaths to be scheduled at certain points in the music to avoid making them audible.

But what were all of these sustained notes and crescendos trying to accomplish? I had no idea. And this style of music was extremely atypical for the time period, which meant I'd have to prove it wasn't a forgery. The libretto for this section was written in the Greek alphabet, and I assumed it was this text that had been sent to the translator in Greece. I'd have to check with Seth to see if there had been any progress on it.

In addition, there were odd symbols I couldn't identify interjected into the musical notation itself. They were somewhat like Greek characters, but I knew they weren't part of the standard Greek alphabet. They were inserted in a seemingly haphazard manner, sprinkled throughout all the vocal parts. Always, a Latin character would be written alongside the symbol, but if it was meant to be a translation of the symbol, I was still lost. The Latin characters were all consonants, with no vowels at all, such as MCMGHPD.

What the hell did that mean? Of course some Semitic languages, such as Hebrew, don't write out the vowel sounds, though Modern Hebrew has a system for clarifying them. But if the symbols were from some other alphabet, it was one I wasn't familiar with.

I couldn't figure out where these strange symbols fit into the piece, or if they fit at all. Ignoring them seemed to work, somewhat. They were generally below or above the staff, so it was unlikely they represented notes. But the harmonies in the piece often seemed odd, as if there were notes missing. For instance, the music would sometimes pause on a chord, with four voices, but the tenor doubling the bass—that is, on the same note as the bass, but an octave higher—and the soprano doubling the alto, leaving a chord that ultimately consisted of two notes. Two notes do not a chord make. Not in western music theory. Our ears are trained to expect a third note. Two notes leaves us feeling unsettled, and uncertain which chord we're actually listening to.

Sunset was heralded by another deep, resonant church bell ringing out over the Temple grounds.

Bowyn set his book down on the bed and stood to stretch. Then he began performing Resh, facing the bedroom door, which was roughly the west. I joined him, figuring I might as well fall into the routine for as long as I was staying there.

After we finished, we went down to dinner. Breakfast, lunch, and dinner were always after Resh, even though that meant eating close to nine o'clock in the evening in June, and around four thirty in December. It was part of the discipline. Don't ask me which one of us thought that up over a decade ago. It just seemed like a good idea at the time.

Bowyn was still distracted, which bothered me. He gave me a quick peck on the mouth as we left the room, but his mind was clearly elsewhere. When we joined the others in the dining room, he immediately wandered off.

Frustrated, I decided to take my plate back up to the bedroom. Alex would kill me if I didn't return it to the kitchen, but I could bring it down later. As I climbed the stairs, however, I found my way blocked by Rafe.

"Brethren," he said smoothly, somehow managing to make the word sound sexy. I could feel his eyes scanning my body as he smiled at me. "How are things in the Renaissance?"

I wasn't sure if he was being sarcastic or merely playful, so I replied, "All right, I guess."

"You guess?"

I shrugged, the plate of risotto starting to feel heavy in my right hand. "There are some symbols on the staves that I can't make much sense of. I mean, they look familiar, but I can't place them."

"Symbols?" he asked, taking a step closer. His hand on the banister brushed against my left hand. I was tempted to pull it away but couldn't think of a compelling reason to do so. He *was* dead sexy, after all. And certainly Seth and Bowyn wouldn't mind me flirting with him. Or doing other things with him, for that matter.

"I'm not sure what they are. Some sort of occult alphabet, perhaps. But nothing I recognize. They're always paired with a Latin letter, but even those don't make sense, because they're all consonants. No vowels at all."

Rafe was looking at me intently with those penetrating, dark eyes. There was something grave in his expression, even as his fingers lightly traced the length of mine in an unmistakably seductive gesture. "I remember seeing them on the manuscript," he purred. "I can show you what they are."

"You can?" It was enormously arrogant of me to assume that, just because Rafe looked as if he belonged on a fashion runway, he couldn't possibly know something that I, Herr Professor, didn't know. So I mentally slapped myself and asked, "What are they?"

He smiled and bent down to bring his lips close to my ear. "Come to the chapel after midnight."

His breath was hot against my earlobe, and my voice quavered a bit as I responded. "I'm not going to fuck you in the chapel."

He laughed and kissed me lightly on the neck, causing me to shiver. "You can have me whenever and wherever you want, Brethren. But I'm not asking you to come to the chapel for sex. There are better places for that."

Then he slid his rough, razor-stubbled chin along my cheek and finished by delivering a firm kiss to my mouth. He was a damn good kisser.

Rafe chuckled and pulled away, a smirk on his lips, before slipping past me to continue down the stairs. After a moment of standing there like an idiot, with my plate still in one hand and the beginnings of an erection tenting the cloth of my robe, I climbed the steps again. Regardless of what happened in the chapel, I was seriously tempted to take him up on that offer.

BOWYN FAILED to return to the bedroom after dinner. By this point I'd given up trying to be reasonable about it. Where the fuck was he? He'd been so attentive yesterday. What could have changed since then? Was there something going on with Marianne? Could she be seriously ill? If so, why not tell me about it?

I felt the hair prick up on my scalp as another possibility occurred to me. What if the little bit of pudginess I'd observed on Marianne that morning was more than just a few extra pounds. Could it be a baby bump? Bowyn's baby?

*Oh Christ.* That would certainly complicate things. Of course, that was a pretty big leap. And probably just my jealousy talking.

Too many possibilities and not enough data. It was pointless to fret about this when I knew nothing about it. I would simply have to get Bowyn to open up about whatever was bothering him. In the meantime I had a fifteenth-century manuscript demanding my attention.

By the time the chimes rang out midnight, I'd gotten no further in interpreting those bizarre symbols, and Bowyn hadn't shown up either. Frustrated, I performed Resh and then headed downstairs to meet Rafe in the chapel. Hopefully he really did have some information. Though why he couldn't have told me at dinner, I had no idea.

If this was just a ruse to get me alone for sex, I'd be very annoyed. I'd fuck him, of course. But I'd be annoyed about it.

# Chapter Eight

As I walked down the path to the chapel, the cold wind whipped my robe around my legs and cut through the fabric to raise goose bumps on my skin. In winter they would be made of wool, with a cotton lining. But the one I was wearing at present was just a moderately heavy cotton. Okay during the day, but not so great on an October night.

In addition to being cold, it was fucking creepy out here. I was the only one outside right now, as far as I could see. The night was cloudy, so the moon was mostly hidden, and the faux Victorian streetlamps didn't give out as much light as I would have liked. I had to dart through patches of darkness between them. My muffled footsteps on the cobblestone, mixing with the sound of the wind and the faint buzzing of the flickering lightbulbs, produced a soundtrack suitable for a horror movie.

Damn it, I should have been smart enough to bring a flashlight!

I was relieved to finally reach the chapel, but my relief was short-lived. After pushing the creaking metal door open—*of course* the hinges had to creak!—I was confronted by utter darkness. Or maybe not entirely "utter." Just below the domed ceiling were seven stained glass windows, containing the alchemical symbols of the seven planets of astrology—the Sun, the Moon, Venus, Mars, Mercury, Jupiter, and Saturn. The anemic gray moonlight faintly illuminated these from outside.

I reached to my right, where the light switch had been years ago, but found nothing but smooth wall.

"Seth had the switch removed," Rafe's voice said out of the darkness, startling me.

He switched on a flashlight, sweeping the beam across me for a second, before diverting it away from my eyes. It was still annoying, because I couldn't really see him at all. Just a spot of light in the center of the chamber.

"Why the hell would he do that?" I said, willing my voice not to sound nervous. I failed.

"There are fake gaslights, controlled by a switch hidden behind the altar. You know how he likes to give the illusion we're contemporaries of Crowley and the Golden Dawn."

I did, but that didn't explain why Rafe was toying with me. "Fine. Could you turn the lights on, please?"

"Not yet."

The flashlight beam swept up to the ceiling while I debated whether I trusted Rafe enough to step inside. I was still standing in the doorway, so my exit wasn't blocked. I could probably escape if I had to. That is, unless he had a gun. The idea was ludicrous, of course. Why *would* he have a gun? I was just letting the creepy setting get to me.

Still, I backed up a step, reaching out to hold on to the doorframe. Rafe remained oddly quiet for a long time, sweeping the light around, illuminating all the stained glass windows, one after another.

This was getting me nowhere fast, and my ass still had ice-cold wind blowing up it. "Look, Rafe, if you don't have anything to tell me about the symbols in the manuscript, I'd just as soon get back inside where it's warm."

"I told you I would help you and I will." The flashlight swung down to illuminate the floor between us, forming a path of light to where he was standing. "Come here."

I was still nervous about being alone with him as long as he was playing this silly game. But I took a breath to calm my nerves and walked across the marble floor. When I reached him in the center, I felt his hand grip my shoulder. It was all I could do to keep from screaming as he pulled me close and slid his arm around both my shoulders. Our faces were suddenly so close that I could smell the faint scent of his cologne and feel the heat coming off his skin. When he spoke, his breath brushed my ear.

"What did the symbols look like?"

This annoyed me. If he was claiming to know what they were, he should know what they looked like. But I played along. "Like letters from the Greek alphabet. But I know the Greek alphabet—a little, anyway— and those symbols are different."

"Different," he said, softly, in affirmation. "But still Greek."

He swung the light of the flashlight upward and I watched it climb one of the marble columns to the level of the ceiling, where the column joined a circular cornice. Above it, smaller columns continued up to a second cornice, with the stained glass windows set in between the columns. Above that was the dome. The dome itself was glorious, with a Renaissance-style painting of the fall of Prometheus. I'd been at the Temple when Seth commissioned it from an artist he knew in Boston, though I could no longer remember the woman's name.

But what drew my attention, at this moment, were the symbols carved into the small column the flashlight was illuminating. Seven symbols in a vertical line. They were about forty feet above me, but there was no doubt in my mind. "That's it!" I practically shouted while Rafe laughed gently in my ear. "Or some of it, anyway."

Not all the symbols I remembered from the manuscript were on that column, but Rafe swung the light around to another column and said, "Is that it? Or is *this* it?"

The symbols on this column were different from those on the first—at least, some of them were.

Rafe swung the light again. "Or is *this* it?"

He laughed when I grabbed his arm in my excitement and began guiding the hand that held the flashlight from one column to the next, examining the entire circle above us. Each column had seven symbols, and as I moved around the circle, I could see that they were in a pattern. The first symbol of one column became the second of the one next to it, and the third of the one next to that. The order of symbols remained constant, so as I moved clockwise around the circle, I got the impression of a steady stream of symbols flowing upward.

One thing I was absolutely certain of—those carvings hadn't been there eight years ago. Seth must have had them added. "What are they?"

"What do you think?" Rafe asked, infuriatingly. "Seven lines of seven symbols? Seven *ancient Greek* symbols?"

"Well, fourteen symbols," I corrected. That was why no one column had all the symbols on it.

By this point, Rafe wasn't even trying to be subtle about nuzzling my ear. As he nibbled my earlobe, I could feel my cock stiffening, but I ignored it. A nagging feeling in the back of my mind was telling me I should know exactly what the symbols were.

Then suddenly it hit me. Of course.

"Notes," I said. "The symbols are notes. These," I added, indicating the carvings, "are Greek musical scales—Lydian, Phrygian, Dorian, Hypolydian, Hypophrygian, Locrian, and Mixolydian." Each scale consisted of seven notes, separated by a whole step or half step in the scale. Fourteen of them simply meant the scales were traversing two octaves, an average range for the human voice.

Rafe's hand found my cock and began kneading it through my robe. "Good boy. Now let me give you a reward."

It felt good, but I pushed his hand away. Even though our doctrine incorporated open—some might say rampant—sexuality into our basic beliefs, the chapel was sacred space, and it still felt disrespectful to receive a quick and dirty hand job in it.

"Not tonight," I said, finding his mouth in the dark to give him a kiss by way of thanks. "We'll find time to play tomorrow."

"Promise?"

"Yes." But there was still one thing bothering me. More a matter of pride, really. "If you already knew the symbols were notes, why didn't you transcribe them?"

"I don't know anything about music," Rafe said. "If you came here every day, you'd have these symbols etched into your brain, just like the rest of us."

"Seth must have known the symbols were notes."

"Obviously," Rafe agreed, sounding as if he were already growing bored with the conversation now that he knew he wasn't going to get laid. "And he assumed you would recognize them. You are a musical expert, after all."

Ouch.

"Ancient Greek notation was never my field of expertise," I protested.

Rafe waved a hand dismissively. "Well, you know them now. As for Seth, he might know what the symbols are, but that doesn't mean he knows what they're for or why they're scattered all over the manuscript."

No. Of course, he wouldn't. That was for me to decipher.


BOWYN WAS in the room when I returned, already undressed and in bed, reading. He positively glared at me when I walked in.

"Did you have fun?" he asked.

I didn't like the tone of accusation in his voice. "Fun?"

"With Rafe. In the chapel."

Of course, the bedroom window faced out on the chapel. He could have seen us coming and going. But it wasn't like Bowyn to be jealous.

"We didn't fuck around in the chapel if that's what you mean. Though it wasn't for lack of him trying."

He didn't respond to that, so I slipped out of my shoes—moccasins, really—and pulled my robe over my head. Then I draped it over the back of the desk chair. "If you really want to know, we did arrange to fool around a bit sometime tomorrow."

Bowyn sighed and set his book down on the nightstand. "I'm sorry. You're right. I'm being childish."

Naked, I crawled onto the bed and straddled him. He was under the blankets from the waist down, but I planted a kiss on his bare chest before raising my head to kiss him on the mouth.

"It's not like screwing Rafe is one of my life goals," I said. "I'll tell him no if you want me to."

"I'm sorry. That isn't what I want. Go ahead and have fun with him, or anyone else you like. I'm just in a pissy mood. And frankly, there are plenty of other guys here I could point you at. You can do better than that self-centered prima donna."

That seemed oddly judgmental, coming from Bowyn. He generally had a live-and-let-live philosophy. Had there been some bad blood between him and Rafe? "I wasn't planning on running away to the Casbah with him. It's just a fuck."

Bowyn laughed, though his eyes still looked troubled.

"I wish you'd tell me what's been bothering you all day," I said softly. "It's only our second day together, and already I feel as if we've been fighting."

Bowyn reached up and brushed his fingers along the side of my face. He hesitated for a long moment, clearly wanting to say something but not knowing how. I waited patiently, afraid anything I said might derail whatever it was he was trying to get out.

At last he said, "Marianne's pregnant."

"With your baby."

He looked surprised I'd already guessed but simply responded, "Yes."

Even though I'd suspected it, hearing him say it out loud made my heart sink. After last night part of me had been hoping we might find a way to be together again. Now that hope was fading. "So you're a couple, then?"

He shook his head. "No, it's not like that. Ever since Jack passed away… she's been regretting they never had a child together. They tried, and she did get pregnant, but there was a miscarriage."

That, I'd never been told.

Bowyn continued, "She was devastated, of course, so she refused to try again for a while. Then Jack was diagnosed, and, well… it just never happened. She blames herself now, for not trying again while they still had the chance."

"So you offered to be a sperm donor?"

"Basically." Bowyn rubbed a hand through his thick blond hair. "Frankly, I'm beginning to wish we'd gone to a clinic so I could have just jerked off in a cup."

"But you had sex instead?"

He nodded. "I didn't think it would be a big deal. I wasn't all that into it—I really just don't find women very interesting, sexually. But with a little prepping, I was able to pull it off."

The image that brought to my mind was amusing, but I forced myself not to laugh. Something was clearly upsetting him, and we hadn't come to that part yet. I doubted it was the sex in and of itself. Bowyn had had sex with a lot of men over the years, and he'd confessed to me in the past that some of them really hadn't been attractive to him. But he'd gone through with it to avoid hurt feelings.

"We did it nearly every night," he went on, "for a couple of weeks. Then we gave it a rest. Fortunately it took. I was really not looking forward to doing it again."

"So what's the problem?" I pressed.

He laid his head back, thumped it gently against the headboard, and moaned. "Everything. She's been weird ever since we had sex— kind of possessive. I was stupid when I thought we could fuck around without it affecting our friendship. It's kind of cool to think I might be a dad. I'm excited about that part. But when we started this… well, it's going to mean a lot more changes than I expected. And there's a chance she might lose the baby."

"What? How?"

"It's called Rhesus isoimmunization. After the first miscarriage, her body developed antibodies—antibodies against Rh positive blood. And thanks to me, that's the blood type the baby has." He rubbed his face with both hands. "They gave her a shot of something called anti-D immunoglobulin right after the miscarriage to try to prevent the condition, but it didn't help. She probably shouldn't have tried to get pregnant again or… she should have had my blood tested first. But she didn't do that, and I didn't know it could be a problem. So now she's pregnant, and her body is producing antibodies that are attacking the new baby."

I'd never heard of anything like that. It sounded horrifying. I took his hand in both of mine and stroked it, not really sure what I could do to comfort him. And poor Marianne must have been going through hell with the threat of another miscarriage looming over her. I couldn't even imagine how rough this would be for her.

"Is there anything they can do?" I asked, certain that sounded incredibly lame.

"They've been monitoring her, and it doesn't look like the baby's in too much danger yet." Bowyn shrugged. "She just passed four months and so far so good. But her doctor decided to give her some of the anti-D immunoglobulin intravenously today, and it made her feel pretty sick."

"Is she all right?"

"I guess so, apart from feeling crappy. Beyond that, we've been making offerings to Eileithyia, and we'll just have to hope for the best."

Eileithyia was a Greek goddess of childbirth. Yes, in addition to the ceremonial aspects of the Order, we also believed in and worshipped the ancient Greek gods. Well, technically we believed in *all* gods. But the ones we worshipped were generally from the Greek pantheon. Not that the Temple would throw anyone out for worshipping Odin, as Christopher seemed to, or any other god, including Yahweh or Christ. But the Order was focused on Greek deities. This was one of the differences between our Order and Crowley's occult order, the Ordo Templi Orientis—they were largely focused on Egyptian deities.

I got up briefly to turn the lights off and then slipped under the covers so I could snuggle up to Bowyn. This time he seemed to welcome it. We put our arms around each other and held each other close. Even though we were both naked, neither of us made any move to get the other aroused. I wasn't feeling particularly sexual at the moment and neither was Bowyn. We simply held each other.

I still had a lot of unanswered questions, but they would have to wait. Tonight Bowyn needed comforting, so that was what I would give him. Tomorrow we could talk about all this, and I could hopefully find a way to be there for Marianne as well.

I WOKE in the middle of the night with a vague feeling I'd just heard something—something not quite right. Bowyn was curled up against my back, sound asleep, his soft, regular breathing tickling the back of my neck. The room seemed completely still, lit by the pale light of the waning moon.

Then it came again. A brief, faint rustling noise that seemed somehow to be inside the room and outside at the same time. I sat up, hoping that would make me hear better. It did, to some extent, since one ear was no longer buried in my pillow.

There it was again. This time the rustling was accompanied by a faint thump, as if someone had stepped down a bit too hard, but it also sounded a little farther away. I could tell now that it was coming from the other side of the wall, where the servants' passage was. Somebody was sneaking around back there.

I wasn't alarmed. As I said, Bowyn and I had used those passageways when we first moved into the house. They had seemed cool and mysterious back then. No doubt they appealed to the neophytes for the same reason.

Still, it was unsettling to know someone was skulking about inside the walls of your bedroom. I slipped out of the bed and moved silently to the servants' door, hoping to get a look at whoever it was. But when I opened it, nothing but darkness greeted me on the other side. Whoever it had been was gone now.

I closed the door and slipped back into the comforting warmth of the bed and Bowyn's arms.

# Chapter Nine

BOWYN AND I ran into Marianne at breakfast the next morning, and the three of us went off to sit in the gazebo in the west garden, where we could talk without being disturbed. Marianne looked awful, as if she hadn't slept at all the night before.

"I'd appreciate it if you kept this to yourself," she admonished me as she sat on the wooden bench that ringed the inside of the gazebo. "Alex and Seth know about the baby. I suppose Seth has told Rafe," she added, making a face. "But nobody else."

She was playing idly with her tarot deck, the standard Rider-Waite deck she preferred, drawing cards seemingly at random, though she may have been posing questions in her mind. I couldn't tell.

"Why are you keeping it a secret?"

Marianne looked out over the garden, and I was struck by how pretty she was in profile, her fiery red hair glowing in the morning sunlight. She drew the eight of Swords and frowned at it. The card was startling and somewhat disturbing, featuring a woman bound and blindfolded, standing in a ring of swords. I'm not good at tarot myself, but I recalled some of its meanings being illness and jealousy. I had no idea what Marianne saw in the card.

"If I have another miscarriage," she commented, losing interest in the deck and wrapping it up in a blue silk cloth with yellow stars and moons on it, "I'd rather nobody knew I was pregnant to begin with. It's hard enough to deal with losing a baby without everyone constantly going on about how sorry they are."

I didn't really know how to respond to that, so I merely sat down beside her and put my arm around her shoulders. "My lips are sealed. But I demand to be named godfather."

Marianne turned to look at me, a mischievous smile lighting up her face. "Don't you mean *fairy* godfather?"

Bowyn and I both groaned at that, but it was nice to see her smiling again.

"Did Bowyn tell you what we named him?" Marianne asked me.

"You already know it's a 'him'?"

"Of course. The wonders of ultrasound. His name is Jay."

"Short for Jason?" I asked.

Marianne smiled and winked at Bowyn. "You tell him."

"Well," Bowyn said, looking oddly uncomfortable, "Marianne wanted to name him Jack, but… well, I wanted to…."

For some reason he had trouble finishing, so Marianne clucked at him and said, "Bowyn wanted to name him Jeremy. So we compromised on Jay—the first letter in both your names."

Bowyn had turned beet red and looked away, embarrassed. I was stunned. Touched, yes. But in a way, it just made things more painful. I tried to hide my discomfort by smiling and asking, "What are your plans for after the baby's born?"

Marianne and Bowyn exchanged a look before Bowyn cleared his throat and answered, "Neither of us feels this is a good environment for a child. I mean, maybe it would be okay for the first year, but after that…."

I had to admit, I'd been thinking the same thing. I wasn't opposed to children being exposed to casual nudity. Not that I was qualified to say, but there were psychologists who claimed it was healthy for children to learn about the human body before they got hit with all the confusion of puberty, and that had always made sense to me. Certainly a lot of parents took their children to nude beaches and resorts. But there was a lot more than casual nudity going on at the Temple. If neophytes were required to be legal adults before joining, it was foolish to think of raising a child there. Never mind what Child Services would have to say about it.

"So you'll be leaving the Temple, then?"

"My parents have some property in upstate New York, in Shokan," Marianne said. "They said we can build a house there, or maybe just get a small trailer. And my father is willing to take Bowyn on as a supervisor in his hardware store."

Bowyn? Working behind a counter?

My expression must have betrayed my surprise, because Bowyn hastily added, "He's offering a good salary."

I knew at that moment just how much I'd been longing for things to go back to the way they'd been before—Bowyn and I together again, working through the conflicts that had separated us, perhaps even living together there at the Temple—because I felt that dream shatter in an instant. And it was as if my heart had been riddled with broken glass. Whether or not Bowyn loved me, he was going away. He was starting a new family, far from me.

And our time together was finally, truly done.

"Wouldn't Seth pay you to continue managing the Temple, even if you moved off the grounds?" I asked, struggling to keep my voice light.

Marianne interjected, "We talked about it. But we both feel it would be good to get away from… all of this. At least for a few years. Seth has been dominating our lives for way too long."

Something in Bowyn's expression—perhaps just the way he seemed to be so carefully controlling it—made me wonder if he really agreed with that sentiment, or if he was simply going along with what Marianne wanted.

The idea of living in a trailer in New York didn't sound appealing to me. It might not be *that* bad. I grew up in a trailer park in Gorham, New Hampshire. As a kid I liked it well enough. But I also remembered the crap insulation in the winter, and the way it felt like it was going to blow over in wind storms. My family had been glad to get out of it.

The elephant in the room, of course, was the fact that they weren't at all a happy newlywed couple. It wasn't unheard of for a gay man to set up housekeeping with a woman to raise a child together. But would either of them really be happy with that life? Bowyn would probably continue to have sex with men—I couldn't imagine him *not* doing it—but it wasn't going to be the easy, casual sex available at the Temple.

And it wouldn't be with me. Even if Marianne didn't mind me being Bowyn's partner, New York was too far away from Durham to make the commute practical. Certainly we could see each other now and again. And perhaps we'd sleep together. But this pretty much blew away any chance Bowyn and I had of becoming a permanent couple. At least, in the way I'd always hoped. No house with a little white picket fence for us. I'd visit, we'd fuck like bunnies, perhaps, and then I'd leave him to go back to my life while he stayed behind to change diapers and struggle to work a baby stroller and family medical insurance into the budget. I'd been foolish to get my hopes up again after just one night of glorious sex. We still cared for each other, but that was as far as it could go.

I shoved the thought to the back of my mind. It hurt, but there was nothing to be done for it, and their problems were more urgent than mine.

Had they mentioned the idea of leaving to Seth yet? He wasn't going to be happy about losing both of them. Ultimately he'd always depended upon Bowyn, Alex, and even me to keep him grounded. And with Marianne gone, he'd never be able to manage the Temple finances without bringing in an outside accountant. She even managed his personal bank account, since he hated being bothered with financial details.

Bowyn's expression had clouded over and he seemed to be avoiding looking directly at me. After a brief, uncomfortable silence descended upon the three of us, he said abruptly, "We should get to morning service."


THE SERVICE was about Pythagoras that morning—his musical theories and his belief that the world was based upon mathematics. The sermon touched upon the Music of the Spheres, the idea that the entire cosmos resonates harmonically, and the theory that musical harmonies imitated the harmony in the cosmos. Certain harmonies and melodic patterns affect us emotionally because they resonate with the harmonics between the human body and our spirit. Renaissance philosophers like Ficino believed the body could be healed—or harmed—through music, through harmonies that strengthened or weakened the bond between body and spirit.

Certain groups of fundamentalist Christians have been on a kick about the harmful effects of rock music—above and beyond the content of the lyrics—for decades, and their theories tended to echo the theories of the Renaissance, even though they tried to phrase it in medical terminology. A doctor in Australia claimed that the anapestic beat—two short beats followed by a long beat, like the drum beat in Queen's "We Will Rock You"—actually destroyed the symmetry between the hemispheres of the brain, causing everything from feelings of panic, to sexual excitement, to aggression, to a complete breakdown in the ability to distinguish harmful from healthy stimulation. No doubt it might even lead to the horrors of masturbation. Another of these so-called studies claimed that "voodoo music" caused rats to cannibalize other rats.

Did I believe music had that kind of power? Obviously, I found most of these claims ludicrous. But I'd always been fascinated by the power music had to stir our emotions. That was why I'd dedicated my career to its study. And that which stirred our emotions also touched our spirit. I'd always held on to a secret desire to see Ficino proven correct in his belief that music could heal both body and spirit.

THE SONG the choir sang after the sermon wasn't one of my compositions, but a beautiful madrigal called "Tempro la cetra" by the Renaissance composer Claudio Monteverdi. Once again it featured a solo by Christopher, and again I was nearly brought to tears by the pure beauty in that voice and the sorrow that seemed to be underlying every note he sang. The young man had a gift. And I hoped he would one day share that gift with the world beyond the confines of the Temple.

After services I rushed back to the room to continue my work on the mass. With everything going on with Bowyn and Marianne, I hadn't had a moment to put the information Rafe had given me to use.

Now that I knew the symbols were ancient Greek musical notation, it was short work to find a reference online to translate them into notes of the musical scale. The Greeks had different symbols for sung notes, as opposed to those played on an instrument, so I knew the part had been written for voice. But it still made little sense. There was a note here and a note there, but nothing resembling a coherent melodic line, and nothing to indicate how long a note was to be held. Instead there appeared to be random notes inserted into each of the four standard parts. Some filled out the gaps in the chords I'd found puzzling, but other chords still seemed to be left open. After struggling with it for a couple of hours, I had all the notes written out in the software but was once again stuck. So I decided I needed to take a short walk to air out my brain.

The grounds of the Temple cover about twenty acres, including some forest around three sides of the sprawling lawn. There were cobblestone paths interconnecting the gardens, and many of these were bordered by hedges and fruit trees. It meant more maintenance chores for the neophytes, keeping those cobblestones clear in winter and the hedges trimmed during the rest of the year, but it was a very peaceful, meditative environment to walk in.

As beautiful as they were to look at, though, cobblestone paths weren't necessarily pleasant to walk on. Especially in moccasins. So I veered off the path to walk across the grass, forcing my thoughts away from Renaissance musical notation. It was a gorgeous day, sunny and warm for the season. Red and gold maple and oak leaves had fallen across the grass since the last time it was raked, and the air had that crisp, earthy smell so characteristic of a New England fall.

Behind the chapel I passed a small cemetery. There were a number of graves in it from the early half of the twentieth century, and I'd been told, a few newer ones since the founding of the Temple. I'd read in the annual newsletters about a woman who'd passed away from leukemia and another elderly initiate who'd had a heart attack. I hadn't known either of them. I did wonder if Jack was buried there, since he hadn't been close to his parents after he'd turned away from Catholicism. But I wasn't in the mood to take that path down memory lane right now, so I passed on by. If Jack was there, I'd pay my respects before leaving the Temple in a few days.

Somewhere off to the left, on a slight rise, a huge flock of black birds mulled about on the grass, pecking at something. It seemed an unusually large gathering and the interest they were showing in whatever was in their midst made me curious enough to investigate. So I climbed up the hill for a closer look.

They were definitely ravens—much larger than crows, with heavy, curved black beaks and a distinctive ruff of feathers at the neck. There were so many of them, it was hard to tell at first what they were gathered around, but my approach agitated them and they scattered a bit, revealing something that made my blood run cold.

It was a human body.

It was naked and lying flat on its back upon the grass and leaves. Definitely male—*that* part was clearly exposed—but there were so many ravens walking on the upper body and head, I couldn't see the face. My first thought was it might be Christopher—that somehow he'd passed out, or worse, while feeding the birds.

Perhaps he was just unconscious. He might have had a seizure or a heart attack. Young people did occasionally die from things like that. I froze for a moment, chilled, the hair pricking up on my scalp. Should I call for help? Run back to the house to call 911? Perhaps the most sensible thing would be to check for vital signs first....

Steeling myself, I took a step forward, and suddenly the ravens decided I'd come too close. With a chaotic fluttering of wings, they swarmed into the air in a black cloud, croaking at me angrily for disturbing their breakfast.

Then the corpse sat up.

It *was* Christopher. And he looked furious. "What are *you* doing here?"

*Christ.* I should have known lying motionless with ravens walking all over his naked body and face would be his idea of meditation or something. "*I* was minding my own business, taking a walk," I snapped, starting to grow tired of his attitude. "What were *you* doing? I thought you were dead."

"I'm fine."

He got to his feet and reached for his robe. I couldn't deny his body was delightful to look at close up. He was smooth and boyish, but with enough muscular definition to avoid making me feel creepy just for looking. But the ravens had left scratches all over his skin and even drawn a little blood here and there. "Why did you let them crawl all over you like that? Didn't it hurt?"

Christopher shrugged and pulled his robe over his head. "I like the way it feels. The pain is my offering to the Allfather."

Allfather is one of the many names of Odin. I wasn't actually surprised by his answer. People who worship Odin often find themselves playing the submissive in a sort of BDSM relationship with the god, reveling in pain because they believe it pleases him. Not so much because the Allfather enjoys making his followers suffer, but because he is pleased by strength, and their ability to endure pain pleases him. It's not the path I would choose, but if Christopher felt it brought him closer to the divine, that was his choice.

But I saw something else, as he was dressing, that I did feel I had a right to question.

His arms were covered with tiny scars—needle tracks caused by hundreds of injections of… something. Most likely heroin. Marianne had already mentioned he'd been an addict before coming to the Temple.

What bothered me more than the evidence of a past addiction was the fact that several of the needle marks looked recent—certainly more recent than nine months ago. "Christopher," I said calmly while he cinched his belt about his waist, "may I see your left arm, please?"

He stopped what he was doing, looking at me in alarm. He turned so his left side was farther away from me. "I already told you, I don't want you looking at me."

Nice try. But I wasn't going to let him guilt me into letting him off the hook. If he was still using here at the Temple, we had a problem. It wasn't that we were completely prudish about drugs and alcohol. Seth and Alex had spent years in a commune, after all. They didn't smoke pot like they used to, but it wasn't impossible to find at the Temple. Yet unless things had changed considerably since I'd last been there, harder drugs were still frowned upon.

"Christopher," I said firmly, using my best professor-talking-to-a-student voice, "let me see your arm."

He hesitated a moment longer, but he must have regarded me as an authority figure because at last he obeyed, sticking his arm out. His face looked defiant, but I could see the fear in his eyes. I reached out to take his wrist, but he flinched, so I stopped shy of actually touching him. When he turned his arm over, several marks looked fresh.

"Where are you getting it?"

He drew his hand back then and gritted his teeth. "Look, if you really want to fuck me—"

"Jesus!" I cut him off. "I don't want to fuck you. I want to know who's giving you the heroin, or whatever the fuck it is you're shooting up with."

"If you don't want to fuck me, then why won't you leave me alone?" His voice was trembling, and he suddenly seemed much younger than his eighteen years. Tears pooled in his eyes.

Before I could think of a response, he turned and ran into the woods.

"Christopher!"

He ignored me.

Those woods continued straight up into the White Mountains. I ran after him, but I stopped a few yards into the forest. There was no trace of him. The birch and aspen trees stretched away for miles in all directions, except the way I'd come in, with a dense undergrowth of hemlock, witch hazel, and dying ferns blanketing the forest floor. A slight breeze was making all the trees and shrubs sway back and forth, obscuring the path he might have taken. Christopher could easily have dropped to the ground and out of my sight. I called his name a couple of times but received no answer. If I wandered much farther in, I'd probably get lost quickly, and at this time of year that could be fatal once night fell. I'd just have to hope he knew those woods well enough to find his way back.

But it was time to find Seth.

# Chapter Ten

"WHAT DO you want me to do about it?" Seth asked, leaning against the wooden railing as he looked out across the grounds toward the forest.

I'd seen him standing on the widow's walk on top of the house when I'd returned, so I'd come up there to join him. The view was breathtaking, though supposedly a widow's walk was for looking out to sea to watch for the return of a husband's ship, and there was no ocean in sight. Just miles of forest rolling over the White Mountains in the south and the Mahoosucs in the east, across the Maine border. Far to the west, the Green Mountains of Vermont were barely visible.

"Do you want me to throw him out?" Seth continued.

"No!" I was annoyed he seemed so blasé about this. "But he's an addict, Seth. As long as somebody keeps supplying him with that shit, he's going to keep taking it."

"Don't you think that's his choice? He's an adult, isn't he?"

I bit back an angry retort and forced myself to respond rationally, knowing nothing else would work with him. "Yes, he's an adult. And yes, it's his choice to keep shooting up. But he came here looking for help, didn't he?"

"He came here looking for a spiritual education," Seth corrected. "And he's getting it. We're not a drug rehab program."

I couldn't deny that, so I tried another tack. "Seth, somebody here is supplying him with hardcore drugs. There is nothing spiritual about someone pushing heroin at the Temple."

He considered that for a moment, one eyebrow quirked up in a way I'd always found sexy. At least, when I wasn't arguing with him. "No, I suppose not."

"Is there anybody here that he trusts?"

"Me, to some extent. As long as I keep my distance physically."

"Then see if you can get him to confide in you about who's giving it to him."

"And then kick out the dealer?" he asked, giving me an odd smirk, as though he still thought I was being unreasonable.

"Maybe. Find out who it is, first. Then we can deal with him. Or her."

Seth nodded, his gaze returning to the woods where Christopher had disappeared. "This isn't the first time he's run off. The last time he was gone for three days."

I hoped he was smart enough to come back before night fell. Three days in the summer was very different from three days in October.

"How is the transcription coming along?" Seth asked, changing the subject.

Despite my frustration with the odd notation, I considered my progress to be fairly good. After all, it had only been two days, and I had a fair-sized portion of it sorted out. I gave Seth a brief rundown of where I was at and he rewarded me with that perfect, brilliant smile. "Excellent! I have faith in you, Jeremy. If anyone can have it ready in time for the new moon, you can!"

I hated to promise that, but I'd more or less agreed to it already. "I'll get back to work on it right after lunch."

"Well," Seth replied, giving me a highly suggestive look, "make sure you leave yourself a *little* time to enjoy your stay."


I WAS relieved to see Christopher back at the house for lunch, so I knew he wouldn't die of hypothermia that night. But he avoided making eye contact with me and skittered away as soon as he could. I let him go.

Marianne still wasn't feeling well after the drugs the doctor had given her, so she skipped lunch altogether. Bowyn and I took our bowls of sweet potato orange soup—a heavenly dish reminiscent of hot pumpkin pie with just a hint of citrus—up to the room. We had a quick tumble after eating, and then Bowyn settled down to read a book while I went back to the Ficino.

It was on about the tenth time I had the program play the transcription through its speakers, using a generic "string section" instrument to avoid the horrible synthesized choral voices the computer had, that I noticed something. The interpolated notes from the Greek notation seemed to be forming a melodic line, of sorts. It was choppy, since I had no idea how long each note should be sustained, but it occurred to me now that perhaps the idea was to sustain each note until the next one in the sequence. It would be a challenge for the singer, since some of the notes would be pretty long, but it wouldn't be impossible. Not if he or she figured out appropriate places to breathe.

Excited by this possible discovery, I went back through the transcription and altered the durations of each note. It took a couple of minutes, but when I was finally able to hit Play again, I knew I'd found the solution. At least in part.

The melodic line stood out now, creating an eerie resonance throughout the piece. Even played back on mediocre "violins" and "cellos," the melody added something that made me shiver as I listened to it. Bowyn, who'd been ignoring all the tedious replays until now, looked up from his book to listen, and after the piece ended, he asked, "What the fuck was that?"

"Hmm?" I responded, wanting him to explain the question before I said anything more coherent. I needed to know if he'd sensed the same strange quality in the music I had, or if he merely thought it sounded like crap.

"What did you do to it?" he asked, putting his book down and getting up to come over to the computer. He peered at the screen, even though I knew his ability to read music was limited. "I suddenly felt chilled all over."

*Excellent.* I felt like wringing my hands and chuckling like a mad scientist. Except I hadn't created this. It was something Ficino had coded into the music. And as yet I hadn't a clue what it really was.

"Those notes that I said looked random," I said. "They're not. Of course. They form a fifth melodic line, weaving through the other four."

"But what made it feel so strange?"

I shook my head. "I'm not sure yet. Ficino believed the right combination of notes and harmonies could manipulate the human spirit. This part of the mass might have been an attempt to put his theories to the test."

I no longer had any doubt Ficino had written this. Not because I had any real proof, but because of an intuitive sense of his genius shining through in the music. It *had* to be by him.

Bowyn gave up trying to make sense out of what he was seeing on the screen and straightened up, raising his arms over his head in a stretch. We were both still naked after our postlunch activities, and as I watched the way his nude torso flexed, I started to stiffen again. I had a strong desire to lick that delicate line of blond hair running from his navel down to his pubic hair.

"Those voices sounded like ass," Bowyn commented, distracting me from my lascivious thoughts.

"They're MIDI soundcard voices," I said with a shrug. The standard electronic instruments on the soundcard were much improved over the original instruments developed in the late 1980s, but they were still pretty awful. "I can't wait to hear what it sounds like when it's sung by the choir."

"If it gives me a chill played by computer, the choir will probably make me piss myself." Bowyn laughed.

I laughed too, but I was actually a little concerned about that. The effect was bound to be more intense when the piece was properly performed, and at the moment I still had no idea what its intention was. Knowing Ficino, it was likely to have been designed as a piece of musical magick, aimed at healing the body. But that was just a guess. It could also have been designed with any number of other goals in mind. Judging by the effect it already had on us, the music might have a powerful effect on the body—beyond the possibility of inducing involuntary watersports. Was it really safe for people to listen to?

I was also uncertain how to arrange it properly. Ficino had inserted that fifth melody into all four parts. Was it intended to be performed that way, with one note sung by a soprano, followed by a note sung by a tenor, and so on? Or had that simply been a way of obscuring a part intended for a soloist? Again, I wasn't sure. But it did seem as though several high notes on the bass staff would strain even a baritone. If I looked at it as a single melodic line, it seemed to make sense as a high tenor part.

There was a knock on the door and Bowyn went to answer it, not bothering to cover himself or worry about the fact I was also exposed. But when he opened the door, I saw that our visitor was naked too.

Rafe.

# Chapter Eleven

RAFE LOOKED stunning leaning against the doorframe. His chiseled gym body didn't affect me the way Bowyn's natural beauty did, but it was still a pleasure to look at.

"Don't tell me you've run out of lube again?" Bowyn asked him, clearly irritated.

"Not at all," Rafe responded. Then he opened his hand to show the small bottle of lube he had concealed there. "Will you be joining us?"

Oh yes. I'd forgotten my promise to him last night. Inconvenient timing, to say the least.

Bowyn raised his eyebrows and glanced over at me.

"Sorry." I gave them both an embarrassed smile. "I forgot I told Rafe he could come by to play this afternoon."

"You aren't changing your mind, are you?" Rafe asked. He looked surprised, as if it were inconceivable to him that anyone *wouldn't* want to fuck him.

And it wasn't that I wasn't horny at the moment. I'd just been getting myself worked up over Bowyn, not Rafe. But it seemed rude to throw him out after the promise I'd made last night. Of course, I could simply ask him to come back later.

Bowyn stepped back from the doorway and made a sweeping gesture with his hand to indicate Rafe was free to enter.

"Would you like some time alone?" Bowyn asked me.

The way he was quirking his eyebrow at me seemed to indicate he didn't *necessarily* have to leave, so I replied, "No. You're welcome to stay if Rafe doesn't mind."

Rafe cracked a smile and said, "I never mind an audience."

"Uh-uh," Bowyn said, shaking his head. "I'm not just going to watch."

He was already growing erect, and Rafe glanced at his stiffening cock for a second before saying with a slight bow, "I'm yours to do with as you will, Brethren."

His smile took in both of us.

I stood, my own cock rising to attention. It had been too long since I played with two men at once.

"Give me that," I commanded, indicating the lube he still held in his hand.

Rafe tossed the bottle to me and I caught it. It was a highly concentrated lube that didn't require a large amount, so I put a few drops on my first two fingers, then walked up to Rafe and pulled him into an embrace. As those expert lips melded with mine and his aggressive tongue penetrated deep into my mouth, I slid my fingers between his ass cheeks and quickly found his sphincter.

Rafe moaned into my mouth as I massaged his hole to thoroughly moisten it. Then, with little warning, I slid both fingers inside. His stomach muscles contracted against mine as he grunted. But he didn't pull away. Instead he pulled me closer and shoved his tongue even deeper into my mouth. I'd judged correctly—this puppy liked it rough.

Bowyn came up behind me and began nibbling my ear, which he knew always drove me wild. I whimpered into Rafe's mouth and shoved my fingers farther into his willing hole, wishing it was my cock plunging into him instead. But Bowyn was doing wonderful things to my own ass with his hands, massaging my cheeks as his lips surrendered my earlobe and began kissing down my neck. He moved down my shoulder and then my back, sending shivers along my spine, until at last Bowyn's mouth and tongue slipped between my ass cheeks. There they sought out my hole and plunged in without hesitation.

I can't deny I'm basically a bottom. I enjoy being on top now and then, but a warm tongue probing into my depths is the closest I ever expect to come to heaven on earth. There had been times when Bowyn was able to make me come just with his passionate ministrations to my hole. But as much as I loved what he was doing down there, I had Rafe to take care of. I wanted to be inside him. Now.

I spun him around and pushed him forward toward the bed. "Give yourself to me!" I hissed.

Rafe laughed in delight and crawled onto the bed, arching his back to present me with that perfectly sculpted ass, his hole wet and open.

Bowyn grabbed my hips as I tried to move forward. "Wait."

He stood and went over to the nightstand and then opened the drawer. I was embarrassed to realize he'd remembered what I'd forgotten—

condoms. He ripped open a package and tossed its contents to me while Rafe watched in amusement. I strongly suspected he never bothered with them…, which was all the more reason for Bowyn and me to do so.

I slipped the condom on quickly, lubed my cock, and then wasted no more time claiming the ass being offered to me, thrusting myself in to the hilt. Rafe grunted. "Yes! Don't hold back!"

I had no intention of holding back. I pulled out, nearly all the way, and then shoved in hard. Rafe groaned.

As I pounded into Rafe, over and over again, Bowyn climbed onto the bed and shoved his cock into Rafe's mouth. He hungrily swallowed it down to the base and began sucking on it ravenously.

But it wasn't long before Rafe let Bowyn's cock slip free, and while he rubbed his cheek against Bowyn's golden pubic hair, he gasped, "More. I need more."

"I'm giving it to you as hard as I can," I laughed.

But Bowyn gave me a smirk. "I know what the little piggy wants." He leaned forward and gave Rafe a hard slap on the ass. "All right. You want more, we'll give you more. Where did that lube get to?"

Apparently I'd dropped it, though I didn't remember doing so. I pulled out of Rafe to go retrieve it from where it had rolled under the desk. When I returned to the bed, Bowyn had unrolled a condom over his erection and was sitting on the edge of the mattress, stroking himself.

"Put some on me," he ordered, and I obliged by tipping a few drops of the lube onto the head of his cock. He slid his hand up and down the swollen shaft to spread the lube and then told Rafe, "Sit down."

Rafe locked eyes with me, allowing me to see the sheer pleasure on his face as he lowered his ass onto Bowyn's dick. Bowyn placed his hands on Rafe's hips to guide him slowly up and down the length of his shaft several times. Then he slid his hands under Rafe's thighs and leaned back on the bed, pulling Rafe backward down on top of him and lifting the man's legs upward as he did so. I was presented with an amazingly hot view of Bowyn's cock embedded deep in Rafe's asshole.

"Come on," Bowyn said, spreading his legs to give me room to approach. "He wants us both to fuck him at the same time."

Was that possible? I'd heard of guys getting fisted, as revolting as that sounded, so I supposed two dicks wouldn't be unheard of. But *I'd* certainly never seen it. "Won't that hurt?"

"No," Rafe moaned. "Do it! Tear me wide open!"

Tearing him wide open wouldn't hurt? Well, it wasn't my asshole. If he wanted us both in there, I supposed I could give him what he asked for. Obviously this wasn't the first time for him.

I spread some more lube on myself and stepped between Bowyn's legs. Rafe's asshole was in a good position for me to slide in, on top of Bowyn's cock. Perhaps "squeeze in" would be more accurate, since it took a lot of patience and slow, steady pressure before the head of my cock breached his entrance. The ecstatic moan Rafe gave out as I slid my cock in a bit farther reassured me he wasn't in distress. It was incredibly tight, but the feel of Bowyn's erection sliding against the underside of mine drove me wild.

By the time I was all the way in, my balls pressed tight against Bowyn's, Rafe was practically drooling, the way he was writhing and moaning on top of Bowyn. I slid out of that tight ass as far as I could without popping out, then shoved myself back in, eliciting a cry of ecstasy from the man. It felt good, especially when Bowyn began to move too, so that we were both churning that asshole in rhythm with each other. Rafe hadn't bothered with a condom and he was beginning to leak copious amounts of precome all over his taut stomach. I grabbed his cock and started pumping it as I continued to plow into him.

It wasn't long before I felt him spasm in my hand and he was splashing white come all over his jet-black pubic hair, his stomach, and even his chest. Watching him writhe under me while he shot was enough to send me over the top, and I pumped one or two more times before burying myself to the hilt and erupting. I could feel Bowyn's cock pulsating against mine and I knew he was coming too. It was amazing.

I fell forward onto Rafe's chest, loving the feel of his semen, slick and warm between us as we panted. My hand found Bowyn's and we intertwined our fingers in the afterglow of our orgasms. For one brief moment, the three of us basked in the false feeling of love one gets after an orgasm. I did love Bowyn, and I thought he loved me. But neither of us loved Rafe, and I suspected we were mostly trophies to him. He'd now been taken by all the Brethren. Well, all the men. Perhaps not by Marianne or Alex.

Eventually Rafe and I had to climb off Bowyn before we suffocated him. While Bowyn caught his breath, I dug a towel out of the dresser and used it to wipe Rafe off and then myself. Then I forced him to give me another of those marvelous kisses before sending him out into the hallway, stark naked and sweating, his dick and ass red enough to make it obvious to everyone he passed what he'd been up to. Somehow I didn't think he minded parading around like that.

"Better watch that one," Bowyn said, still lying on the bed, panting. "He's the biggest slut at the Temple, and he's not exactly safe."

"We're all sluts at the Temple," I said.

"True enough."

"And you have to admit, he's pretty fucking hot."

Bowyn gave me a wry smile. "I'm not telling you that you can't fuck him. Just be careful."

I crawled onto the bed to stretch out languidly beside him. "I will be. Not that I intend to keep fooling around with him. He was just being really insistent."

"You've only been here two days," Bowyn laughed. "Not exactly playing hard to get, are you?"

I didn't even pretend to be offended. I just smiled at him affectionately. "I never said I was hard to get. I'm enjoying the chance to let loose again. It's been way too long since I've had great sex."

"Really?" he asked. "When was the last time?"

"None of your business."

"True. But I still want to know."

I thought about the question for a moment; thought back over all the encounters I could remember having since leaving the Temple. And truthfully, none of them had been all that wonderful. "If you must know... I think the last *great* sex I had, before this week, was eight years ago with you."

His cheeky smile faded and he regarded me solemnly. "Why did I ever let you leave?"

Ah, that was the question, wasn't it?

For a long moment, I couldn't answer. Then at last I said, "You couldn't have stopped me. I had to get away from all this. It was fun, in small doses. But I needed something saner. And I needed to get back to my degree. Why didn't you come with me?"

Bowyn sighed and looked away. "I wasn't like you. I didn't have any clear idea what I wanted to do with my life. The Temple needed me. Seth is... insane," he said with a laugh, "and Alex barely has time for anything outside the kitchen. Jack was good at the accounting, but otherwise he and Marianne were pretty wrapped up in each other. I was the only one who could make sure things got done. This was where I belonged."

"I know," I said, though it hurt to say so. It was the first time I'd acknowledged, even to myself, that there might have been reasons beyond whether Bowyn loved me or Seth more. "So here we are again."

He nodded. "Here we are."

"Am I at least allowed to say I still love you?"

Bowyn pulled me close for a long, tender kiss. When I raised my head, I saw his eyes had misted up. "I love you too. But I've fucked it all up again, haven't I?"

"Well," I said, cautiously, "I wouldn't exactly say wanting to have a child was 'fucking it up.' But I think it does mean we're not going to be able to make this work. Not for us."

Bowyn sighed and nodded. "I just wanted to make her happy. We didn't really think it through. I was picturing a little kid running around the grounds here. I never thought we'd have to leave."

"I suppose you could just give her child support," I suggested. But I didn't really think that was a great option, and I was glad when Bowyn shook his head.

"He's my baby too," he pointed out. "I can't just dump all the hard stuff on her and pat myself on the back because I send her a check once a month."

"I guess that's one of the reasons I love you." Was this all that much different than the situation had been eight years ago? Then, Bowyn had known the Temple couldn't survive without him, but I could. I'd convinced myself it was about whether he loved me more than Seth, but it hadn't been about that at all. At least not entirely. Now the baby needed him more than I could claim to. And he was making the only choice he could make.

Still, he looked miserable. I laid my head on his shoulder and draped my arm across his smooth chest. He brought his hand up to stroke the back of mine, and we lay there for a long time, neither of us speaking.

Then Bowyn suddenly perked up and said, "Hey! Do you want to see a picture of him?"

"A picture?" I asked, baffled.

He slid out from under me and went to his dresser. Pulling open the top drawer, Bowyn drew out a manila envelope and brought it back to the bed.

"Look," he said, his face brightening as he sat down cross-legged beside me on the mattress and opened the envelope. He drew out three gray "photographs" and handed them to me.

They were ultrasounds. I had no experience looking at them, so to me they just looked like swirls of gray and black. "Um… he has your eyes."

Bowyn laughed and pointed with his finger. "The doctor had to show us what to look for. But here's one of his hands." He indicated a spot that did look vaguely like it might become a hand someday. "And that's his penis."

"You're kidding."

"No, it is. See? Right there?"

I couldn't really see it, but I nodded as if I could and smiled at him. I was glad he was excited about the baby. Hell, *I* was excited about the baby. Two of my favorite people in the world were going to have a son, and that was wonderful, regardless of any problems the situation created.

"He's going to be beautiful," I said. "Just like his mom and dad."

# Chapter Twelve

I RAN into Seth at dinner and discovered Rafe had already given him all the gory details of his encounter with me and Bowyn. Not that I was surprised.

"I have to say, my love," Seth told me, slipping on a phony look of wounded pride that wouldn't have fooled his own mother, "I'm hurt that you've already given Rafe a taste while you continue to snub me."

I had to admit, I was beginning to enjoy feeling fought over. As I've said, I'm okay to look at but not gorgeous. And I suspected Rafe had simply wanted to have me because he knew Seth wanted me. But it was still nice. The gay dating scene back in Durham had been tepid, to say the least—for anyone over thirty, anyway—and that took a toll on one's ego.

I leaned in to give Seth a lingering kiss on the lips. "You know I'm not snubbing you. It's just the way the dice fell. You'll get your turn before I leave."

"Tonight?" he asked hopefully.

"Tomorrow night. Maybe. I think Bowyn and I need some private time right now."

At the mention of Bowyn's name, Seth glanced across the room at the corner where Bowyn and Marianne were hiding out, engaged in some kind of intense conversation.

"Yes," Seth said, thoughtfully. "I think that boy needs you right now. Things have been getting far too serious for both of them."

I wasn't really in the mood to dwell on that at the moment, so I changed the subject. "I've made some significant progress on the Ficino. I was hoping we could arrange for a choir rehearsal tomorrow evening. I'd like to hear the Credo sung by actual human voices in order to tweak some parts of it."

Technically that section was unlikely to be a Credo, unless the Greek libretto turned out to be nothing more than the Latin Credo translated into Greek, but it seemed as good a name as any for now.

This seemed to delight Seth. His face lit up with that perfect smile and he said, "Wonderful! Timothy is our choirmaster. I'll have him track you down tomorrow, right after the service."

"How does Timothy do with Christopher?" I asked.

"*Do* with him?"

"I mean, does Christopher listen to him?"

"I suppose. Why?"

"Because Christopher has taken a dislike to me. With good reason, I guess. But I want him to sing the fifth part."

"I seem to recall you were quite an accomplished tenor several years back," Seth said smoothly.

I had been—in my twenties. But my voice had dropped a note or two with age. "I'm not sure I can hit those high notes without straining," I replied. "Christopher can. Not to mention the kid has the sweetest voice I've ever heard."

Seth smiled. "I'll make sure Christopher is available to you."

I had no doubt he dropped the double entendre on purpose, but I wasn't about to complain. I had what I wanted.


I SPENT the rest of my evening wrestling the Credo—or whatever it was—into shape for the choir. It was almost there, but it needed a little polishing. Plus I had to extract the fifth melody line and write it up as a separate tenor solo. The rest of the mass was in worse shape since I'd devoted so much time to this section, but that didn't matter at the moment. It was this part I wanted to hear Christopher sing.

Eventually I came out of my music-induced coma and realized it was nearly eleven, and I hadn't seen a trace of Bowyn since dinner. Telling myself it was just because I needed a break and absolutely *not* because I was checking up on him, I shut down the laptop and headed downstairs.

I found Bowyn in the kitchen, sitting at the table with Marianne while Alex bustled around making one of her famous herbal tea concoctions.

"Have a seat," Alex cheerfully ordered me the moment I entered the room. She grabbed another earthenware mug from the overhead rack before rushing to take the boiling kettle off the burner.

I had to admit a hot cup of tea sounded good, so I obeyed and took the empty chair next to Bowyn.

"You do remember I'm on meds now?" Marianne asked, dubiously eyeing the tea Alex dropped in front of her.

Alex laughed as she brought two more mugs to the table for me and Bowyn. "There's nothing in there that will harm you, sweetheart. Just spearmint to settle your stomach, with a little catnip to help you sleep and a touch of jasmine. I double-checked for possible interactions with your new medication online earlier."

Alex never served store-brand bagged tea. Her cabinets contained jars of just about any herb you could name, and you were unlikely to ever get exactly the same brew twice. But they were always wonderful. And her knowledge of the medicinal properties of herbs was extensive— she'd been working with them for a long, long time.

As Alex took a seat at the table, settling in for a chat with a steaming mug of tea for herself, Rafe sauntered in. Technically he wasn't naked— something that would have gotten him immediately ousted from the kitchen—but the skimpy bath towel he had wrapped around his waist earned him a sour look from Alex just the same.

"Is there something you need, Raphael?" Alex asked. Her voice had a stern, parental ring to it.

Rafe opened the stainless steel industrial refrigerator and peered in before responding, "Do we have any whipped cream?"

The corners of Alex's mouth tightened ever so slightly, but her tone was almost sweet when she said, "Of course. There's cream right in front of you. You'll find a mixing bowl and a whisk hanging from that rack above the island."

"I have to whip it myself?" He looked scandalized.

"Surely you don't expect me to stock whipped cream in a can," Alex replied. I knew she would rather die than serve anything in her kitchen that wasn't organic and homemade.

Marianne had to lift her teacup to hide the smile forming on her lips, and the twinkle in Bowyn's eye told me he was enjoying this little scene immensely.

"Couldn't you whip it for me?" Rafe asked smoothly.

He was giving Alex that same smoldering look I'd fallen for on the stairs. Had he directed it at me, I probably would have been suckered into making the whipped cream for him, but Alex was made of far sterner stuff than I. She looked at him coolly and simply said, "No. I'm done with work for the day, and now I'm relaxing with old friends."

"Please?" He was pouting now.

I cringed. It was like watching a train wreck about to happen, knowing you could do nothing to prevent it.

"I will not be coaxed into making sex toys for my husband and his current twink-of-the-month," Alex said, calmly. "If you're too lazy to make it yourself, drive down to the 7-Eleven and buy some."

Rafe shut the refrigerator door a bit too loudly and stalked out of the room without another word. As soon as he was gone, Marianne gave in to the giggles she'd been holding back, and Bowyn rolled his eyes and shook his head.

"Jesus," Alex muttered, taking a sip of her tea.

"Are you okay?" I asked. I'd never heard her say a word about Seth's dalliances before. Perhaps she was more upset by it than I'd realized.

But Alex waved a hand dismissively. "I'm fine. I just get fed up with that pompous little twit. He thinks fucking Seth gives him some kind of special privileges around here."

"Worse than that," Bowyn corrected. "He's been fucking his way through all the Brethren like we're merit badges. Jeremy was the last to fall."

Marianne looked at me and her jaw dropped. "Jeremy! You slut! You've been here less than a week."

I groaned and buried my face in my hands. "I know, I know. But… come on!" I looked up and waved a hand toward the door Rafe had just walked out of. "He's fucking gorgeous."

"True," Marianne replied.

"And," Alex added, "he *is* really good in the sack."

I raised my eyebrow at her. "You too?"

"Well, just once. The first month he was here."

Marianne groaned and drained her cup. "Me too. I was a sucker for that charming 'Greek lover' act. But I should have known better than to screw around with anybody that vapid and self-absorbed. Five seconds after he came, he was out the door."

Alex laughed. "I don't think he really likes women," she said, blowing on her tea to cool it. "Like Bowyn said, he was just bound and determined to fuck all the Brethren."

Bowyn slapped me on the back. "Congratulations! You've just helped him complete his collection."

"Maybe we should get our pictures put on bubblegum cards!" Marianne exclaimed cheerfully.

"You might have warned me," I grumbled. I wasn't quite sure why it bothered me, but I felt... I don't know. Manipulated. Used.

"You had fun, didn't you?"

"Well... yeah."

"Then don't worry about it," Bowyn said. "It's just his kink."

"Well, I don't like men with too many muscles," Marianne said, puzzling me for a moment until I recognized the quote from *The Rocky Horror Picture Show*.

I replied with my best imitation of Tim Curry, "I didn't make him for *you*!"

Bowyn groaned while Marianne and I burst out giggling like high school kids.

Alex smiled affectionately at the three of us. "I can cope with him sleeping with everybody. What I can't deal with is the way he struts around like he's the official Temple mascot or something. He's in for a rude awakening someday when Seth dumps him for something younger and cuter."

But I was no longer thinking about that. Something Marianne had said was just bubbling to the surface of my consciousness. "He's Greek?"

"Didn't you notice the accent?"

"Well... sort of," I said defensively. "But Bowyn just said he was European. I guess I just didn't think too hard about where in Europe he'd come from." Now I recognized the musical lilt to his voice. The accent was subtle, but it was obvious now that they'd pointed it out to me. "Does he know the translator, then? The person in Greece who's translating the Greek part of the Ficino text?"

Of course, being Greek didn't mean Rafe knew everybody in Greece, any more than being gay meant I knew every gay person in New Hampshire. But it wasn't far-fetched to think he might have directed Seth to someone he knew.

"It's his uncle," Bowyn said. "If you ask me, that's why Seth has put up with Rafe's constant preening for so many months."

"Seth," Alex added with a hint of bitterness in her voice, "is also not above using sex to get something he wants."

I nodded absently. But I was wondering now just how much Rafe really knew about the manuscript. Had his uncle passed along anything to him about the libretto yet? I'd begun to feel a bit possessive of the manuscript after working with it so closely. After all, I was the one who supposedly knew more about Ficino than anyone else here. It irritated me to think Rafe, and hence Seth, might have more information about the document than they were telling me.

Still, I wasn't about to go storming into their room right now while they were probably going at it—sans whipped cream—and demand whatever information they might have about the libretto. I could ask Seth about it tomorrow.

"That uncle is bilking us, if you ask me," Marianne was saying. "His stipend for the translation is adding up. It's cost the Temple almost five thousand dollars so far!"

Of course, she would know, since she'd been doing the accounting for the Temple since Jack passed away.

Bowyn whistled. "It probably would have been cheaper to send our charming Greek lover to take some classes in ancient Greek."

"And Seth isn't paying you a dime, is he?" Alex asked me.

I felt like a prime idiot now, but I had to confess, "I never asked for compensation. Except the right to publish a paper on the manuscript."

Alex raised her eyebrows as if to say, "You're a sucker." But she just sipped her tea and said nothing.

After I'd finished my tea, I decided to return to the room so I could put in a little more work on the manuscript before bed. Bowyn, Marianne, and Alex were still engrossed in conversation, but Bowyn assured me he'd be up in a short while. I snagged a couple of poppy seed muffins off the side table in the dining room, which Alex kept stocked with snack-type foods, coffee, and juice for those of us who needed something to nibble between meals, and then I climbed the stairs to the third-floor landing and let myself into the room.

Christopher was there, sitting on the end of the bed.

# Chapter Thirteen

As soon as he saw me, Christopher jumped up. I stepped back involuntarily. Not that I really thought he was going to attack me, but it happened so fast I didn't have much time to figure out my reaction.

"Jesus!" I gasped. "You scared the crap out of me!"

"Sorry."

I quickly went from startled to angry. "What the hell are you doing in our bedroom, Christopher?" The door hadn't been locked—nobody locked their doors in the Temple—but it was still considered inappropriate to wander into someone's room without permission.

"I'm sorry," Christopher said, nervously. "I just… I needed to talk to you."

As I stepped closer to him and closed the bedroom door behind me, I noticed something. His robe had cobwebs on it and a few spots of dust he hadn't yet brushed off. "You came in through the servants' door."

He glanced over at the door by the fireplace and nodded. This was getting weirder by the second.

"Hasn't anyone told you that you can't just go into other people's rooms?"

"I'm sorry."

He made a move as if to leave, but I stepped between him and the door.

"Why don't you tell me what you're here for, Christopher?" I asked, trying to take some of the edge out of my voice.

He had a difficult time looking me in the eye. He wiped the palm of his right hand nervously against his hip, but his left hand seemed to be deliberately hidden in the folds of his robe. The first thing that jumped into my mind was he was hiding a weapon—a knife, perhaps. I immediately felt guilty for thinking it. Was I jumping to the conclusion he was dangerous because he had a problem with drug addiction? I hated to assume that. But he was being careful to keep that hand out of sight, and I knew I'd be foolish to ignore my instincts.

"Do you have something in your hand?" I asked, hoping it was a book or something equally innocuous.

Christopher hesitated for a moment, glancing furtively at the doorway, as if he were afraid someone else might enter. Then he pulled his left hand from the folds of his robe and thrust it out in my direction. I took another step back, but Christopher didn't appear to be striking out at me. He just stood there for a moment, looking uncomfortable, as he held his hand out. There was a ratty old washcloth clenched in his fist.

"What is that?"

"Take it," he said.

Uncertainly, I held out my hand and Christopher dropped the bundle into it. The washcloth unfurled to show me a hypodermic needle, a tarnished spoon, and a small glassine bag with a tiny amount of whitish powder in it. Though I'd never actually seen it before, it seemed a safe bet the bag contained heroin.

I looked at it in shock for a long time, until Christopher said, "It's all I've got. I swear."

When I looked up at his face, I saw he was eyeing me carefully, waiting for my reaction. Both his hands rubbed nervously at his hips as he shifted from one foot to the other.

"Are you stoned right now?" I asked.

"No."

I assumed he was telling the truth. From what I knew of heroin, it made you lethargic—not antsy. His eyes didn't look dilated. Although I wasn't sure if heroin did that anyway.

"Why did you bring this to me?"

"I don't want you to kick me out," he said. "I thought if I turned it over, you'd see I was serious about trying to clean up."

"Where did you get it?"

"I brought it with me when I came here."

*Bullshit.*

"I'm sorry," I replied, shaking my head. "I don't buy that. You've been here nine months. How long does a bag this size last you? A week, maybe, if that? You didn't come here with nine months' supply, I'm pretty certain. And you didn't hold off for a year before shooting up again."

Christopher looked stricken. His eyes darted to the door, but I was still blocking it. I wasn't letting him go until he told me the truth.

"Somebody here is giving the stuff to you," I insisted.

"No! No, I swear." He glanced at the servants' door, but he didn't attempt to move toward it. "Look... okay, you're right about me getting more since I've been here. But it's nobody here giving it to me."

"Who, then?"

"One of my... friends... from before I came here," he said. "When I get desperate, I can call him, and he meets me down at the rest stop on Route 2."

"Where you have sex with him," I finished. I knew the rest stop he was referring to. It was a long walk—two or three miles at least—but not too far for a teenager jonesing for a fix.

Christopher shifted uncomfortably. "He's not too bad. He just likes to suck me off. I don't mind."

*Terrific.* Not only was he still using, he was still turning tricks.

Oh, I know. We were standing in the middle of Sex City, and I was one of its founders. I wasn't exactly in a position of moral high ground. But a few Temple residents smoking pot was *not* the same as shooting up heroin, damn it. And "free love" wasn't the same as prostitution. This kid was taking us somewhere darker than we'd ever intended.

"Christopher—"

"I know!" he interrupted, his eyes wide with panic. "I know I fucked up! I broke the rules and I lied to you. I just... I need you to give me another chance. Please! Don't throw me out. I'll do anything you say. I won't call that guy ever again. You can take away my phone privileges. You can punish me. I don't mind being hit. You can *have* me—"

"Stop!" I practically shouted it. "Stop right there!"

The young man recoiled as if I was going to strike him.

"Jesus Christ, Christopher! For the last time, I am *not* trying to fuck you!" I was furious that he kept looking at me as if I was just as sleazy as one of his tricks. "I don't want to hit you; I don't want to whip you. I don't need to use you to satisfy any of my sexual kinks, goddamn it! Get that through your fucking head!"

That did it. He started crying.

*Christ.*

"Look, I'm sorry I yelled at you...."

To my surprise, Christopher stepped forward and leaned against me, his tear-filled eyes pressing into the crook of my neck as his arms wrapped tightly around my waist. "Help me," he sobbed weakly. "Please. This is the only place I've ever felt safe. I know I screwed up. Just give me a chance to make it right."

I couldn't help but hug him back. I'd always been a sucker for tears. He was a bit shorter than me, so I was able to rest my cheek against his soft blond hair. I held him and shushed him. "I don't want you to leave either. We'll talk to Seth and Bowyn and see what they have to say about it…."

While I was talking, I gradually became aware that he was caressing my back. It felt okay at first—just the type of gesture people made when they were being hugged. But it wasn't long before it began to feel more caressing; sexual. About the time I noticed that, I also noticed he was grinding his crotch into mine, and it was easy to tell through the robes that he was growing hard.

Well, to be honest, so was I, though I'd barely been aware it was happening.

Unbelievable. I didn't buy for a second that he really desired me. The kid was *playing* me. Again! Was he incapable of relating to older men in any way that wasn't manipulative? Perhaps. Maybe this was the only way he knew to get what he wanted. Knowing what I did about his past, I supposed I couldn't really blame him.

I sighed and pushed him away—gently but firmly. "It's late, Christopher. I'm going to talk to Seth about this tomorrow." I still had no desire to venture up to his room tonight, whipped cream or no whipped cream. "We'll see what we can work out."

I nearly mentioned that I would see him in choir tomorrow, but under the current circumstances, it might have come across as if I were offering some kind of deal. So I stopped myself.

"Thank you." Christopher smiled at me through the tears and wiped his cheeks with the back of his hand. "I knew I could talk to you about this, Jeremy. I knew you'd understand."

*Yeah, right. We're simpatico—practically soul mates. Whatever, kid.* "Why don't you get to bed?"

I saw him out—through the main bedroom door, this time—then closed the door behind him and set the hypo on the desk. I hoped Bowyn would be up soon, because there was no way in hell I could focus on the manuscript now.

# Chapter Fourteen

"HE TRIED to fuck you?"

Bowyn seemed to find this much more amusing than I did.

"What he was doing," I said with exaggerated patience, "was offering me a deal so I wouldn't rat him out."

"Well, so much for that, tattletale," Bowyn teased. But as he picked up the hypo from the desk, his expression grew more serious. "I really thought he'd gotten free of this shit."

"What do you think we should do with him?"

"We? I thought you weren't part of the Temple anymore."

I frowned at him, not interested in playing that particular game again. "Fine. But you are. I already know what Seth will do, and that's nothing. As far as he's concerned, sleaze is a virtue. He'd love to see that kid remain a prostitute and a drug addict."

"That's pretty harsh," Bowyn replied, frowning. "Seth may be raunchy and self-centered, but he's not totally lacking in compassion."

I was in too pissy a mood to hear it. I stripped off my robe and tossed it on the floor. Then I crawled into bed. "I want to know what *you're* going to do about it."

"I," Bowyn said, putting the hypo back on the desk, "am going to talk to Seth, Marianne, and Alex about it tomorrow. Christopher broke the rules, but it's not really about that, is it? It's about whether the Temple can help him, or if he'll just drag us down with him."

I watched as Bowyn stripped off his own robe, some of my foul temper fading at the sight of his beautiful golden body. I was rapidly growing hard as my eyes followed the lines of his abdomen down into his sandy pubic hair.

"We all like Christopher." Bowyn crawled onto the bed and straddled my hips. "We'll do what we can to help him."

He leaned down and kissed me, his soft blond hair falling down on either side of us, blocking out the world, and soon I lost track of anything other than the smell and taste and feel of Bowyn. Everything else would have to wait until tomorrow.

THERE WAS no way to get the Brethren together in the morning—not with Alex supervising breakfast and Seth giving the daily sermon. Bowyn and I let them and Marianne know we had something important to discuss that afternoon, then got out of their hair.

There was a laser printer in the office downstairs, and Bowyn helped me connect my laptop to it through the Wi-Fi so I could print out parts for the choir. Then we joined Marianne in the dining room for breakfast.

The sermon that morning revolved around the story of Odin and Balder. Balder was Odin and Frigga's son, killed through the machinations of Loki.

"The grief among the gods," Seth told us, his deep voice reverberating against the marble walls of the chapel, "was so great that Balder's wife's heart burst with sorrow and she was laid upon his funeral ship beside him. Gods and beings from all over the nine worlds came to see the ship lit afire. After the funeral, Odin loaned his eight-legged horse, Sleipnir, to his son, Hermod, and commanded him to bring Balder back from Hela's kingdom.

"Thus Hermod rode Sleipnir for nine days, until he came to the river, Gjoll, that borders the kingdom of Hela. There, the guardian of the bridge confirmed that Balder had passed that way nine days earlier. Hermod crossed the bridge and rode on until he came to the enormous iron Hel-gate. Hermod spurred Sleipnir onward, and the magnificent steed leaped over the gate.

"Hermod rode into the palace and entered Hela's great throne room. There he found his brother, Balder, seated upon one of the high seats with his wife, Nanna, at his side. When the goddess, Hela, asked him why he'd come, a living man into her kingdom, he replied, 'I have been sent by Balder's father to bring his son back to him.'"

This was a loose interpretation of the myth from what I could recall. In Snorri Sturlusson's account, it was Frigga who sent Hermod to retrieve her son. But there was little point in challenging Seth when he was on a roll.

"When Hermod told her that all the gods were weeping at the loss of their beloved Balder, Hela told him, 'We shall see if Balder is as beloved as you say. If all things in the worlds, alive and dead, weep for him, then he shall go back to the gods. Otherwise he shall remain with me.'

"So Hermod rode across the nine worlds, asking everything he came across to weep for the return of Balder."

Here Seth paused for dramatic effect. Of course, all those present—even those who might not have heard the myth—knew Hermod's efforts were doomed to failure. That was *always* how these stories went.

After everything in the nine worlds, including the rocks and trees, agreed to weep for Balder, Hermod came upon a giantess in a cave. He pleaded with her to weep, but she was in fact the trickster, Loki, in disguise, so Hermod's pleas fell upon deaf ears. Loki refused to weep.

"Betrayed by his own blood-kin," Seth said ominously, referring perhaps to the fact that Loki and Odin are blood brothers, "Balder remained in Hela's kingdom."

He paused again, and it seemed to me he looked deliberately at Christopher, who was listening intently to the story from his seat in the front row of the choir. "Yet all is not lost for the son of Odin. One day the armies of Hela will rise up and attempt to destroy the nine worlds in a blaze of fire, and Odin will lead his army of gods and men out to meet them on the field of battle. He knows he will die. But his sacrifice will halt the destruction of the worlds and at last put an end to Loki's treachery.

"And when the worlds rise up out of the flames, Balder will live again, and he will sit upon the throne of his father."

# Chapter Fifteen

I MET with Timothy, the choir director who'd taken over when I left, after the service and found out he'd already scheduled an impromptu choir rehearsal for after lunch at Seth's request. We stood in the center of the chapel while the members of the choir wandered out to get lunch. The short bald man took the choir parts I handed him and flipped through them with a look of dismay.

"*La, la, la?*" he asked, referring to the "lyrics" I'd transcribed.

"That will be replaced by a phonetic transcription of the ancient Greek once we have it back from Rafe's uncle."

Timothy flipped through until he came to the Credo. "And what about this part? *MaCaMa GaHa PaD ZaR*? What the hell is that supposed to mean?"

I looked at him apologetically. "That's what the manuscript says— sort of. I'm guessing on the vowels."

Timothy sniffed. "Not much of a guess. They're all *A*."

"I don't know which vowels to use," I confessed, "and I have no idea what it means, or if it means *anything*. It could be a code that only Ficino and a few friends knew. But you don't have to worry about that— it's only in the solo, and I'd like to work with Christopher on that part myself, if you don't mind."

Timothy made a gesture that indicated he wasn't particularly concerned about it. "Be my guest. He's a sweetheart, but he can be a bit... challenging at times."

"Thanks," I responded. "I think I can handle him." *I hope.* "Just focus on the Greek part with the choir. We'll get you the phonetic transcription of those lyrics as soon as we have one."

Timothy sighed, looking unimpressed, but waved a hand disdainfully and said, "*La, la, la* it is, then."


WHEN THE choir gathered after lunch, we ran into another snag— Christopher was a no-show. We waited fifteen minutes for him, but finally Timothy said, "We might as well get to work. This isn't the first time he's skipped out on us. Fortunately he's a quick study, so he can usually catch up later."

But I wasn't in the mood to deal with a lead tenor who wasn't going to know his part when my main purpose had been to hear that part sung. I took the pages for the solo tenor part and picked up my laptop. "Would you mind working with the choir on the rest of it? It's fairly straightforward. I'm going to see if I can find out where Christopher's gone to. The piece won't work without the solo."

Timothy looked skeptical. "I can do that, but I hope the kid isn't in one of his 'moods.' If he is, he's liable to run off the moment he sees you coming."

"I'll take that chance."

I WASN'T sure where to look for Christopher, but he turned out to be easy to find. As soon as I began walking down—or rather, alongside— the cobblestone path from the chapel to the house, I noticed ravens circling at the top of the hill, near the forest. Figuring Christopher might be feeding them, I headed that way.

Lo and behold, there he was.

Christopher stood in the middle of at least a hundred of the squabbling black birds, tossing bread scraps at them from a stash he had in a fold of his robe. Last I'd heard, there weren't supposed to be as many as a hundred ravens in all New Hampshire, but... well, apparently there were now.

Christopher looked down at me as I climbed the hill. The ravens croaked indignantly, scattering out of my path, but he made no move to run away.

Instead he smiled. "I knew you'd come looking for me."

"Did you?" I made no attempt to hide my annoyance. "Did you think it would be amusing to make me chase after you?"

"Don't raise your voice. It upsets them."

He meant the ravens. I glanced around at the noisy scavengers as Christopher tossed out another handful of bread scraps. I don't hate ravens, but I can't say I've ever had any real affection for them either.

I tried again, lowering my voice. "Timothy asked you to come back to the chapel after lunch for a rehearsal, didn't he?"

"Yes."

"Then why aren't you there?"

Christopher shrugged and gave me a shy smile that seemed apologetic. "I needed some time alone, that's all. The sermon really got to me today. I didn't mean to make you mad, Jeremy."

"Will you go to the rehearsal, then?"

"I'd rather not." He saw me looking displeased at that and quickly asked, "You can work with me out here, can't you? I don't mind being with you. I just don't want to deal with everyone else right now."

He was manipulating me again, I felt sure—implying a personal relationship between us that didn't really exist. But I'd brought along his sheet music and my laptop, which would allow me to play him the MIDI version of his part, so I just went along with it.

I handed the music to him. "Do you read music?"

"Not much," he replied, eyeing the sheets curiously. "Enough to follow along, once I know the part. What are these words?"

"I have no idea what the words are," I admitted. "They might just be phonetic syllables that Ficino felt resonated musically and magickally, in some way. I'm sure the vowels aren't correct, anyway, so don't worry about it too much. Just try to sing the syllables as best you can."

I sat down cross-legged on the grass, set the laptop in front of me, and flipped it open. While it booted up, I said, "I have a cheesy electronic version of your part on here. You can listen to it and see if you can learn it from that."

I was skeptical. The notes weren't really what I would consider to be a melody. In other words, without the rest of the choir to support them, they sounded somewhat atonal, jumping from note to note without any real connection. An untrained singer would generally have difficulty remembering where the next pitch was without a coherent melody line to lead him through the piece.

But Christopher had almost no problems with the piece at all. I was surprised, after playing the first few notes, that he was able to sing them back exactly as he'd heard them, despite a diminished fifth going down followed by an upward leap of a major seventh. Not an easy passage.

"Excellent!" I said, but he just nodded briefly, as if uncomfortable with the praise. I played him another segment.

Again he sang it back perfectly. We went through several short passages like that, until Christopher said, "This is kind of boring. Can we just do the whole thing at once?"

"Um... If you like. It's pretty long."

"Just play it a few times and I'll see if I can remember it."

So I did. He listened intently, following along on his pages of music and sort of half singing under his breath. We did that four or five times, until Christopher said, "Okay, I want to try it without the computer now."

"Go for it."

He sang it with the phonetic syllables, and once again I found myself enthralled, not only by the music, but also by the perfection of his voice. There was an indefinable purity and richness to the tone that musicians often call "sweet," but more than that, Christopher had an instinctive feel for the rhythm of the piece, such as it was. He added crescendos and decrescendos, held notes at just the right moments, and paused for dramatic tension. Somehow he managed to string those seemingly random notes into something coherent and sublime, and the strange phonetic "words" felt as if they *were* words, as if he were singing of something both magnificent and heart-wrenchingly beautiful.

When he finished, I found myself staring at Christopher in awed silence, profoundly moved. He seemed to have gone somewhere deep inside himself, and as I watched, he blinked and focused his eyes on his surroundings.

Christopher whispered, "Don't move."

I lowered my eyes from the young man's face and saw what he was looking at. Ravens still surrounded us on the hillside, but there were many, many more of them than I remembered being there when I'd walked up the hill. Now they were eerily motionless, squatting down in the grass in silence, their heads cocked to one side or the other, pebble-like black eyes watching Christopher intently. The effect was unsettling.

Then from somewhere far off, Bowyn called my name.

Startled, the ravens leapt into the air, and for one terrifying moment, Christopher and I were engulfed by a tornado of black fluttering wings. Christopher covered his ears against the birds' indignant screeching, pinching his eyes shut and screwing up his face like a little boy frightened by someone yelling at him. I glanced away, uncomfortable, as if I were seeing something he hadn't meant to show me.

"That was… odd," Bowyn said as he drew near, looking up at the departing cloud of ravens. "I thought you were under attack for a minute there."

"We were fine," Christopher said. He looked sullen now, all traces of fear gone from his features.

Bowyn glanced at me, but I just shrugged as I bent to pick up the laptop. We *were* fine, after all.

"Did I interrupt something?"

"We're done," I replied. I turned to Christopher. "You did a great job. Can I count on you to be at the rehearsal tonight?"

Christopher nodded, but he was watching Bowyn suspiciously. I wasn't sure why until I turned to leave. Then Christopher looked at me and asked, "You're having a meeting about me, aren't you?"

Bowyn and I both stopped in our tracks. I could tell Bowyn was annoyed, but I didn't see any point in lying about it. "Yes, we are, Christopher."

"You're going to tell them to kick me out."

"I'm going to tell them about the conversation you and I had last night," I replied. "Since I'm no longer living here, it isn't my place to tell Seth and the others what to do about the situation."

But of course I *did* still have some influence at the Temple, whether I liked it or not, and Christopher knew that.

"I thought I could trust you."

I turned to face him head-on again and looked him in the eye. He didn't look away this time, and the hurt I saw in his eyes seemed genuine. "Christopher… let me be absolutely truthful with you. First of all, I don't really know you. I think you have an amazing vocal talent, and I find you interesting to talk to, but that's the extent of it. I've been told a little bit about what you've been through, and I don't think I can blame you for having a drug problem after all that. You've had it rougher than anyone should. But I'm concerned about heavy drug use going on in a place I helped create."

"I said I would give it up!" Christopher practically shouted. "I have!" He was pleading with me, on the verge of tears.

"And I believe you'll try. But I don't think many people are able to simply 'give up' heroin without help."

"You already told us once that you'd kicked it," Bowyn pointed out.

"Just keep me here on the grounds. I won't be able to get more if I can't leave. You can lock me in at night." Christopher was crying now, making no attempt to wipe away the tears that spilled down his cheeks. "I'll do it this time. I swear. Don't kick me out. Please. I don't have anywhere else to go."

The tears were getting to me again. "Look, Christopher, for what it's worth, I'm not going to suggest you be forced to leave. But Seth and the others need to know you're still having trouble. I know that's not very reassuring, but try not to panic about it. We'll see you this evening at choir, and I promise to let you know what we've decided then. Okay?"

Christopher frowned but mumbled, "Okay."

As I turned and walked down the hill toward the house, Bowyn caught up to me. Glancing back to make sure we were out of Christopher's hearing, he leaned in close and said, "You do realize, he cries like that whenever anyone tries to make him do something he doesn't like."

"I figured as much," I said ruefully. "Just about everything he does—crying, hugging, confiding in people, even having sex with them—he's learned how to use it all to manipulate and survive. God knows what he's really feeling under the smoke and mirrors."

"So now you're a psychologist?"

He was teasing me, I knew, but I still groaned in frustration. "No. None of us is. That's the problem."

# Chapter Sixteen

THE MEETING with the Brethren, once we'd chased a group of initiates out of the dining room and locked ourselves in, was short. Seth would hear nothing of sending Christopher away from the Temple, and the rest of us all liked—or at least sympathized with—the young man, despite his issues. So we weren't inclined to do so either.

"What about outpatient drug counseling?" Alex suggested. "I think the program in Berlin offers it. And that way Christopher wouldn't have to leave the Temple."

Bowyn gave a sharp laugh. "Do you mean a counselor would come *here*?" he asked incredulously. "To the Temple?"

The idea did seem ludicrous. There probably wasn't anything the counselor could really do about it if he or she was offended by what went on here. None of it was illegal—provided nobody was caught smoking pot. But things could get ugly, especially if the counselor became convinced the Temple was part of Christopher's problem.

"Perhaps not," Alex replied. "But maybe Christopher could go to their offices once or twice a week. It's worth looking into, isn't it?"

"How expensive would that be?" Marianne asked dubiously.

Since I still had the laptop with me, it was easy enough for me to go online and look up the website for the counseling center Alex was referring to. They didn't have prices listed, but they did have a phone number, and Marianne agreed to call them and get more information.

AFTER THE issue of Christopher had been decided, at least for now, Alex announced she absolutely *had* to get back to the kitchen, and Marianne went to the office to make the phone call. But I cornered Seth at the door leading into the front hall before he could escape.

"I hear Rafe speaks Greek."

The sex kitten in question hadn't been invited to the meeting.

"Yes."

"Can he read the libretto?"

Seth leaned his shoulder against the polished oak doorframe and crossed his arms over his chest. "That part of the libretto, as far as I'm aware, was copied from… Plato or some other ancient Greek source—one which may not yet have been translated into any modern language. Can you read Old English, just because you speak Modern English?" He raised his eyebrow. "Keep in mind, this is poetry, with a heavy emphasis on rhythmic patterns."

He had me there. *Beowulf* had been the bane of my existence one semester when I was a college sophomore. But I persisted. "Rafe can't read a single word?"

"I can," a deep, smooth voice said behind me, and I nearly jumped out of my skin. It was Rafe, of course. He'd come down the hallway while we were talking.

"But only a word here and there," he continued. "That's why I suggested sending it to my uncle Adrian. He teaches history and philosophy at the University of Crete."

I wasn't sure what I was accusing him of, exactly. I just had a vague feeling the two of them had been keeping something from me. But perhaps I was being paranoid.

I decided to change my line of questioning to something more useful. "When do you think he'll have the translation done?"

At that, Rafe held up a few pages of paper and smiled. "He e-mailed them to me this afternoon."

I practically snatched the pages out of his hand. But it did me little good. They were still in Greek.

At my puzzled expression, Rafe explained, "Uncle Adrian doesn't speak English. But he's translated the verses into Modern Greek, so I can translate it into English."

"How long will that take?" It took all my self-restraint not to whine like a spoiled six-year-old.

Rafe moved around to look at the pages I was still holding and read out loud, "For you who rules all things, this… libation… and… soup…? I bring, Zeus or Hades, as you prefer to be called." He stopped reading and looked at me, his demeanor oddly apologetic for a man who normally exuded arrogance. "I should take some time to work out a more… poetic translation."

Bowyn had been waiting near the staircase for me to join him. Now he wandered over to us. "Have you already read it?" Rafe nodded. "Yes, of course."

"What is it about?" I asked.

"I believe it's a summoning—of the spirits of the dead."

*Charming.*

I handed the papers back to him. "As much as we need to know what the libretto says, we'll also need to come up with a phonetic translation of the original Ancient Greek, so the choir knows how to pronounce it."

"Uncle Adrian sent that as well. Though he wrote it out in the Greek alphabet, of course, so I'll have to translate it into the Latin alphabet."

"How long do you think that will take?"

"I can do it tonight."

"All right. We'll deal with that tomorrow. For this evening, the choir will have to content themselves with 'la, la, la.'"

Seth moved to take Rafe's arm and lead him away—no doubt to some midafternoon acrobatics—but I stopped them. "What about the solo part?"

"What about it?" Rafe asked.

"The libretto for the solo is distinct from the choir's libretto. It's written in Latin characters, but I was wondering if it might be spelling out Greek words phonetically."

That caught Seth's attention. "Can you show us?"

I hadn't shut the laptop down yet, so I went over to the dining room table and brought Christopher's transcribed part up on the screen. The others drew near and leaned in close to examine it.

"That isn't Greek," Rafe said after a moment. "Even if it was ancient Greek, spelled phonetically, I would expect to recognize a word or two, but nothing sounds familiar. '*MaCaMa GaHa*'? That's nonsense."

"Well, I've just been guessing at the vowels," I said. "They could be anything."

But Seth's eyes suddenly went wide. "Wait a minute…. *MaCaMa GaHa PaD ZaR*…." He read it a couple times more, saying it under his breath, his brow furrowed in concentration. "It's distorted, but… I think I might recognize it."

The rest of us all stared at him blankly. Seth frowned as he leaned in closer to read more of the text, and then he nodded, as if he was certain. "Come on. Let's go up to the library," he ordered. "Bring the laptop."

FORTUNATELY IT was still the middle of the afternoon and there was plenty of light in the library, so I wasn't treated to another episode of Follow the Bouncing Flashlight. Seth told the three of us to wait by the faux fireplace while he disappeared into the stacks. I took the opportunity to set the laptop up on the same mahogany desk I'd used the day before and plug it in, since its batteries were now running pretty low.

"Damn it!" Seth called from within the stacks after several minutes had gone by. "Why haven't we put in a card catalogue yet?"

Bowyn shook his head and shouted, "Maybe if you told me what you were looking for, I could help search."

When Seth didn't answer, Bowyn sighed and disappeared into the stacks after him. They started arguing about something, but the conversation was unintelligible from where I was sitting. That left me alone with Rafe, and when I looked over to where he was sitting, spread-eagle in one of the large leather chairs, he grinned at me and then proceeded to lift the hemline of his robe up to expose his substantial endowment. From the look of it, he had to be thinking some very dirty thoughts.

I groaned. "Not now," I said, though I had to admit, the sight of his erection *did* arouse me. But this was hardly the place or the time.

After a few minutes, Bowyn and Seth returned, and Rafe had enough sense to lower his robe, perhaps realizing neither of the other men would appreciate sexual flirtation when there was serious magickal work to do.

"Unfortunately," Seth said to me, "there are no first editions of John Dee's diaries available for purchase, as far as I can discover, so we'll have to make do with Casaubon's slanderous *True and Faithful Relation*."

He was referring to a book published by the English cleric Meric Casaubon in 1659. It was called *The True and Faithful Relation of What Passed for Many Yeers Between Dr. John Dee (a Mathematician of Great Fame in Q. Eliz. and King James Their Reignes) and Some Spirits* and it reproduced some of the diaries of John Dee after they'd come into the author's possession. The full title is five times as long.

Frankly, I really didn't care whether we got the information from a dusty old tome or looked it up on Wikipedia—or perhaps something a *little* more authoritative. I could understand Seth's book fetish, but there was no point in being ridiculous about it. What concerned me at the moment was the mention of John Dee. "Seth, John Dee wasn't even *born* until almost thirty years after Ficino died. There's no way Ficino could have been aware of Dee and Kelley's work."

"Who, pray tell, is John Dee?" Rafe interjected.

Seth, Bowyn, and I all turned to look at him and, for a moment, I felt sorry for the arrogant peacock. This was one area in which sex appeal wasn't going to impress anyone.

"Perhaps, my oversexed pet," Seth responded coolly, "you should be spending a little more time with your occult studies and a little less time with your pretty ass in the air."

Ouch.

But Rafe didn't rise to the bait. He ran his hands up his inner thighs, underneath his robe, and purred, "Couldn't you teach me *while* my ass is in the air?"

Bowyn groaned and rolled his eyes while Seth clucked at his "pet" and said, "John Dee was the court astrologer for Queen Elizabeth the First and one of her most trusted advisors. He was also rumored to have raised a magickal storm that saved the English fleet from the Spanish Armada."

"More importantly," Bowyn said, "he and his channel, Ned Kelley, claimed to be receiving communications from the angels, which Dee wrote about in his diaries. The angels dictated an entire magickal language to them, which could be used to communicate with the divine."

I knew all this. The language was called, by Dee, the Language of the Angels and later occultists had dubbed it Enochian. Dee claimed it was the original language spoken in the Garden of Eden before man's fall from grace. Since the Order wasn't a particularly Christian-leaning organization, we hadn't really done much work with angelic spirits, though many people claimed Dee's system was incredibly powerful.

Seth flipped through the pages of the book until he found the page he was looking for, and then he thrust it in front of me. There it was—the first line from the tenor solo, spelled differently but phonetically similar to what I'd written—*Micma goho Piad....*

*Behold, sayeth your God....*

It was the third of the Enochian elemental calls—summonings of the angelic spirits.

# Chapter Seventeen

"IT ISN'T possible," I insisted. "Ficino never met Dee and Kelley. Enochian didn't even *exist* when he was alive."

"Unless Ned Kelley was telling the truth," Bowyn replied. "And it really was the first language—or some kind of spirit language, at any rate—passed along through him to John Dee by the angelic spirits."

Edward Kelley had been a rather seedy character. Three decades younger than Dee, the twenty-seven-year-old Kelley had already been pilloried for counterfeiting and forgery by the time he approached Dee, claiming the ability to communicate with angels while in a trance state. Dee had, by this point, been dabbling in spirit communications for a while and had received a prophecy about a great medium who would be working with him soon, so he was more than willing to accept Kelley's claim at face value. Their relationship went on for decades. It ended shortly after Kelley convinced Dee the angels had commanded he have sex with Dee's wife—a woman closer to Kelley's age than Dee's. After they'd parted ways, Kelley ended up imprisoned for false claims that he could produce gold from base metal. He died trying to escape prison at the age of forty-two.

So there was reason to suspect his communications with the angels were entirely fabricated.

"*Partially* fabricated," Seth corrected when I pointed this out to him and Bowyn. "I don't believe the angels suggested wife-swapping either—though, as a whole, European culture might have benefitted from the practice. But I've worked with Enochian magick, and it's a very powerful system. Kelley may have believed himself that he was making it all up, but if he was even partly in a hypnotic state, something real may have come through."

"Like spirit writing?" I asked, referring to a process of making random scribbles on a piece of paper while focusing on a question. Some people who are sensitive to the spirits often find words appearing in the scribbles of their own volition—words that provide an answer to the question.

"Exactly."

"And Ficino may have tapped into the same spiritual current in his own magickal workings," Bowyn filled in.

It seemed possible. Oh, I know, it all seems absurd to someone who doesn't believe in magick. But those of us who do—well, *some* of us—see the physical universe as merely the visible, tangible surface of something that runs much deeper—an ocean of spiritual undercurrents that have a profound influence upon the physical world. These currents contain the entire storehouse of human and divine knowledge—something referred to as the "akashic records" by Theosophists—and someone who is sensitive to spiritual influences can often receive some of that knowledge, either deliberately or accidentally.

"Okay," I said, shifting in my seat as I eyed the screen of the laptop warily. "So I'm thinking now that maybe it isn't such a good idea to hold a rehearsal of the mass tonight."

As I feared, Seth raised an eyebrow and asked, "Why not?"

*I knew it. My life really* was *a horror movie.*

"Because," I explained slowly, as if to a small child, "we have no idea what we're invoking or why. This is why your mother said it was bad to play with Ouija boards, Seth."

Seth laughed. "If I recall, I played with Ouija boards despite what my mother wanted. And, I suspect, so did you."

Well, he had me there.

"Magick spells and incantations," he went on, "don't work unless you know how to raise and direct energy while casting them. If that weren't the case, every thirteen-year-old who picked up *The Lesser Key of Solomon* in middle school would cause massive death and destruction, or at least rid the world of a few bullies and abusive teachers."

"Christopher *does* know how to direct the energies in the mass, Seth, whether consciously or unconsciously. I've seen it."

I quickly recounted the experience I'd had with Christopher that afternoon, the way his singing had enthralled not only me, but also the birds surrounding us. But rather than make Seth fearful or cautious, this information delighted him.

"Excellent! I suspected the boy had some magickal ability."

"More than 'some,' if you ask me. Though it may be he only realizes it through music."

"It's too bad you won't be staying with us, my love. Christopher could benefit from your coaching."

Nice try. But I had a life to get back to. "My point is we're handing a young man with some inherent ability a piece of magickal invocation that might as well have been designed explicitly for him. And we have no idea what it does. This strikes me as unwise."

Bowyn nodded in agreement. "Just a bit."

But Seth would hear none of it. "Both of you, please! You know it's in Enochian now, and you have reference material. So *find out* what it does. You're mages, aren't you? Stop acting like superstitious peasants in a bad horror film and put your skills to good use."

With that he left, taking Rafe with him.

I sighed and turned to look at the libretto, still displayed on the laptop. "I knew he'd say that."

"Well, what do you think?" Bowyn asked, smiling, his usual good humor returning. "Are we about to open up a gateway to hell and unleash Armageddon?"

"I… don't know…."

He laughed and bent down to kiss me. For a moment my anxiety was lost in the warm softness of his lips. Then he pulled away. "You could always refuse to translate the Enochian."

"What good would that do?" I was feeling peevish once again. "Seth would just go ahead and have the mass performed regardless. He pretty much has all the pieces now. As tempting as it is to tie him up and gag him—which I'm sure he would enjoy—my only real choice is to do the translation and find out exactly what the spell does."

BOWYN HAD me pack up the laptop and take that and the Casaubon book down to our room, though I doubted Seth would have approved of its removal from the library, so he could toss me onto the bed for a little stress relief before I went back to work. It was much needed for both of us.

But I wanted to have a better idea what the libretto was saying before the rehearsal tonight. At that time of year, sunset was at about quarter to six, so it didn't give me much time to work before dinner.

Bowyn went back to the book he was reading—a collection of H.P. Lovecraft stories—while I went back to the laptop. Unfortunately, after about an hour and a half, I had to admit I was stymied.

"Goddamn it," I mumbled to no one in particular, though of course Bowyn heard me. "These aren't Enochian!"

Bowyn closed his book, putting a finger between the pages to hold his place. "What's that? I thought we'd established that it was."

"Certainly big parts of it are," I admitted, "but there are passages with just a few Enochian words here and there. The rest consists of words I can't find in any of the references."

Bowyn got up off the bed and came over to look at what I'd accomplished so far. The first two-thirds had been a fairly close approximation of the third Enochian call of the elemental tablets—the one used for invoking the senior angelic spirits of the tablet of Air. There were numerous variations in phonetic spelling—apart from me using *A* for all the vowels—and grammar, but I'd been able to work the kinks out of these fairly easily. The final section, however, was extremely problematic. There were Enochian words interspersed throughout the text, but I was unable to find a good percentage of them in Dee's work.

"Please tell me you looked up an online reference guide to Enochian."

I rolled my eyes at him. "Of course. I'm not an idiot." The Casaubon text was invaluable as a primary source but failed to lay out a coherent Enochian dictionary. Additionally it wasn't the only source for the language, as Casaubon had only published some of Dee's writings. Fortunately there were several Enochian dictionaries that could now be found online. "I'm sure some of the words in the libretto are just obscure, because of the way they're spelled out, and I'll probably find them eventually. But I'm just as certain some of them aren't in any reference I've found. I've tried every variation on pronunciation I could think of."

"That doesn't mean they're not Enochian," Bowyn pointed out. "They may just be words Dee never had revealed to him."

I mentally kicked myself. Of course. However Ficino had arrived at his version of the Enochian language, he hadn't been in communication with Dee or Kelley. So there were bound to be words that were unique to it.

"In that case, we're screwed," I said. "Without a translation key, we'll never figure out what this means."

Bowyn looked up at the window. It was cool outside, but warm enough that he'd opened it just a crack, and now the night breeze brought the sound of the church bell to us, signaling Resh and dinner.

"I wouldn't be so sure," he said. "If the choir rehearses the mass tonight, with Christopher participating, we may get a pretty good idea."

# Chapter Eighteen

WE RAN into Marianne at dinner, and she took us aside to tell us about the phone call to the Berlin rehab center.

"They agreed to see him," she told us, her voice low. She glanced around to make sure nobody was listening and then took another sip of some kind of tea that had a strong spearmint aroma to it. "I already spoke to Seth and Alex about it, and they think we should pay for it out of Temple funds if you two agree."

"Sure," Bowyn said.

I wasn't crazy about having to approve anything the Temple did, but I supposed I'd asked for it. There was no point being contrary, especially when Christopher needed our help. "Okay. But what about you? You're the Temple accountant."

Marianne grimaced. "Well, it's a little expensive. But nothing like Seth's library acquisitions. And it's nice to see Temple funds going toward actually *helping* someone for once."


I HADN'T yet seen the inside of the chapel at night, with the lights turned on. The outer wall of the chapel was cylindrical, with large columns spaced evenly along the wall, though the columns weren't actually flush against the wall—there was a gap of about two feet. The lights, looking like Victorian mantle gas lamps, were attached to the columns. There were also similar lamps on the inner circle of columns that supported the dome cornice. Apart from a faint electrical hum, audible when one stood close to the lights, the impression of stepping back in time to the Victorian era was perfect.

I was pleased to see that Christopher had shown up for the rehearsal. He looked sullen, but he was there. In fact, nearly everybody was there. Even though this was just supposed to be a rehearsal, rather than an actual performance, the chapel was packed with initiates and neophytes who had been hearing rumors about the mysterious musical project. They were all dying with curiosity about it, and they weren't going to miss this chance to hear what all the fuss was about.

I thought at first Seth would be annoyed, but I should have known better. Anything that focused attention on him or one of his projects was good in his book. He was delighted, hopping from person to person, chatting everyone up as if he were trying to persuade them to buy stock in the production.

While everyone was busy jabbering away, I took the opportunity to approach the choir and have a brief talk with Timothy and Christopher. Motioning them both aside, I told them, "I think you both should know we've had some more luck translating the libretto."

"Please don't tell me you're going to shove new lyrics at my choir five seconds before showtime," Timothy groaned. He was eyeing the size of the crowd anxiously, wringing his conducting baton in his hands.

"No. But… did you notice anything odd this afternoon when the choir performed the Credo?"

Timothy shrugged. "No. It was a fairly easy piece, and I confess I found it somewhat dull."

"It won't be dull with Christopher singing the solo," I assured him. "The choral part is designed to support the soloist, and if this afternoon was any indication, it's pretty powerful." Christopher was listening to this conversation, so I threw him a bone. "Christopher really nailed it."

The young man glanced down at the floor, as if uncomfortable being praised.

"Good," Timothy said.

"Not necessarily."

I explained what we'd discovered about the libretto and watched Timothy's expression go from cynicism to wide-eyed horror in the space of about thirty seconds. Being a member of the Temple, he was not only the choir director, but also a magician himself.

"You're not serious! Calling angelic spirits without having any idea what we're asking them to do? Have you lost your mind?"

Christopher seemed a bit lost. No doubt his experience with ceremonial magick was still limited. "Why is that a problem?" he asked us. "Angels are good, right?"

"No!" Timothy and I said in unison.

"If you pay close attention to the mentions of angels in the Bible," I explained, "you'll see them described as massively powerful beings, occasionally appearing as benevolent messengers, but much more frequently as fearful harbingers of destruction. If you're in good with the Judeo-Christian God—which most of us here are *not*, I might add—you might be able to order them around by invoking his name. Otherwise, you might want to avoid them."

Our philosophy at the Temple included the belief that all gods were real and should be treated respectfully, including the God of the Old Testament. Where we differed from Christians and Jews was in the way we viewed him. We didn't believe Tetragrammaton, a common name for him in ceremonial magick, was the only god, and we didn't believe he was all-powerful. But we did believe he deserved our respect. And the angelic spirits were his minions. Only the followers of Tetragrammaton had the right to invoke them.

Christopher shrugged. "I didn't sense anything dangerous when I sang this afternoon."

It was true the experience had been beautiful and awe-inspiring to me, as well, rather than frightening. But that didn't change the fact that we were messing around with powerful forces when we had no idea what we were doing.

"I would recommend," I said directly to Christopher, "just singing a generic 'la' for all the notes in your solo. Don't try to sing the syllables I gave you."

"I sang them this afternoon and nothing bad happened."

"You were mispronouncing them this afternoon, thanks to me having no idea what I was doing. There's no point in compounding the error by mispronouncing them again tonight."

He rolled his eyes but muttered, "Whatever," which I took to be acquiescence.

"Can we at least do some warding before the performance?" Timothy asked.

I nodded and jerked my thumb in Seth's direction. "I'll see if I can talk P.T. Barnum over there into it."

I turned to go, but Christopher snagged my elbow. Waiting until Timothy had moved away, he lowered his voice and asked, "So? What happened at the meeting?"

I mentally kicked myself for leaving him hanging. "We all want you to stay, Christopher. But we'd like to arrange for you to see a drug counselor. If we set it up for you, will you go?"

He looked delighted. "Sure! Anything you want, Jeremy!"

Then he startled me by hugging me again. It was bizarre he would go from not wanting me to touch him at all to what seemed like overenthusiastic hugging so quickly, and I still suspected the hugs were his way of getting what he wanted from me. But I hugged him back regardless.

"Do you think you can follow along with the other tenors for the choral parts?"

"Oh yeah. Timothy went over them with me about an hour ago. They're easy."

Christopher broke away and ran to rejoin the choir.

I found Seth surrounded by neophytes, enthralling the newbies with tales of Aleister Crowley. He wasn't particularly pleased by my interruption, but when I explained what Timothy had asked for, Seth's face lit up.

"Excellent!" he replied, never one to pass up an opportunity for showmanship. "I think that could be most instructive to our neophytes." He lifted his arms and raised his voice. "People! People! Listen up! Could I have order, please? Thank you. Before the performance, we're going to perform the LBRP...."

I let him ramble on about it, as if the entire evening had some sort of carefully planned itinerary, while I found my seat beside Bowyn, Marianne, Alex, and Rafe. It was nice that Alex had been able to take some time away from the kitchen, but I was concerned about Marianne. She was looking pale. "Are you okay?"

She shook her head slightly. "I'm pretty nauseous, actually. And my head is killing me."

"Do you want to go back to the house?" Bowyn asked, concerned.

"I don't want to miss the first performance of the fabulous Ficino requiem," she replied with a laugh. "I should be able to last that long, if Seth ever shuts up so the music can start."

"I can't believe he's turning a simple rehearsal into such a circus," Alex muttered. "Poor Timothy must be having a stroke."

Seth led the congregation through the Lesser Banishing Ritual of the Pentagram. This was one of the most elementary rituals of ceremonial magick—at least for those following the Golden Dawn tradition—and one of the very first rituals everyone learned at the Temple, so even the neophytes were able to follow along easily. The purpose of the LBRP was to mark out an area of magickal space and prevent hostile energies from entering and interfering with magickal workings. Not, in this case, the angelic spirits themselves, since those were being invited in, but any other spirits that might take advantage of the situation to cause trouble. The Victorian version of the LBRP called upon the angels to protect the four quarters, but as I've said, we weren't particularly in sync with the Judeo-Christian tradition. Our version invoked the magickal elements instead—air, fire, water, and earth.

At last Seth took his seat beside Alex, with Rafe on his other side, and the music began.

The first two pieces were choral arrangements with no soloist. Up to this point, I'd heard them only in horrible MIDI renditions. Now, even with "la, la, la" substituted for their proper librettos, the beauty of the music was astonishing. It wasn't beautiful in the same way something written by Mozart or Beethoven was beautiful—it wasn't the genius of a master composer shining through. It was a sort of mathematical beauty. Ficino had determined the precise combination of notes and chords that would evoke a powerful emotional and spiritual response in the listener, and the effect could be felt in the body. In places, the choir held chords with a dissonance that was palpably disturbing, finally resolving them into something harmonic that left the listener with an immense sense of physical relief, only to find the process beginning again in a slightly different way.

Toward the end of the first piece, I started to notice something. I was almost certain I could hear the melodic line that Christopher had sung that afternoon as a solo, not in any one voice or part, but somehow interwoven throughout the melody. But I couldn't be certain before the piece ended. Wondering if I might hear the same thing in the second piece, I listened for it and this time I was certain. I could hear that melody coming through as sort of a *cantus firmus*—a preexisting melody, used as a foundation for a musical piece—though it was much more hidden in the composition than a *cantus firmus* would be, spread out among all of the choral parts. The sopranos would hit one note, followed by two notes sung by the altos, and so on. If you didn't know the melody was there, you wouldn't hear it. It was brilliant.

Though I noticed a slight "charge" to the air during these performances—something I could easily have imagined—nothing seemed particularly out of the ordinary. That is, until Christopher's solo.

With the chorus supporting him, and likewise bolstered by the magnificent acoustics in the chapel, Christopher's voice achieved a new level of beauty and power that touched upon the sublime. All those present in the audience were clearly riveted, unmoving, their eyes fixed upon Christopher. I was enthralled as well, but part of me was anxious now that I knew something—but not nearly enough—about the magickal intent of the music. I was watching the audience as much as the choir, aware of a strong visceral sensation building up in my body as the core of my being seemed to resonate with the music.

Something fluttered past my ear, and my eyes darted after it. As I followed its erratic path upward, the shadows high up in the dome of the chapel seemed to be writhing and swirling. Something was obscuring the painting on the inside of the dome and the moonlight coming in through the stained glass windows—something with a thousand fluttering wings.

Bats.

I couldn't tell how many bats were up there, but it was far more than I had ever seen before. I'd never been afraid of them, until that moment, but there is something primordially frightening about enormous swarms of small creatures, the hair on the back of my neck pricking up at the sight. I watched them, entranced by their frenetic swirling and fluttering high above me and the unearthly spell Christopher was weaving with his voice, until at long last the final note swelled throughout the chapel and slowly faded.

There was a long silence, during which nobody appeared to be breathing.

Then Marianne screamed.

# Chapter Nineteen

MARIANNE WAS doubled over in her seat, clutching at her stomach, clearly in severe pain. Bowyn reached out to her, but she shoved his hand away, lurched forward, and vomited on the marble floor. Where she'd been sitting, the pew was covered in blood.

While the rest of us stared blankly at her in shock, Alex leapt in to take charge.

"Somebody call 911!" Then when she realized that wasn't likely to accomplish much in a room full of people without cell phones, she pointed at one of the nearby neophytes and ordered, "You! Run back to the office and call! Now!"

Despite the Temple's relative seclusion, Route 2 was just down the hill, and it was less than fifteen miles to Androscoggin Valley Hospital in Berlin. We could have driven Marianne there, but an ambulance would hopefully get here faster, and the EMTs could begin treating her all the sooner, without the danger of us trying to move Marianne to a car. Bowyn and Alex stayed by Marianne's side while I ran down to the front gate to direct the ambulance to the chapel.

The next hour was chaotic and unpleasant. The ambulance arrived and EMTs did what they could for Marianne before strapping her to a stretcher and spiriting her away. Bowyn insisted on riding in the front of the ambulance while Seth drove Alex, Rafe, and me to the hospital in one of his more practical sedans. He left orders for a few of the senior initiates to see to it that the mess in the chapel was cleaned up and everybody stuck to their scheduled chores.

The ride to the hospital was one of the most unpleasant ordeals of my life. I had no idea what was wrong with Marianne, though Alex kept going on about a possible miscarriage. Seth and Rafe were, for once, mercifully silent, while I fretted about the mass. Had the music caused this? Or was it just a coincidence? I was probably being superstitious. Marianne had been feeling ill before the performance, after all. But I couldn't shake the feeling that we'd been foolish to allow the performance to go on that evening.

WE ARRIVED at the ER only to discover the intake nurse wouldn't tell us anything since we weren't immediate family. The fact that we were dressed like time travelers from a medieval monastery probably didn't help. There was no sign of Bowyn, so presumably he'd been allowed into the ER as the father-to-be. The rest of us had to fret in the waiting area while incoming patients gave us suspicious looks out of the corners of their eyes, and the widescreen television tormented us with an unpleasant reality makeover show and interminable ads.

Three hours later, we'd still learned nothing, and the only thing to interrupt the drone of the television had been a scruffy young college student who chatted with us, thinking we were doing Shakespeare in the Park or something. Rafe had been eyeing him like a fresh kill, so I was relieved when the young man was taken into the ER proper for someone to attend to his twisted ankle.

It was another couple of hours before Bowyn finally came out to the waiting area, looking haggard. I'd never seen his expression so lifeless, and I immediately knew the news had to be terrible.

"How is she?" I asked.

Bowyn looked surprised to see us there. I learned later that he'd been kept isolated in a room for several hours once Marianne had been taken into the Intensive Care Unit. He'd received updates now and then, but for the most part his ordeal had been worse than ours because he'd endured it alone.

"They think she'll be all right," he said, "but it's too soon to say for sure." He was so exhausted he seemed to have trouble speaking.

"What made her sick?"

"I don't think they know yet."

"Can we see her?"

Bowyn shook his head. "Not tonight. We might as well go home. They have the number if anything changes."

"What about the baby?" Alex asked, her voice shaking.

Bowyn replied dully, "There isn't going to be any baby."

WE RODE home in complete silence. Bowyn sat wedged into the backseat between me and Alex. I held one of his hands, and I think Alex took the other. But none of us could think of anything to say.

We pulled into the garage at close to four in the morning, exhausted. Alex and Seth insisted upon hugging Bowyn when we left them in the kitchen, and Bowyn even endured an insincere hug from Rafe. Then we went up to our room.

I was out of my robe and stretched out on the bed before I realized Bowyn had taken the envelope of ultrasounds from the dresser drawer. He brought it over to the bed and sat down beside me, and I watched as he opened it up and found the one where the baby's hand was visible.

"Maybe they shouldn't show you these," he said quietly, brushing the tiny hand with his finger, "until the baby is born."

And then the tears came. I held Bowyn while he sobbed for Jay, that small, helpless little boy his father would never have a chance to hold, and I wept for both of them.


SOMETHING AWAKENED me later in the night. Bowyn was sound asleep at last, after hours of tossing and turning, and I had an odd feeling of déjà vu, remembering the rustling in the walls two nights earlier. A light rain was falling outside, clouds darkening the sky, so even the pale moonlight from two nights ago was absent. Because of that, I was able to see the faint glow around the edges of the servants' door fade in briefly and then out again. It was so dim, I doubt I would have caught it had there been any moonlight.

Curious, I slipped out of bed and padded across the cool hardwood floor. The door opened with just the smallest sound of wood popping out of place, and I poked my head in. Off to my right, the narrow passageway came to the outer wall of the house and took a left-hand turn. A faint glow faded as whoever was carrying the flashlight moved away, and the soft footfalls of moccasined feet climbed the stairs, with an occasional quiet creak of the wooden boards. Or perhaps descended—the stairs went in both directions, so the visitor might have been climbing up or going down to the second floor.

I thought about pursuing him, but my curiosity wasn't great enough to venture into that dark, dusty rat maze. Already the light had faded to nothing, and I would have been walking in darkness unless I turned back to find a flashlight. By then, he or she would be gone. And I had a warm bed with Bowyn in it beckoning to me.

I closed the door and went back to crawl between the sheets. But these nighttime forays through the walls of the bedroom—coupled with Christopher sneaking into the room via that door—were beginning to creep me out a little. If I'd been planning on staying much longer, I would have insisted on putting a lock on the door.

# Chapter Twenty

NEITHER BOWYN nor I heard the morning bell. I suppose we were both exhausted, physically and emotionally, so we overslept by a good hour. It's possible we might have slept longer, but we were awakened by a gentle knock on the bedroom door.

Still groggy, Bowyn hoisted himself up on one arm and called out, "Who is it?"

"Christopher" came the muffled voice from the hall. "Is Jeremy there?"

Bowyn groaned and fell back onto the mattress. "Your troubled teen wants to talk to you."

I gave him a sour look but got up and went to the door. It was a reflection of how quickly I'd grown accustomed to life at the Temple—with a bit of sleepiness lumped in, perhaps—that I didn't realize until I'd opened the door that I didn't have a stitch on. But Christopher didn't seem fazed by it.

He himself was dressed in street clothes—battered old blue jeans, a plain T-shirt, and a leather jacket. I looked at him in confusion, wondering if he was leaving the Temple after all.

"Sorry if I woke you," he said. "I didn't see you at breakfast, and Alex told me you might be leaving the Temple before I get back. So I wanted to say good-bye."

None of this was quite making sense to my sleep-addled brain. "I'm not going away for at least a few more days."

"I know. But I won't be back by then."

So he *was* going away. "Where are you going?" I asked.

"Rehab." He didn't seem bothered by the idea. If anything, he seemed unusually cheerful this morning. "I have to spend a week in Berlin, so they can keep an eye on me." He rolled his eyes at that. "After that I can come back and just go in three times a week for counseling."

"Oh."

"I'll have to get drug tested every time I go in, and I'll get kicked out if the tests come up positive. They're pretty hardcore."

I was still trying to clear the cobwebs out of my head, wishing I had a cup of tea, but I smiled at him. "That's great, Christopher. I mean, that part might suck, but I think this will be good for you in the long run."

Christopher shrugged. "Yeah, I guess. Anyway, there's a cab waiting for me out front. I just didn't want to leave without saying good-bye."

That part still seemed a little odd. I supposed it was possible Christopher had actually taken a liking to me, but it still felt as if we'd gone from a hostile relationship to being friends way too quickly. But when he opened his arms for a hug, I went along with it.

The kiss was another matter entirely. I wasn't even quite sure how it happened, but somehow his mouth found mine and he was kissing me. Not just a friendly kiss, either—there was passion in it. I accepted it, too startled to think of a more appropriate reaction, until he pulled away with a gentle laugh and gave my stiffening cock a playful squeeze. He turned and walked away before I could figure out if I wanted to protest.

I closed the door and heard Bowyn laugh behind me. "I guess I wouldn't mind if you wanted to bring *that* one into our bed."

Heading back to the bed, I frowned at him. "I didn't tell him to grab my dick," I grumbled. "Or kiss me, for that matter."

"You didn't fight very hard."

"No," I admitted. "I mean, he *is* cute, and I guess I liked it, to some extent...."

"I didn't say I had a problem with it."

"Well, *I* had a problem with it," I replied, crawling onto the bed to straddle him. "It made me feel like one of his lecherous old tricks."

Bowyn reached up and gripped my erection, which, annoyingly, hadn't subsided. "Don't worry about it," he said, as he began to casually jerk me off. "I'd be willing to bet he did it just to fuck with your head."

"Probably." And he'd succeeded. But I couldn't think straight anymore with Bowyn's hand drawing all my focus to my crotch. I leaned forward, and this time there was no doubt at all in my mind about whether I wanted the kiss.

WE WENT to see Marianne after lunch—Bowyn, Alex, Seth, and I. Fortunately, Rafe was busy—presumably with something involving sex, since I wasn't aware of anything *else* he did at the Temple—and couldn't come along. Not that he was all that horrible, but I doubted Marianne would want him there when she was going through something this traumatic and deeply personal. We were family. Rafe was not.

Marianne was out of danger now, the hospital staff had told Bowyn when he called, and she'd been moved to a single room. Not being in a rush this time, we dressed in street clothes. I don't know if the staff would have given us a hard time or not if we'd worn our robes, but there was little point in tempting fate. We checked in at the reception desk, and they allowed us to go right up to her room.

We found her after a small amount of confusion—they had just moved her to a double-occupancy room to free up space. The double room was barely big enough for two beds, and we had to push our way past the bed of an elderly woman—Marianne's roommate—and numerous pieces of equipment to get to Marianne's side of the room. Bowyn had to sit on the bed while Alex took the only chair, leaving Seth and me to stand around feeling awkward. Overcrowding is one of many reasons I loathe hospitals.

"How are you feeling?" Bowyn asked, keeping his voice low. The woman on the other side of the curtain was asleep, but it still felt as if we had no privacy.

Marianne shrugged. "I guess I'll live." But her expression was anything but flippant. Her eyes were dark and haunted as she watched the drizzle coming down outside the sealed window. The total lack of fresh air is one of the *other* reasons I hate hospitals.

"Do you need us to bring you anything?" Alex asked.

"I don't know. Maybe… some books or something. Something cheerful. I have some old Leo Buscaglia books in my room."

Seth wrinkled up his nose. "Would you like us to bring you some cheap bodice rippers while we're at it? Or perhaps something about Christmas angels?"

Dr. Leo Buscaglia had been a popular writer and motivational speaker in the eighties and nineties. His stories about love overcoming adversity were one of Marianne's guilty pleasures. I had to admit, I found his stuff to be a pleasant diversion whenever I stumbled across it, but I think Seth would rather have had open-heart surgery without anesthesia.

Alex shut him up with a look. "Whatever you need, sweetheart. Do you know how long they want you to stay?"

"My doctor says they want to do some tests. Not only because of… the baby… but they aren't sure why I was so sick last night. I'm still nauseated. Plus, I'm still bleeding a lot. So they're doing a bunch of blood work to see if they can find anything. I should be able to go home in a couple days."

We stayed for about an hour, talking about everything except the baby. Marianne didn't seem ready for that, and the rest of us took our cue from her, keeping the conversation light. The question of how the hospital and the tests would be paid for came up, but only in passing. Apparently Seth had Marianne on a family insurance policy, along with Alex and Bowyn, so there were just some minor details to work out about what was covered. Bowyn assured her he would handle that end of things.

We left when Marianne said she was tired, but as we were on the way out of the room, she asked Bowyn, "Would you mind staying for a moment?"

So the rest of us waited for him out in the hall for what we expected to be just a minute, but which turned out to be several. When Bowyn finally joined us, his expression was troubled, but all he said was, "Let's go."


IT WASN'T until later that afternoon, when we were once again alone in our room, that I found out what Marianne had talked to Bowyn about.

"I think she wants to try again," Bowyn said quietly.

"Huh?" I was sitting at the laptop, once more wrestling with the Ficino manuscript. I turned to face him. "Isn't it a bit soon to talk about that?"

"She didn't really say it," he amended. "She mostly cried about the… about Jay. But she made a point of saying that the doctor had reassured her this didn't mean she'd never be able to have children. That's what some of the tests are going to try to find out."

An unpleasant, selfish thought flitted into my head—the thought that it might be better for me and Bowyn if Marianne didn't get pregnant again—and I pushed it away violently, ashamed of myself for thinking it. "What do *you* want to do?" I asked him.

"I don't know."

I stood and went over to join him on the bed. Taking his book out of his hands, I set it aside and drew him in for a long kiss. When we pulled apart, I said, "Maybe that's something to think about later."

Bowyn nodded and sought out my lips again. For the next half hour—well, more like an hour—I did my best to distract him from his troubled thoughts.


LATER IN the afternoon, Rafe came by the room to deliver his English translation of the Greek libretto, although he was still working on the phonetic transcription of the ancient Greek.

"As you requested, Brethren," Rafe said, bowing a bit too dramatically.

"Okay, thanks." I took the notes from him and ignored the performance.

Bowyn and I hadn't bothered to dress yet, so Rafe lingered in the open doorway, looking at us both with obvious longing. "Is there anything else I can do for you, Brethren?"

"The notes are good for now, thanks. Please finish up your phonetic transcription as soon as you can and give a copy to Timothy." I gave him a smirk. "We'll call you if we think of anything else we need." That wasn't going to happen—not with all the crap going on right now—but part of me enjoyed teasing him.

He bowed and I bowed back; then I closed the door.

I took the notes over to the bed and sat cross-legged beside Bowyn to read them. The translation didn't seem bad, considering it had gone through an intermediary translation. I couldn't really tell if much had been lost in that process, but one thing was immediately clear to me.

"This isn't Plato," I said aloud.

Bowyn looked up from his book and tried to peek over my leg at the pages. "How do you know?"

"Well, listen to this—*Ia! Ia! Cthulhu fthagn!*"

"What?" Bowyn laughed. "You're so full of shit."

That particular chant, as any fan of horror author H.P. Lovecraft knows, was supposedly used by the insane followers of the Old Ones to summon the god Cthulhu from the depths of the sea.

I smiled at him. "True. But I'm serious about it not being Plato. It's an invocation to Zeus or Hades. Odd that it doesn't seem to care which. If Plato wrote anything like this, I've never heard about it. Not that I'm really an expert on Plato, but I've had to read a lot of his works, since Ficino worked with them so much."

"Could it be a lost work?"

I shook my head and frowned. "I really doubt it. This is a magickal invocation, which isn't something I've ever known Plato to write about. But the ancient Greeks certainly believed in magick and had spells for all sorts of things, so I can believe it's a text from his time period, or thereabouts."

"What does it say?"

I read Rafe's translation aloud:

"For you who rules all things, this libation and broth I bring, Zeus or Hades, as you are content to be called. From me accept the sacrifice, the unburnt offering of all fruits that complete has been poured forth for you, out of the gods and the sons of Ouranos, take in hand the scepter of Zeus, and with Hades share the rule of earthly things, send to the light the souls of those below, those willing for a contest to know beforehand from where will sprout the root of evils, what must be offered up for the blessed to find rest from toil."

Bowyn leaned forward to look at Rafe's notes and placed his chin on my leg, reminding me of the way my Labrador used to curl up with me when I was a kid. I couldn't resist reaching down to stroke his hair.

"More summonings?" he asked.

"I think so. Or at least a request that the gods open the gates between the land of the living and the land of the dead."

Bowyn raised his eyebrows. "That's nice. Why?"

"Your guess is as good as mine," I replied. "And I'm beginning to grow very concerned about what could happen when we apply both the Greek libretto to the choir and the pseudo-Enochian libretto to the solo. You felt it, didn't you? The way things were resonating during Christopher's solo?"

"I felt it," Bowyn admitted. "But what does that mean? What was it trying to do?"

I didn't want to say out loud that I feared the mass had had something to do with Marianne's miscarriage. I didn't really know that. Miscarriages happen all the time without metaphysical intervention. Marianne hadn't been feeling well to begin with, and the pregnancy had had its own issues.

But as a magician, I really didn't feel comfortable plowing ahead with a magickal operation I knew very little about. How many horror movies began that way? *"Why, looky here! It's a book called 'The....*

*Book… of… the…. Dead'… and it's bound with human skin. Let's open it up and read from it!"*

No, I don't get my magickal knowledge from B horror films, but if you believe in magick, casting spells without having any idea what the effects could be is plain stupid. And, of course, we'd just done it.

On the other hand, one doesn't undertake the study of magick without a certain amount of arrogance and a high degree of inquisitiveness, and these were traits Bowyn and I had always had in common with Seth. For all that I had reservations about the mass, part of me still desperately wanted to know what it was for. And even if I found out the answer to that question, would I be able to go back to Durham without ever finding out if the mass *worked*?

"I don't know… anything… right now," I said at last. I set Rafe's notes aside. "And as much fun as it is to research what demonic forces we may have unleashed upon the world, I'm hungry. Let's see what we can dig up for lunch."


IT WASN'T more than a couple of hours until supper, but Alex took pity on us and set Bowyn and I up with some leftover *solyanka,* or what passed for it in the vegetarian cookbooks—a delicious casserole made with potatoes, ricotta cheese, and cabbage. Alex herself was too busy to talk much, so we ate while she rushed around the kitchen, preparing dinner and barking at staff, as usual.

"Chop that up finer, please. Sam! Do these forks look clean to you? Well, they don't to me! Colleen, I need another… say, four eggplants! Now!"

Bowyn and I knew her well enough to know she didn't mean anything personally—she just needed to get food prepared for about a hundred people, quickly, and make sure it was delicious, healthy, and unlikely to give anyone food poisoning. A little schmutz on a fork might not seem like a big deal to the dishwasher, but it certainly was a big deal to the person eating with it.

"Do either of you need anything?" Alex asked, breezing by the table.

"I'm all set," I responded.

"Would you like some tea?"

Bowyn shrugged. "You're busy. We can get it ourselves."

"Don't be silly."

Alex went over to the cupboard where her alphabetically labeled canisters of dried herbs were laid out in tidy rows and took down several of them. She placed them on the counter in front of her and retrieved a ceramic teapot from another shelf. This type of teapot had a mesh filter that sat inside the top, where she could mix the tea and then allow it to steep in the hot water she poured into the pot.

Alex had tossed in several mints and a bit of ginseng—which was a good overall tonic, though it smelled and tasted enough like dirt to need its flavor masked—when she suddenly hesitated. She looked down at the handful of herb she'd taken from the container labeled "Spearmint," running it through her fingers for a moment, a bewildered look on her face. She sniffed it and her eyes widened in horror.

"Who's been fucking around with the teas?" Alex shouted out to the neophytes scurrying back and forth in the room.

Nobody answered, so she whirled to face them, still holding the spearmint in her hand. "Answer me! Who's been in the teas?"

All activity ground to a halt, and all the neophytes were looking at her, terrified but baffled. Not one of them answered her. Bowyn and I glanced at each other, equally puzzled.

"This," she shouted, holding up the herb in her hand, "isn't spearmint! Not all of it. Who put something in the 'Spearmint' canister? Answer me!"

When all she got was silence, Alex turned back to the canister and picked it up. She peered into it, shaking it and angling it so the light could better expose its contents. After a minute of that, Alex slammed the canister down on the counter and braced herself, as if she might fall over. Her eyes closed and she was breathing heavily.

"What's wrong?" Bowyn asked.

She shook her head and took a very long time to answer. "Somebody mixed something in with the spearmint." Her voice sounded choked, and when she raised her hand to return the herb she was holding to its canister, it was shaking.

Bowyn's eyes went wide. "Wasn't that what Marianne was drinking last night? It smelled like spearmint."

"It's not spearmint," Alex repeated slowly. "Not all of it. Somebody mixed pennyroyal into it."

I don't have an extensive knowledge of herbs, but I knew one thing about pennyroyal—it's often used to bring about abortions.

# Chapter Twenty-One

IT WAS Alex who ordered one of the neophytes to call the police. Then she ordered everyone out of the kitchen but me and Bowyn. "Take everything off the burners and you"—she pointed at someone—"put up a sign on the dining room door to tell people dinner will be delayed for at least an hour or two. Then I want everyone out of here. Understood?"

Alex collapsed into a chair beside me and put her head in her hands. "Oh gods...."

Bowyn was looking at her with an expression that was more hostile than I'd ever seen on him. "Are you telling me," he said, slowly... quietly, "that my son died because of the tea Marianne was drinking? Tea that *you* made for her?"

Alex raised her face and looked at him with tears beginning to well up in her eyes. "I... I don't know."

Bowyn stood up so quickly that his chair fell over, clattering to the floor. He grabbed the chair in a fury and stood it upright, slamming it into place at the table. Both Alex and I jumped while Bowyn stormed off, muttering, "I'm going to get Seth before the police arrive."

I didn't know who needed my comfort more, but since Bowyn was storming out, I opted to put my arm around Alex. I still didn't know what had really happened. The thought of someone with as much experience as Alex making a mistake like this was almost inconceivable. But she wasn't denying it. She lowered her head and sobbed while I rubbed her shoulders and utterly failed to think of anything I could say to her.

THE POLICE didn't really know what to make of the situation. No matter how many times Alex tried to explain to them that there was no way that pennyroyal could have ended up in that canister by accident, the two officers seemed convinced that it was nothing more than a mistake. One with tragic consequences, perhaps, but they couldn't believe anyone had deliberately done anything wrong.

"Ma'am," the older officer said reasonably, "you said yourself that it was chaotic, and you were being pulled in twenty different directions at once. Did you make the tea, or did Mrs. Truitt—"

"*Miss* Truitt," Bowyn corrected.

The officer—his name was Westcott—looked over at Bowyn. "Are you the boyfriend?"

"More or less."

The man nodded and turned his attention back to Alex. "Did Miss Truitt make the tea herself?"

"No," Alex said adamantly. "Nobody touches the herbs in that cupboard besides me."

"Then isn't it possible that you were too rushed to notice that the wrong herb was in the container? You say—" He checked his notepad. "—pennyroyal smells like spearmint, right?"

"Somewhat," Alex said. "One of my kitchen helpers cut herself and…. Look, officer, I admit that I made the tea and that I must have put the pennyroyal into it, thinking it was spearmint. If I'd been paying closer attention, I might have noticed it didn't look right. Spearmint is dark green, and pennyroyal looks greenish brown when it's dried. But I never would have put it in the tea canister in the first place! That's what I'm trying to tell you. I don't fill them while I'm in the middle of meal prep. It's something I do at night, when things have calmed down. And those two herbs don't look anything alike, even dried and crushed. Someone had to have mixed it in with the spearmint to hide it."

The officer's partner was younger and didn't seem terribly bright. He wasn't even pretending not to be weirded out by the Temple and everyone who lived there. Nobody had been walking around naked in front of the police, to my knowledge, but we were all in our robes, and this guy was blatantly staring, probably wondering exactly what we had on underneath. Had Rafe found him to be cute, he might have let the officer have a peek, but fortunately for all of us, that didn't happen.

Seth was standing over Alex with one hand resting protectively on her shoulder while Westcott questioned her. It was the first time I'd seen Seth touch his wife since I'd arrived, and it was reassuring to me to see the small sign of affection between them.

"Officer," Seth said coolly, "my wife is an expert in herbal medicine. She's published four books on the subject. She would not have made a mistake like that."

Westcott sighed, clearly not convinced. As far as he was concerned, Alex had made a simple mistake and mixed up the teas. Case closed.

"And another thing," Alex said, getting up and walking over to the sideboard, where the tea canister was still sitting, open, among the others she'd taken down earlier. "Smell this."

Reluctantly, the officer went over to lean over the canister and take a sniff. "Smells like spearmint," he said, unimpressed.

Alex reached into the cupboard and pulled down another canister. Then she opened it and placed it under his nose. "And this?"

Westcott sniffed at it, but seemed a little less certain. "Spearmint?"

"No," she said, showing him the label on the canister. "Pennyroyal. You can see that it doesn't look much like spearmint at all. But you'll also notice this one doesn't smell nearly as strong as the other canister."

"Because the other one also has real spearmint in it."

"No." Alex shook her head emphatically. "Dried pennyroyal isn't guaranteed to cause a miscarriage—not in small amounts. But if whoever mixed the pennyroyal in with the spearmint wanted to be certain it would work, they would have mixed something else in as well."

She turned back to the cupboard and began rummaging through several small bottles made of brown glass with black rubber stoppers. After a moment, she found what she'd been searching for. "The oil would have left a residue floating on top of the tea and Marianne probably would have noticed it, but… here it is. Pennyroyal tincture." She held the bottle up to the light. "It's half empty now."

"Are you sure it wasn't like that before?"

"Positive."

"Why is that better than oil?"

"It's alcohol based, so there wouldn't have been any residue from it. If someone applied it to the herb and let it dry before mixing it in with the spearmint, it would have been far more concentrated than just the herb itself."

I couldn't really blame Westcott for looking skeptical. The whole thing was starting to sound more and more far-fetched. In order to do what Alex was proposing, the pennyroyal would have had to be prepared at least a day or two in advance.

Westcott frowned and nodded at his partner. "All right, Mrs. Harriman. We'll write up a report, and call the hospital to see if they ran some toxicology labs. If they didn't find evidence of this, we'll ask them to check for it specifically. We'll take some pictures while we're here, and see if we can lift any fingerprints. Are you sure nobody but you ever touches these containers?"

"Until now."

"Then we'll take your fingerprints too. Of course, you've just been touching everything again," he added, annoyed. "But if anything turns up that isn't one of your prints...." He shrugged, noncommittally.

Bowyn was standing off in one corner of the kitchen, watching all of this, his face clouded. I tried to say something to him while the police went about their business, but he merely held up a hand for me to be silent, so I left him to his dark thoughts. It upset me to see him closed up like that, but I'd never been through the loss of a child, and I could only imagine how he must feel to learn that someone in his own home may have deliberately caused the miscarriage.

And that was what made all this truly horrific to me. I believed Alex. She might have made the tea, failing to notice the pennyroyal mixed in with the spearmint and the stronger-than-usual smell while she was in the middle of trying to coordinate everything else in the kitchen. After over a decade of nobody—and I mean *nobody*—ever touching those canisters but her, she had no reason to assume they contained anything other than what they were supposed to contain. I also knew she hadn't made a mistake and mixed pennyroyal into the spearmint. Despite what the police might have thought, this wasn't an accident. Somebody had deliberately put the herb there, knowing that it was likely to find its way into Marianne's tea—somebody who wanted Marianne to lose the baby.

And that somebody lived here at the Temple.

AFTER THE police left, Alex went to the sink to wash off the ink they'd used to fingerprint her. Seth seemed to feel the need to comfort her, so he said, "Nobody blames you for this, Alex."

His wife didn't respond. Over in the corner, Bowyn finally roused himself and announced, "I'm going to the hospital to tell Marianne what we've found." Even though all this had begun at "dinnertime," by Temple standards, it wasn't even eight o'clock yet. Hospital visiting hours went until nine.

"Won't that just upset her?" Seth asked.

"More than thinking her own body rejected the baby and she might never be able to have another child?" Bowyn snapped. "I don't think so."

Alex turned off the water and said quietly as she wiped her hands on the towel by the sink, unable to look at him, "You're right. She should be told. Now, rather than wait for a doctor to tell her."

When I offered to go with him, Bowyn said, "I think I need some time to myself on the ride over there."

I was worried about him and Marianne both. Marianne would be devastated. But Bowyn…. He had darkness in his expression I'd never seen before. More than anger—rage. But it wasn't in his nature to lash out at Alex, the most convenient target for his fury. I didn't know if he blamed her, or if he believed someone else tainted the tea. But he clearly needed to get away from all of us to work it out. There was nothing I could do—not right now.

So I let him go.

Alex replaced the towel on the rack, her hands shaking slightly, and then said, "I need my kitchen staff in here. People aren't going to wait all night to eat."

# Chapter Twenty-Two

AFTER DINNER I decided to take the laptop up to the library. Bowyn still wasn't back, and hanging around the empty room was depressing me. Besides, I wanted to look at the Ficino manuscript again. Not for any particular reason, but I'd been staring at digital copies of it for days when the actual manuscript was just two floors above me. It was hard to put into words, but I had a strong desire to *connect* with the real manuscript again, in person.

I couldn't touch it, of course. But as I slid its wide drawer out of the case, I marveled at the craftsmanship in its pages. Even damaged and faded, the meticulously hand-notated musical staves and the careful calligraphy amazed me, as it always did when I examined ancient manuscripts. The printing press was a marvelous invention, but we lost a lot of the art of western manuscripts when we began typesetting. Not that I had any desire to go back to the days when books had to be copied by hand if they were copied at all. John Dee had spent much of his lifetime gathering a mere 3,000 manuscripts, less than I have on my personal eBook reader, to assemble what was then considered to be the largest library in England.

As I looked over the pages of the manuscript, laid out in tidy rows under the glass lid, I couldn't help but notice that there were more pages than I'd remembered. I don't mean that someone had added pages, but the image files Seth had put on the laptop weren't all the ones laid out in the display case—two had been left out. I remembered one from the first night I'd seen the manuscript—the beautiful frontispiece Seth and I had examined. The other page contained an illustration with very little text—mostly abbreviated notations on parts of the image and a few brief lines in Latin at the bottom. The drawing style matched that of the frontispiece.

I could read the Latin with a dictionary handy, but these abbreviations weren't immediately obvious to me. The illustration appeared to show an altar with a hole or pit in the floor in front of it. Rectangular objects—

perhaps platforms—were laid out in a circle around both, possibly indicating where the choir was supposed to stand. In the center of the pit was a drawing of a man dressed in a robe. I assumed this represented the magician. Magickal symbols adorned the floor in several places.

I grew curious as to what Seth had made of this, so I set off through the house in search of him.

The first stop, of course, was his bedroom, but for once he wasn't there engaged in some kind of circus act with Rafe. I did come across a couple—male and female—having all-out intercourse on the plush carpet in the hall, which was pretty ballsy even for the Temple, and made me wonder how often the carpets were steam cleaned. I stepped past them, politely turning down their invitation to join in, and continued downstairs.

The Temple was huge, and it was housing over a hundred people at that time, so finding Seth turned out to be a challenge. I almost gave up and went back to my room, but I ran into an initiate out on the grounds who told me Seth was in the chapel, so I detoured out that way.

By now it was well past sunset, and the rain was coming down again—not hard, but in a relentless, dull drizzle that chilled me and settled into my robe and hair. I liked the crisp fall odor of damp leaves and grass that accompanied it, but I was glad to finally reach the shelter of the chapel.

Seth was there with Rafe and Timothy, engrossed in conversation while four neophytes shifted wooden platforms around the room. Seth was waving a piece of paper around, and as I approached, I could see it was a copy of the illustration I'd seen.

Rafe noticed me first and bowed, which caused Seth and Timothy to turn and see me. Timothy bowed as well, but it was only the half bow that I was beginning to recognize among the senior initiates—a subtle indication of rank. It was yet another sign that this organization I'd helped create had gone on without me, developing nuances that hadn't been there eight years ago.

"Ah, my love!" Seth said with a broad smile.

I didn't return it. "What's all this?" I nodded toward the neophytes as they adjusted the position of a wooden platform they'd just dropped into place.

"Just a little redecorating."

"Based upon one of the illustrations in the manuscript."

"Yes," Seth replied, extending the paper to me.

I didn't take it from him. "I've seen it."

"Then why are you acting so… petulant?"

Truthfully I wasn't sure, apart from a vague feeling he was hiding something from me. But being talked down to did nothing to improve my mood. "Why didn't you include that page in the image files you gave me?"

Seth clucked at me as if I were a difficult child in need of a nap. "Jeremy, my love, I gave you the pages I needed you to work on. Since the page in question contains no music, I saw no need to waste your time on it."

I supposed that made sense. "Fine," I replied grudgingly. "But what have you learned from it?"

"As you saw for yourself, the frontispiece gives the necessary astrological correspondences for the operation. I confess I'm still baffled by much of the other symbols on it. This page"—he held up the paper in his right hand—"gives us the most auspicious layout for the choir and altar. Very little else. We still don't know what the operation *does*, until you can translate the Enochian part of the libretto. Have you made any further progress with that?"

I had to admit that I hadn't. "There are too many words in the final portion of the libretto that Dee and Kelley apparently never encountered in their work. Without some kind of dictionary, I'm at a loss to translate them."

"Frustrating," Seth agreed. His attention was momentarily caught by Timothy issuing orders to the neophytes to slide the platform to the left by a few inches. He consulted the illustration to verify the positioning.

"If Ficino learned this language from the same spirits that Dee spoke with," Rafe said to me, "why don't you just ask those spirits what the words mean?"

Seth and I both turned and stared at him blankly for a second. I'm ashamed to admit I'd already filed Rafe under the "not terribly bright" category in my mind—or at least, not interested in much other than getting laid—and that made me slow to recognize a good suggestion when I heard it.

"That might be our best option," I agreed.

"Of course!" Seth exclaimed, delighted. "We can hold a séance!"

The word "séance" often conjures up an image of people sitting around a table holding hands while the medium moans and her assistant in the back room pulls a lever to make the table levitate. But séances in ceremonial magick are a little different. More of a group magickal working, where one person allows the spirits to talk to the rest of us through him or her. Nobody in the room is simply a bystander—everybody participates.

But one thing is still essential—a medium.

"Who here is good with trance work?" I asked.

Rafe bowed low and replied, "I offer my humble services, Brethren."

Perhaps I looked skeptical because Seth immediately added, "Rafe is an excellent trance medium. I've made use of his skills in that area during several operations."

"All right," I said. "When do you want to do this?"

I was hoping Seth wouldn't say tonight. I needed some prep time for ceremonial magick work. Fortunately, he didn't.

"Let me review my notes on Enochian," Seth replied. "It's been a while. But we don't have much time, so it will have to be tomorrow evening."


I LEFT them to their work and returned to the room to find Bowyn had come back from the hospital. He was standing by the window when I entered, staring out at the dismal gray night. When he turned, I was alarmed by how exhausted he looked.

Bowyn looked at me without speaking until I felt compelled to break the silence. "You've been gone a long time."

He nodded but didn't seem to have anything to say in response, so I approached him. "Are you all right?"

He sighed and shook his head, then shrugged. "They said she'll be ready to come home tomorrow morning."

"Good. Do you want me to go with you to pick her up?"

"I suppose." Bowyn hesitated for a moment, before adding, "She's bringing… him… home with her."

I didn't know what he meant at first, but then it clicked. The baby. "Oh," I said. "I… didn't realize they would allow that."

"I guess some hospitals do, now. They cremated him today, and she'll be bringing the urn back with her. We talked about it… and we're planning to have a funeral. You don't have to come if you think it's too weird."

I smiled at him and reached up to brush his cheek. He hadn't shaved since the night Marianne was taken to the hospital, so the stubble had begun to soften a bit on its way to becoming a beard. "Bowyn, I'm dressed like a medieval monk and I've just been planning a séance with Seth and Rafe. I am in no position to call anything weird."

He smiled a little at that and leaned his face into my palm. "I guess it seemed weird to me. But it makes some kind of sense too. You know, to say good-bye...."

"Of course," I said softly. "I'll be honored to be there."

"Thank you." There was something in his tone, in the way he said those two words, that suddenly made it clear just how important it was to him that I be there. I felt certain Bowyn hadn't deliberately tried to manipulate me, but I felt equally certain if I'd been dismissive about the idea of holding a funeral for his miscarried child, it would have put up another barrier between the two of us.

I pulled him close and wrapped my arms around his waist, leaning my face against his shoulder. "It's late. Why don't we get some sleep?"

"Okay."

Since he made no move to undress, I undid the rope belt cinched around his waist and tossed it onto the chair near the window. Then I lifted his robe up over his head. Bowyn gave a short, soft laugh and lifted his arms up to allow me to slip the robe off.

I wasn't sure if he'd be in the mood to fool around, but the sight of his naked body filled me with such a strong desire to touch him, I couldn't resist leaning in close and placing a gentle kiss on his chest. I flicked my tongue playfully at his nipple. I would have understood if he pushed me away, not in a mood to be sexual. But he didn't. Bowyn exhaled raggedly, as if releasing some of the tension that had been building in him over the past several days, and I knew then this was what he needed.

I planted soft kisses down the length of his torso, following the trail of sandy-blond hair from his belly button down to his stiffening cock, and then I took it into my mouth. Bowyn groaned and slipped a hand into my hair, massaging my scalp with his fingers while I worked him up to a full erection with my lips and tongue.

But after a few minutes of this, I heard him whisper, "I need you to take me."

I wasn't surprised. As I said, I'm generally a bottom and quite happy about it, especially when it was Bowyn mounting me. But there had always been times when he needed me to be the "dominant" one. It wasn't exactly that we felt taking a cock up the ass made a man somehow submissive, necessarily—a rather bizarre notion—but there is something about the way it can feel, as if you're being penetrated throughout your body, from his cock in your ass all the way to his tongue in your mouth, as if your lover is extending himself into every part of your being… and accepting all of it. Loving all of it. And allowing you to relinquish control.

I retrieved a condom and the bottle of lube from the bed stand while Bowyn lay back on the bed. After I'd prepared myself, I kneeled between his legs and reached a hand down under him to find his opening. I massaged it with a lubricated finger, watching Bowyn's expression soften, the wall begin to come down. By the time I entered him, he'd begun to feel again—pleasure and love… and grief.

It was when I moved my mouth from his to plant tender kisses along his cheeks that I realized he was crying.

"Do you need me to stop?" I asked him softly.

He whispered, "No. I need to feel you inside me."

And so I let him cry while I caressed every part of his body I could reach, kissed his mouth and face, and moved within him. All of this failed to find and touch the core of his being, but I got as close as a lover is ever able to, and Bowyn knew I was trying.

LONG AFTER we'd finished and Bowyn and I had drifted off in each other's arms, I was awakened by the sound of someone slipping through the servants' passage again. I suppose some part of my subconscious had begun to listen for it.

Bowyn was sound asleep and I had no intention of waking him, but I carefully extracted myself from his arms and climbed out of the bed. My curiosity was getting the better of me. I didn't have any concrete reason to suspect that this person was up to anything sinister, but I was fairly certain now that it was the same person every night—it occurred too consistently around the same time of night, which would be unlikely if it were just random people using the passage. And although the person who'd planted the pennyroyal in the spearmint wouldn't have *had* to sneak into the kitchen through the servants' door, it would have been the best way to avoid being seen.

I tiptoed over to the door by the fireplace, opening it as quietly as possible before slipping into the passage.

My eyes were already well-adjusted to the darkness, but the tiny windows high up in the outer walls admitted no real light into the passage, and I hadn't brought a flashlight. If I had, the light from it would have alerted the person I was trying to follow, anyway. So I felt my way forward, guiding myself along with my hands and bare feet. The walls were narrow, so I was never without a handhold. The only light came from the flashlight the visitor was using, and this was rapidly fading as he walked away from me.

But he wasn't walking very fast, having no reason to suspect anyone was following him. I kept the light in sight, walking lightly to avoid making much noise. I turned the corner and saw the light descending down to the second floor.

Scurrying ahead, I prayed the rough wooden floor wouldn't skewer my foot with a splinter. I was completely naked, since there hadn't been time to fumble around for a robe. There was nothing but an uninsulated outer wall between me and the cold October night air outside, so it wasn't long before I was shivering and beginning to seriously regret my decision. But turning back now would be worse, without any light at all to guide me.

My quarry left the passage on the second floor briefly to cross the main hallway to the servants' door on the opposite side. I hung back a little to avoid being seen by him when I scurried across the hall, which was dimly illuminated by fake gaslights on the walls; then I slipped back into the cold air and darkness of the passage.

As I began to descend the narrow stairs to the first floor, one of the steps creaked under my foot, and I froze. The flashlight beam whipped around to illuminate the steps just below me. Fortunately, the ceiling was low here and the light couldn't quite reach where my foot was. I held my breath, hoping that he wouldn't come back to investigate. It seemed strange to be so panicked about being discovered—after all, *I* wasn't the one sneaking around every night, except for this one. And for all I knew, the person I was following wasn't up to anything sinister. But I held my breath until the light swung away again and I heard footsteps moving away from me. I took the remaining steps more cautiously.

We slipped past a few doors on the first floor, one of which I was certain led to the kitchen, but the visitor moved on until we reached another set of stairs leading down to the basement. Was he planning on taking a shower? At three o'clock in the morning, he might have been able to use one of the upstairs showers. It hardly seemed worth the effort to crawl down through the walls. But the only other point of interest in the cellar was the bathroom—again, hardly worth the effort.

I hung back at the end of the corridor as the visitor opened the door leading into the cellar. He did it slowly and quietly, as if fearing discovery. The shower area was brightly lit, so I glimpsed him, illuminated for just a moment as he slipped out into the basement. But all I could see was someone in a standard robe, with the cowl pulled up to hide his face.

I decided this was my last chance to find out who he was, so I ran forward down the narrow passage and yanked the door open.

I was looking into the showers, brightly illuminated and empty. Curious, I glanced at the outer surface of the door and saw that it had been tiled over to match the walls. But I was in too much of a hurry to give it more than a passing thought.

I stepped out onto the floor, still treacherously wet from the last time the showers had been in use, and crossed it, my bare feet making slapping sounds on the tile. From somewhere I heard footsteps walking faster, but everything echoed in here, and I couldn't tell what direction they were coming from. The bathroom area on the other side of the shower room was also empty. I walked past rows of sinks and mirrors and a few urinals toward the stalls at the far end, ducking my head to look for feet inside a couple that were closed. But even those were empty.

There were three doors to the cellar I could recall, not counting the servants' door—the door leading up to the kitchen, the door to the root cellar, and the large metal bulkhead leading up into the backyard. If somebody had opened the bulkhead, I felt certain I would have heard it.

The root cellar was no longer used as such, Bowyn had told me on my first day back—not since the showers and bathroom had been put in. It was too damp now and not particularly sanitary for storing foodstuffs. But the door was at the base of the stairs leading up to the kitchen, so I opened it. It was pitch black in there, but the light was still where I remembered it being. I flicked it on, revealing rows of shelves stacked high with pots and pans. The door I was standing in was the only way in or out, as far as I could see.

I didn't waste my time there. I turned off the light and closed the door. Then I went upstairs and into the kitchen.

There was always a dim light burning here, as there was in all the hallways and common rooms. Alex insisted on it. She didn't like the idea of anyone wandering around alone in the dark, even in a place as relatively safe as the Temple. I checked the room, found nothing, and then went out into the main hall. If anyone had come this way, he was long gone now.

Cold, tired, and frustrated, I went upstairs and back to Bowyn's warm bed.

# Chapter Twenty-Three

WE DROVE to the hospital the next morning to pick up Marianne, just Bowyn and me. During the short ride into Berlin, I told Bowyn about my adventures in the servants' passage the night before, but he seemed distracted and uninterested.

"You're lucky you didn't fall down the stairs and break your neck," he said, "stumbling around in those tunnels without a flashlight."

"Don't you think it's strange that someone keeps wandering through every night at three a.m.?"

He shrugged. "I don't know. They probably think those passageways are cool. We used to."

"I remember," I conceded. "But why at that time of night? And what were they doing down in the cellar?"

"Taking a shower?"

"No." I'd already told him the visitor had disappeared when I stepped into the basement. "Look," I said patiently, "the fact of the matter is, regardless of what the police might think, somebody tampered with the tea. It wasn't a mistake; it wasn't somebody just horsing around. Somebody wanted Marianne to miscarry."

Bowyn flinched, and I could tell he didn't want to believe it. He didn't want to believe anyone in this idealized world we'd created could ever do something so horrible. But he said quietly, "I know."

There was little else to say after that. We had no idea who had done it or why. But somehow, I was going to find out.

BY THE time we reached the hospital, Marianne was already dressed and packed to go. I was surprised to see her in street clothes—a large, pink sweater and dungarees. She hadn't come in with them. But she hadn't come in with the small suitcase and the Leo Buscaglia book she was reading, either. I assumed Bowyn had brought those over the night before.

The outfit looked pretty on her, but there was something vaguely off about it, and it took me a minute to figure out what it was. Then it hit me—that baggy look had been popular a decade ago. True, Marianne had lost weight since I'd seen her eight years ago, but I didn't think that was the main reason for the loose fit. I suspected she simply hadn't had any reason to go clothes shopping since moving to the Temple.

"Did they give you the urn?" Bowyn asked her uncomfortably.

"It's in the suitcase."

"I have someone preparing a spot next to Jack. I still need to call about a headstone."

Marianne nodded and stood up to follow us out. When she reached for the suitcase, Bowyn took it for her. Then I followed them both out to the car.

It wasn't until we were on the road that Marianne turned to look back at me and said, "Jeremy… I was hoping you'd sing with me at the funeral."

I was surprised, but it certainly wouldn't be a hardship. "What song did you have in mind?"

"'The Awakening of Man.'"

Another piece I'd written in college. The lyrics were my own and not particularly brilliant—there was a reason I generally preferred to use classical poetry for my lyrics or librettos. But the song was appropriate for the situation. "Do you remember it?"

"I think so," Marianne replied with a faint smile. "I spent most of this morning dredging it up from my memory."

"Then of course. I'd be honored."


THE FUNERAL was held after lunch. Seth held a service in the chapel, attended only by me, Bowyn, Marianne, Alex, and Rafe. For once, Seth was subdued. He told the story of Persephone, the beautiful young daughter of Zeus and Demeter, whose mother jealously guarded her from several gods who wished to marry her. In desperation, Hades, the god of the underworld, went to Zeus, who told him the only way to get Persephone away from Demeter was to kidnap her. Hades did as Zeus suggested and spirited her away to his kingdom.

Demeter was so distraught at finding her daughter missing that she searched high and low for her, neglecting her duties as the goddess of the harvest, until all the world began to share in her misery. At last, Helios, the sun, who could see everything, was moved to tell Demeter where Persephone had been taken.

"Demeter demanded the return of her daughter," Seth told us, "and Zeus, moved by her anguish, forced Hades to release Persephone. But Hades would not surrender his beautiful bride so easily. He tricked Persephone into eating some pomegranate seeds. And whoever eats or drinks in the underworld is bound there forever.

"However," Seth added, "the gods decided Persephone would remain with Hades for only six months out of the year—six months, for the six pomegranate seeds she'd eaten. During that time, Demeter's sorrow shrouds the earth in cold and darkness. But for the rest of the year, Persephone is reunited with her loving mother. And when she is, Demeter's joy can be felt throughout the world."

As we filed out of the chapel and around to the cemetery in the back, the bells sounded five times to represent mortal Man—spirit bound to the four elements of the material world—and they echoed forlornly back to us from the nearby mountains. For the first time since my arrival at the Temple, I was able to locate the source of the "bells"—they were coming from loudspeakers hidden just underneath the cornices of the outer pillars of the chapel building.

The sky was overcast and a light drizzle was still coming down, not wet enough for most of us to bother with umbrellas, but still damp and unpleasant.

Jack's headstone was adorned with a *memento mori* in the form of a winged skull design unique to New England. It was creepy but appropriate to the Victorian atmosphere of the Temple. The inscription was a quote from Percy Bysshe Shelley: "He hath awakened from the dream of life."

A small but deep hole had been dug near the head of Jack's grave. While Seth said a few more words at the graveside, Bowyn took the urn from Marianne and placed it gently in the hole. He had to lie down on the grass in order to reach the bottom.

Then I began to sing:

"Darkness is upon me; my body lies still and cold.

Gladly will I wait for my destiny to unfold.

Distant memories of beauty and strength

Come to comfort me like old friends.

My life was a wondrous tale;

Now my story ends."

Marianne answered with:

"My son, you are brave and wise,

Fearing not what fate has chosen for you.

Death is a trial that every mortal must go through.

Though I will mourn your loss,

Grieving for what death has taken from me,

For you I fear not, once earthly bonds have set you free."

And then both of us sang the final refrain together:

"Death is but a moment's rest from life's joy and pain.

In time, when the Fates decree, we shall rise again.

Young and beautiful, we will face the old world

With new courage born of innocence.

Our lives are a wondrous tale,

Never to have an end."

When the song was finished, Marianne turned and hugged me, tears streaming down her face, and I held her tightly, crying myself.

Bowyn stood beside the small grave, looking down into it. "Goodbye, for now, Jay," he said with a catch in his voice. "I never even got to see you, but I hope we meet up again someday, and I hope we recognize each other."

He looked up to see if Marianne wanted to say something, but she was crying too much to speak and she just shook her head. I held out my hand to him, and he came into our embrace. Then his tears came, as the three of us held one another.

After we broke apart, the others joined in, hugging Bowyn and Marianne and whispering soft condolences, while the bells rang six times—the number of Man ascending. But I noticed one person standing apart. Alex was crying too, but she waited off to one side, watching Marianne, perhaps searching for a sign that her offer of comfort would be welcome. Several times, she seemed on the verge of stepping forward, her hand reaching out. But Marianne never once looked at her, though she had to have known Alex was there.

Eventually, after Marianne had accepted a hug from Rafe and returned to stand by my side, Alex turned and walked quietly back to the house.

# Chapter Twenty-Four

THE ENOCHIAN séance was held that evening in the chapel, which had been prepared for magickal work that afternoon, consecrated by Seth, and then locked for the remainder of the day. Bowyn and I went to the chapel shortly after dinner, and Seth admitted us. The air inside was heavy with incense—sandalwood, cinnamon, frankincense, and other odors I couldn't distinguish—and the center of the chapel was illuminated by flickering candles in tall stands. All else beyond that small space lay shrouded in darkness.

Seth himself was dressed in a spotless, white linen robe and looked freshly scrubbed. He smelled of oil of Abramelin, the primary ingredient of which is cinnamon, and he insisted upon anointing our foreheads with the oil before we could enter. I'd always liked using oil of Abramelin in rituals—it made my skin tingle and feel pleasantly warm.

A large square of red silk had been placed on the floor before the altar, and upon this was a chair for the scryer—Rafe—to sit on and the Holy Table. The Holy Table was a table made out of laurel wood, proportioned so it was two cubits square on top and two cubits high. "What's a cubit?" I recalled Moses asking God in the famous Bill Cosby skit. God hemmed and hawed a bit in response and then quickly changed the subject. The thing was, nobody really knew exactly how long a cubit was. It was the oldest recorded unit of measurement, but it varied throughout history. Most commonly, perhaps, it was the length of a man's forearm. I assumed, in this case, that the forearm in question had been Seth's.

The four legs of the Holy Table each rested on metal discs etched with the *Sigillum Dei Aemeth*, "The Seal of God's Truth," containing the seven names of God, the seven planetary angels, and numerous other holy names. The top of the table was draped with silk the same bloodred as the floor covering, with gold tassels dangling from its corners. Underneath this, I knew, lay another copy of the *Sigillum Dei Aemeth*, etched in a square of beeswax, along with numerous other sigils etched on thin metal tablets, all arranged in a particular order. But Enochian magick wasn't my strong point, so I wouldn't have been able to say exactly what sigils were being used or what order they'd been placed in. I just had to assume Seth knew what he was doing.

The scrying mirror was placed in the center of the table, angled so Rafe could gaze into it easily. The mirror itself wasn't what most people think of as a "mirror." It was basically a concave glass disk, about ten inches wide, with a pure black coating on its underside. It was reflective, but not nearly as reflective as a silver-backed mirror. Its intent was not to show the viewer his own face, but something in the darkness beyond the mirror.

Also resting upon the table were a gold ring and another large metal plate with symbols etched into it. This plate was made of gold and had a gold chain connecting two of its corners, so it could be draped around the magician's neck. This was called the lamen, and it protected the magician during the working.

Though we were inexperienced with Enochian magick, Bowyn and I were old hands at ceremonial magick in general, so we knew better than to start jabbering upon entering the sacred space. Rafe was standing just behind Seth when we entered, and we each paused for him to blow incense smoke at us. Then Seth led all of us in a large circle around the space three times, ending with us performing the LBRP before Rafe took his seat in front of the mirror.

Bowyn and I stood silently by while Seth stepped up to the table and began to speak.

"Teach me, oh Creator of All Things," he intoned, his voice echoing in the small chamber, "to have correct knowledge and understanding. For Your wisdom is all that I desire. Speak Your word in my ear and set Your wisdom in my heart."

The prayer went on as Seth placed the ring on his finger and then lifted the lamen to slip its chain around his neck. He then continued, chanting the Enochian letters that were carved into the wood of the table, followed by the names of the angels in the *Sigillum Dei Aemeth* and the holy names of "The Round Table of Nalvage," all of which I'll omit. Suffice to say, it went on for quite a while.

He ended with the lengthy Nineteenth Call, otherwise known as "The Call of the Thirty Aethers." During all this chanting, Rafe sat in the scrying chair, eyes closed, breathing slowly and deeply.

"*Ol vinu od zacam*," Seth intoned. *I invoke and move thee*.... There then followed a lengthy list of Enochian angels, ordered according to their place in the angelic hierarchy, punctuated by the phrase *od dooiap*, which translates to "in the name of."

When the last call was finished, there was a long silence. And then Rafe slowly opened his eyes. They were eerily glazed over, like the eyes of a man doped up on morphine, and he turned his head stiffly to point them at the black mirror, as though they were incapable of moving on their own. His eyes didn't focus on the mirror but continued to look past it, through it.

"What do you see?" Seth asked, his voice barely above a whisper, yet still echoing off the marble walls of the chapel.

Rafe took a long, rasping breath, then replied sleepily, "I am on a mountain... looking down at a plain... stars circling overhead...."

"Do you see ARZL?" ARZL was the angelic spirit we were invoking for this operation. He—or possibly she, since ARZL was supposedly androgynous—could reveal things that had long been kept secret.

"Someone is sitting on the peak of the mountain... looking at me... it could be a boy... perhaps... very thin... with wings...."

"Ask him if he will aid us in our inquiries."

There was a pause. "He will."

Seth reached out to his right, where I was standing, and I handed a piece of paper to him. It contained all the Enochian words I hadn't been able to find translations for. Erring on the side of caution, I'd mixed them up, so Rafe wouldn't be tempted to make sentences out of them, either consciously or unconsciously. Both he and Seth were aware I'd done that.

"Oh ARZL," Seth said, raising his voice to address the spirit directly, "we ask your assistance in understanding several words from an ancient manuscript, which we believe are transcriptions of the Language of the Angels."

"Ask."

"Thank you, wise spirit. The first word is *CAON*."

"Distaff."

"*LINSA*."

"Fiber."

Seth proceeded to work his way through the list, with the spirit providing the English equivalent of each word. Seth was supposedly recording this session, as he always did in case something went by that would require closer examination later, but I hadn't seen any sign of a recording device, so I was quietly jotting the words down on a notepad. Interesting words were going by, such as "love" and "resurrection," but there was no time right now to try to fit them into the libretto.

When Seth reached the end of the list, he began to give the spirit license to depart. "We thank thee, oh ARZL, for your assistance in this matter and bid—"

"Do not thank me," the spirit interrupted him, a sinister smile coming to Rafe's lips, "for these words offer you no comfort. Li matan sol li nor crip tol tox ednas gze teloch."

"What do you mean by that?" Seth asked, his face suddenly looking pale in the flickering candlelight.

But the spirit merely laughed and repeated, "Li matan sol li nor crip tol tox ednas gze teloch."

Then Rafe's head fell forward for a moment, and when he lifted it, his eyes were no longer glazed over. He looked slowly at the scrying mirror and then up to Seth's face. "Did you get anything?"

"Yes, my beauty," Seth replied, though he seemed distracted. He walked over to the podium and reached up and over it to switch something off—the recorder I'd been unable to find. "Do you recall anything?"

Rafe shook his head. "Sorry. I never do."

"I assumed that to be the case. I was merely checking."

I was going over my notes and examining that last phrase. Some of the words seemed familiar, but I'd have to have an Enochian dictionary in front of me to be sure. One of the new words we'd learned—love—was being used in the phrase, but somehow I doubted the spirit had delivered a message about love and peace. Not with that sinister gleam in its eye.

"Do you know what it meant?" I asked Seth. "What that last phrase was telling us?"

"Phrase?" Rafe asked.

Seth fiddled with the recorder a bit, and we were treated to the last thirty seconds or so of the session coming from hidden speakers in the darkness around us. The amplified voices echoed in the chamber, sounding creepier than it had when it had happened, and ending once more with "*Li matan sol li nor crip tol tox ednas gze teloch.*"

Seth switched the recorder off.

"A final dire warning in a dead language," Rafe said with a groan. "How tedious. I suppose I should be grateful I didn't vomit or wet myself."

Seth frowned at him but directed his comment at me. "I'm not certain. Something about fatherly love, I think." Then, almost reluctantly, he added, "And something about death."

"Do you think it's a warning for us to stop working on the mass?" I asked.

"Oh, Jeremy!" Seth threw up his arms in disgust. "Have we been listening to tales of teenagers finding knives in their pillows after playing with Ouija boards? Why would a spirit agree to give us the key to the operation if it didn't want us to use it?"

"Maybe it wants us to fail," Bowyn said. "But it's willing to give us a sporting chance."

Seth rolled his eyes at him but said smoothly, "We have all of the pieces now. Jeremy can complete his translation. All of the ancient Greek has been translated and phonetic transcriptions given to the choir. The chapel has been arranged according to Ficino's diagrams. By tomorrow night, we will be ready to perform the operation with full knowledge of its components. What more do you require?"

"Let me finish my translation before I answer that," I replied. That translation was the key to understanding the purpose of the mass. And until I finished putting the pieces of it together, we *didn't* have full knowledge of what the mass was intended to do.

"Fine," Seth said. "Finish the translation. Then we can perform it tomorrow night at eleven, with Saturn ascending, as it is supposed to be performed."

"Shouldn't we wait until Christopher returns?"

"There isn't time if we're to do this correctly. I realize he's gifted, but I have faith in you, my love. You can sing the solo."

I wasn't so sure about that. Oh, technically I could, with the possible exception of the last high note. Hopefully, my aging voice wouldn't crack on that one. But my biggest concern was the tone of my voice. I'd been a good singer in my youth, but I'd never sung with the precision and purity of tone Christopher possessed.

On the other hand, without Christopher, the power of the mass might be a bit better controlled. I knew now Marianne's miscarriage had been caused by the pennyroyal in her tea, but part of me was still superstitious enough to believe something magickal had been happening during Christopher's solo and somehow that had contributed.

IT WAS still early when we left the chapel—perhaps eight o'clock—but Bowyn and I were both feeling dragged out. We decided to return to our room and call it a night. But we were waylaid by Marianne on the walk back from the chapel. She was bundled up in a knit shawl pulled close around her robe, her red hair blowing loose in the cold evening breeze. "There you are! Is Seth still in the chapel?"

"Yes," Bowyn replied. "Are you sure you're well enough to be out in this weather?"

Marianne shrugged. "He's gone."

"Who's gone?" I asked. "Seth?"

"No, of course not. Christopher."

I was confused. "He's at rehab."

"No," she explained patiently. "He's not. He should be, but I called to see how things were going, and they told me he wasn't there. He was *never* there. He never arrived!"

I felt a sudden chill that had nothing to do with the wind. "We could call the cab company…."

"I already did," Marianne said. "One of their drivers insists she dropped Christopher off right in front of the clinic."

While I stared stupidly at Marianne for a second, the implications of that running around in my head, Bowyn took charge of the situation. "You two get back into the house," he ordered. "I'll go fetch Seth and meet you there."

I nodded.

"You might as well let Alex know too."

# Chapter Twenty-Five

WE GATHERED in the kitchen after chasing out the rest of Alex's assistants. I noticed, as no doubt we all did, that Alex didn't offer anyone any tea. But nobody dared say a word about it. We just sat around the table, looking like a miniature Council of Nicea, arguing apocrypha and finding it distasteful.

"Did he run away?" Alex asked.

Seth shook his head. "I checked his room and spoke to his roommate. He took clothes for a few days' stay and maybe a book or two, but he left a bunch of his favorite books behind—stuff about Norse mythology, Viking history…. If he'd run away, he would have taken those with him, don't you think?"

"What if somebody took him?" Rafe asked. "His father, maybe?"

"He did earn his father a lot of money," Bowyn added. The disgust in his voice was palpable.

Seth scoffed. "So his father somehow knew precisely when and where a cab would drop Christopher off downtown and jumped out from behind a bush with a net? Don't be absurd."

"Maybe he's still here," I said.

Everyone turned to look at me in the silence that followed, as though I'd just said I'd seen Bigfoot in the living room, but I plowed ahead. "I've only told Bowyn about this so far, but for the past few nights, I've been hearing someone walking around in the servants' passages."

"A lot of people use those passages," Marianne pointed out.

"I know. But there's been one person who keeps passing our room at about three o'clock every night. Last night, I decided to follow him. He went all the way down to the showers. Then I lost him."

Rafe chuckled. "If you want to shower with someone, Brethren—"

"That's not the point," I interrupted, not in the mood for his flirtatious silliness. "If it were just someone sneaking between two of the rooms for a late night romp, he would have gone back to his room. But he didn't. He went down to the cellar. Then… I guess he got outside, somehow."

"Maybe he knew you were following him," Bowyn said, "and he didn't want you to find out where his room was."

"I don't think he knew."

I could tell none of them believed me. Or at least none of them thought an initiate skulking about in the servants' passage in the middle of the night was cause for concern.

"To what end, my love?" Seth asked, his impatience obvious. "Even if Christopher had returned, why would he be hiding from us?"

"I don't know," I admitted. "Perhaps he didn't want to go to rehab. Maybe he hitchhiked back here, planning to hide out for a few days and then fake a return."

Marianne shook her head. "Except that the clinic has to bill me— us, the Temple. If he hadn't been there, we would have found out about it. We *have* found out about it, after just two days! He'd never have been able to get away with it, and I'm sure he'd realize that. He might be a little screwed up, Jeremy, but he's not dumb."

I held out my hands in surrender. I'd intended to mention my theory that it could have been Christopher who tampered with the tea, entering the kitchen through the passageway, but there seemed little point now. It was nothing but speculation. Truthfully, I couldn't think of a reason for him to do that, any more than I could come up with a reason for him to sneak around in the servants' passages to begin with.

"Should we call the police?" Alex asked the group. "At least report him missing?"

Seth didn't seem happy about that idea, but he capitulated. "All right. I'll take care of it."


THE POLICE showed up a short time later—the same two as before. All the Brethren, and Rafe, were present for the discussion we had with them in the front parlor, but we let Seth do most of the talking. The young one seemed just as spooked as before by the Temple and its "weird" residents, but I could tell Officer Westcott thought we were probably making a big deal out of nothing. Again.

"So to recap," he said to Seth, "you tried to force a kid with a drug problem into counseling and he ran away instead."

Seth responded coolly, "We don't think he ran away."

"But he might have."

"I suppose anything is possible."

And that's pretty much how it went from there. After about forty-five minutes of that, the two officers left.

"Unbelievable!" Alex snapped, throwing her hands in the air before heading back to the kitchen to make sure everything was in order for tomorrow's breakfast and that the snack table was stocked for the night.

BOWYN AND I finally went up to our room around eleven. I was exhausted—magickal ceremonies and visits from the police can do that to you—but I knew if I crawled into bed now, the bell for Resh would just get me up in an hour. Besides, I had to find out what that "warning," if that's what it had been, at the end of the ceremony was all about. The libretto could wait until tomorrow, but that would bug me all night if I didn't make a pass at translating it.

I sat in front of the laptop while Bowyn opened the Lovecraft book again and stretched out on the bed. It didn't take long to translate the phrase. Enochian does have some grammar to it, but not a complex one, and it's mostly just a matter of looking the words up in a dictionary and plugging them in. I was hampered somewhat by the fact that my phonetic transcription of what Rafe said wasn't perfect, but eventually I announced to Bowyn that I thought I had it.

He glanced up, curious, but not especially concerned. "Really? What does it say?"

I sat back and took a deep breath.

"The father loves the son, but through him finds only death."

# Chapter Twenty-Six

I WOKE up again in the night, just after three thirty, startled as though I'd heard something. Not merely somebody walking around in the passageway, but something far worse—something that made my heart pound in my chest. I could have sworn I'd heard a scream. But all was silent.

Bowyn was also awake, lying beside me in the dark. I could see the glint of his eyes as he blinked, though he held himself still, listening to the silence. He'd heard something too.

After the ornate Victorian clock on the mantle had ticked away a full minute, I whispered, "What was it?"

"I don't know. It… I thought somebody screamed."

He slipped out of the bed and went to peer through the window.

"Did you actually *hear* a scream?" I asked.

"No. I don't know. It just… *felt* as if someone screamed."

That was how it had felt to me too, but like him, I couldn't actually say I'd heard anything.

I got up to join him by the window. The air in the room was chilly, reminding me that Halloween was less than a week away, and without thinking I said, "It won't be long before we have to start keeping the fireplace lit at night."

Bowyn put his arm around me. "Except you won't be here for that."

"Oh. Yeah." I was surprised at how sad I felt when Bowyn pointed that out. I'd been back at the Temple for less than a week, but already it had begun to feel like home again. And sleeping beside Bowyn every night felt more natural than breathing.

I slipped my arms around his muscular waist and pressed my crotch to his hip, hot skin against hot skin, but though we both grew somewhat erect at the contact, this wasn't the time for sex.

Bowyn kissed the top of my head just as something struck one of the windowpanes.

We jumped back from the window, both of us gasping in surprise, but the glass hadn't broken and there was no sign of whatever had struck it. Bowyn's hands clasped my shoulders protectively, as if I were the hapless heroine of a gothic romance.

I glanced out the window at the storm clouds writhing in the night sky. But there was something odd about them, as though they weren't really moving the way clouds should.

Bowyn leaned over my shoulder to peer outside, and he seemed to sense something odd as well. There was movement out there, but with the moon almost new and already set, we couldn't see anything clearly.

We both leaned closer and jumped again as the windowpane was struck for a second time.

"That was a wing!" I said.

"What... the... *fuck?*"

And then suddenly my eyes resolved the swirling mass outside into an enormous, dense flock of black birds, pressed in close around the house, wings and beaks and claws striking the window more and more frequently as Bowyn and I stared at the spectacle in superstitious terror. I'd never seen so many birds! They blotted out the sky. Among the fluttering and clicking and rapping against the glass, another sound came—like thousands of people yelling in the distance. But it wasn't people. It was the screeching and croaking of ravens.

"This is insane," I whispered.

But Bowyn shook off his fear quickly, as he always did. "I'm going outside."

*Why not? Going outside to investigate demonic events always works so well in horror films....*

But I followed him anyway. Since Bowyn didn't bother grabbing a robe, neither did I, and we trotted naked through the hall and down the stairs, passing other naked people as they staggered around bleary-eyed in the dim light of the artificial gas lamps in the hall. Practically all the residents of the Temple were gathering in the lower rooms of the house and the entrance hall, and most had been roused from bed and not bothered to dress, so pushing our way past them was intimate to a degree that felt disturbing, even here.

Outside, we stepped out into a scene from a Hitchcock movie—if Hitchcock had filmed *The Birds* at a nudist colony. Only about twenty people had had the courage to go out into the courtyard, but we found

Seth there, sweaty and panting—either from running down the stairs or from acrobatics, I didn't feel like contemplating—glaring up at the cloud of birds as if it were some kind of personal affront.

"They aren't supposed to be nocturnal!" he snarled.

Bowyn laughed at that. "Should we report them to their union?"

Seth gave him a sour look.

"I suppose," I said, "this is what we get for dabbling in the Dark Arts."

Seth's eyes bulged so much, I thought they might pop out of his head. "Of course," he replied sarcastically. "That's it! After practicing ceremonial magick for two decades, the Celestial Powers have finally decided to punish me by sending an enormous flock of crows to shit on my house."

"Ravens," I corrected. The courtyard was littered with them, dead and broken heaps of black feathers and wings. The corpses of suicide bombers.

"Thank you. A magician should always know the correct identities of the demons that torment him."

"In that case, my name is Jeremy. This is Bowyn."

Seth ignored me and walked farther out into the courtyard to get a closer look at the dead birds strewn across the cobblestones. It was an eerily beautiful scene—a perfectly sculpted naked man, illuminated by faux Victorian gas lamps. Their light flickered against his body and birds flew between him and the lamps as he walked among the small, broken corpses of their companions. Seth's hands were outstretched, making him look as though he were trying to resurrect the ravens. Perhaps he was. He was arrogant enough to try. But they lay still around him, battered and bloody and tragic.

And ominous. As a magician, I don't believe in coincidence. Well, perhaps *some* things are coincidences. People who think powerful cosmic forces are busy arranging traffic lights for their convenience, I find rather laughable. But an enormous flock of ravens attacking your house? That's probably a message.

But what message? Don't dabble in ceremonial magick? I didn't buy that explanation any more than Seth did. I'd been a magician for almost a decade and I knew the dangers. I'd heard of magicians becoming mentally unhinged by working with spirits and not setting up proper wards. But a horde of ravens was odd, even by my standards. There had to be some reason it was occurring at this particular place and time, rather than, say, ten years ago when Bowyn and I first cracked A.E. Waite's *The Book of Ceremonial Magic*.

Something related to the manuscript? Perhaps. But Ficino had wanted future magicians to perform this music, or he wouldn't have written it down. And despite the popularity of spells for vengeance and personal gain in the grimoires of his day, everything we knew about the man indicated he had been focused on the healing arts—not black magick. He'd been a devout Christian. So what was so terrible about us performing the mass?

There was, of course, always the possibility that we were doing it *wrong.* So far, our track record on that hadn't been wonderful.

And then there was Christopher. Was it possible the ravens missed him? Would they go so far as to attack the house because he hadn't fed them for a couple of days? Perhaps that was a more reasonable explanation, but it still seemed ridiculous.

At that moment there was a subtle change in the light, an almost imperceptible brightening, and the flickering shadows faded away. Seth looked up. "They're gone."

All of us in the courtyard lifted our eyes to follow his gaze and saw... nothing. Just a dark night sky filled with pale clouds, breaking here and there to show us the twinkling stars beyond. But no ravens. Not a one.

I looked back down at the courtyard to be sure the dead ravens were still there and it hadn't all been some kind of dream or mass hallucination. They were still there. And the cobblestones were covered in bird shit. There was a streak of the revolting stuff down the length of my forearm. It *had* been real. But the attack, or whatever it was, appeared to be over, at least for now.

"There!" Seth exclaimed, as though he'd orchestrated the ravens' departure personally. "The scary birds are gone. We might as well all go back to bed."

He walked toward us, nodding at one of the low-level initiates. "Ian, please have some of the neophytes clean up the courtyard."

"Yes, Brethren."

"Not this very minute. It can wait until morning."

"Yes, Brethren."

The initiate bowed and went inside, but Bowyn gave Seth a wry smile and said, "Let it not be said the Brethren aren't gracious when handing out shit jobs they don't want to do themselves."

"I'm too tired to discuss the role of class structure in a religious community, my love," Seth told him. Then he gave me an appreciative glance up and down, reminding me this was the first time he'd seen me naked since I'd arrived. "I'm even too tired to suggest we all go to bed *together*."

"Maybe later," I quipped.

Seth smiled and kissed both of us good night, giving me an appreciative pat on the rump, and then he went inside.

I stood there in the courtyard, looking back and forth between the dead ravens on the cobblestones and the quiet night sky, until Bowyn took my arm and said, "You can puzzle it out tomorrow. Let's get back to bed. It's chilly out here."

That was an understatement. Now that the excitement had died down, everybody in the courtyard was becoming aware of the fact that we were standing around naked at four o'clock in the morning in late October, and we were beginning to shiver. Bowyn wrapped an arm around my shoulders and steered me back into the house.

# Chapter Twenty-Seven

THE BELL for Resh rang at seven the next morning, just three hours after we'd climbed back in bed. It was tempting to skip it and sleep in, but Bowyn dragged himself out of bed and I felt guilty enough to follow him. Fortunately, the gestures and recitations were already becoming second nature to me, so my half-asleep brain wasn't taxed.

But when I stepped closer to the window afterward, peering outside at a bleak, gray morning and debating whether I wanted breakfast more than I wanted to crawl back into bed, I saw something that shocked me awake.

"Oh shit," I murmured.

Bowyn came up behind me, and I felt his breath on the back of my neck, exhaling in surprise.

The ravens hadn't left. They'd simply moved. As I looked out at the neatly manicured lawn and cobblestone pathways in the back of the house, the chapel and the grass all around it was covered with them, as if a giant had come along in the night with an enormous brush and splattered black ink all over the landscape.

THE BIRDS were, of course, all anyone could talk about at breakfast. I found out some of the windows in the house had been cracked or even broken last night. One raven had somehow made it through the glass unharmed to flutter around a young woman's bedroom until she'd managed to throw a blanket over it and release it outside.

Some people were attempting to be scientific about the whole thing and suggested that Christopher feeding them all the time had caused the birds to congregate. Perhaps the ravens were stirred up because he'd been away for a few days and they were getting hungry.

But I still found that unconvincing. When Christopher had been doling out crumbs on the hilltop, there hadn't been anywhere near this many birds gathered around him. Where had the rest come from? And no matter how desperate they were for food, it was hard to imagine them slamming themselves into windows and breaking their necks over it. Not en masse. Supposedly the seagulls that attacked houses in Monterey, California back in 1961—inspiring the Hitchcock film *The Birds*—had been driven mad by toxic plankton. But we weren't that close to the ocean, and I didn't think ravens went in for plankton.

I didn't really ask, but from what I could overhear, it didn't seem anyone shared my suspicion that Christopher might have snuck back into the house and hid out somewhere. But even if I was right about that, I couldn't quite make the connection between him sneaking around the passageways at night and the raven attack. Unless he was performing rituals to summon ravens.

Don't think I didn't consider that possibility. An image popped into my head—Christopher standing up in the widow's walk, gesticulating wildly and chanting in Enochian as ravens swirled about him....

*Yeah... right.*

You don't become a magician without being somewhat credulous about paranormal phenomena. But that doesn't mean you have to believe in *everything*. While I was willing to entertain the possibility of a magickal link between the ravens and Christopher, part of my mind was demanding it at least make some kind of sense. And Christopher summoning an evil army of ravens didn't really make any kind of sense. Once again my thoughts returned to the manuscript. We'd nearly finished translating it, and we'd been given some kind of communication that sounded an awful lot like a warning to me. Seth was determined to perform it later that night. Did ARZL not want us to complete the translation or the performance?

If so, he—or she—was probably out of luck, because this close to putting all the pieces of the mass together, even I was no longer sure I was willing to walk away from it. Could I really put the manuscript aside without completing a full translation? And even after I knew what Ficino's intent had been, could I simply go back to Durham without ever testing it to see if the spell *worked*? I doubted it. Not unless it turned out to be a spell to hasten the Apocalypse. We would take precautions, of course—putting up wards, for example—but, as they say in theater, the show must go on.

WITH RAVENS hanging around the chapel like a gang of thugs in leather jackets harassing people on a street corner, nobody was brave enough to walk past them in order to attend the morning service. Bowyn, Marianne, and I found a crowd of initiates and neophytes stopped dead along the cobblestone path, afraid to move any closer. The ravens were all squatting on the grass and the path, not attacking, but watching us silently, as if waiting for us to make a move.

"Should we just walk through them?" Bowyn asked.

Marianne shrugged. "They haven't actually hurt anyone yet, have they?"

"Not yet...."

But we were saved from making a decision by Seth's arrival. He took in the scene with a glance, snorted contemptuously, and then plowed through the crowd and continued along the path. The ravens didn't act terrified of him, but they fluttered or stepped out of his way.

Bowyn trailed after him, and Marianne and I followed Bowyn, clutching each other's hands like Dorothy and the Scarecrow in the Haunted Forest. Marianne must have been thinking the same thing because I heard her mutter under her breath, "Ravens and tigers and bears...."

"Oh my!" I finished, and we both giggled nervously.

The mist had grown heavier since early morning, becoming a heavy fog that obscured anything more than a hundred feet away. Walking through the midst of the ravens, I could imagine a sea of black birds stretched off into the fog forever, with only the chapel rising out of the waves to offer us safe haven. But even that had the great black birds perched on its roof and anywhere else they could find a foothold, peering down at us with those black marble eyes, not so much hostile as simply... cold.

We made it to the chapel without any significant reaction from the birds, so eventually the initiates and neophytes found the courage to follow us inside. Even so, the service was shorter than usual. No one felt comfortable being there, surrounded as we were, and even Seth was distracted and off his game. For the first time since I'd known him, he gave a sermon that was rather dull. We were all glad to wrap it up and head back to the house, even though it meant walking past our creepy squatters again.

I WAS still convinced it was Christopher who'd been scurrying around in the servants' passageways two nights ago, even if I couldn't convince the others. And I wanted to know where he'd gone when he'd disappeared in the cellar. So about an hour before lunch, I went down for a quick shower.

After I'd dried off and dressed again, tossing my dirty robe into the laundry bin and taking a fresh one off the rack outside the shower area, I prowled around a bit, examining the walls closely for any hint of a secret door. Yes, I felt a little silly doing it, but I was convinced the person I'd followed, probably Christopher, hadn't left the basement through any of the doors I was familiar with, and there hadn't been anyplace for him to hide. Well, perhaps in the dirty laundry bin. But this house had a number of "secret" passages I knew about. It wasn't inconceivable that there was one I *didn't* know about.

One possibility was the old root cellar. It had looked empty that night, but perhaps he'd slipped through it quickly. But as I poked around in there, I became convinced any secret door in that room would require one of the shelves to slide to one side or swing out, and I couldn't see any way to do that without a bunch of pots and pans crashing to the floor.

"Are you looking for something?" Alex asked, startling me.

She was standing in the doorway, watching me with curiosity.

"Um… a secret door?"

She laughed and shook her head, causing her silver hoop earrings to jangle. "Good luck with that," she said, reaching for a couple of the large casserole dishes on one of the shelves near the door. "Still convinced Christopher is sneaking around at night?"

"Someone is," I replied. "Maybe him; maybe someone else."

She looked thoughtful for a long moment. "I can't be certain, but… it's possible somebody's been raiding the kitchen."

I forgot about the shelves of pans for a minute, turning to give her my full attention. "Why do you think that?"

"Things seem to be missing," Alex said. "I counted the cartons of orange juice in the refrigerator yesterday because we were getting low and I needed to know if we had enough for breakfast today. This morning one was missing."

"Is that all?" One carton of orange juice could have been snagged by someone making screwdrivers in his or her room, for all we knew.

"I've been noticing other things—a loaf of bread, cheese, a jar of mustard… It's hard to pinpoint. But I never noticed things missing like this until…."

Alex hesitated for a second, and I finished for her, "Until after somebody tampered with the tea?"

She nodded, taking another casserole dish down from a shelf. Since she already had her hands full with the other two, I extended my hand and she passed it to me to carry.

It was possible, of course, that one or more of the initiates was raiding the kitchen at night. They were all warned, upon pain of death, to keep out of there. If they were hungry in the middle of the night, they could get something off the snack table in the dining room. Still, the kitchen was never locked, and some neophyte might be dumb enough to risk the Wrath of Alex.

She handed me another dish. "There's one thing that nobody has really discussed," she mused.

"Motive?"

"Exactly. You've been hinting it could have been Christopher, and maybe he did have the means…."

"Well, him and everyone else who knows about the passageways," I admitted.

"Exactly. But let's consider the possibility it *was* him, for a moment. Why would he do it? He barely talked to Marianne. We don't know that he even knew about the baby. Hardly anybody did. And even if he did, why would he want to hurt her? Or her baby?"

I'd been wondering that myself. It didn't make a lot of sense. "Who would want to do that, period?" I asked.

Alex appeared to mull that one over, but I had the distinct impression she already knew the answer, at least as she saw it. "Well, I can't claim that I'm above suspicion, but it seems to me there are really just three people who might have benefitted if Marianne lost the baby…."

I knew what she was going to say. I'd been avoiding thinking about it myself. The baby had been important to Marianne and Bowyn. Of course, the rest of us were happy about it, but it had been bittersweet, because once Jay was born, both Marianne and Bowyn would be leaving the Temple and moving six hours away. There were three people in particular who'd been unhappy about that potentiality.

"Me," I said quietly.

"And Seth."

"And Bowyn" came a voice from behind us, almost startling me into dropping the casserole dishes.

We both turned around and saw Bowyn standing in the doorway. His face was cold and impassive, but those crystal-clear blue eyes of his were looking directly at me, and they were pissed.

"How could you even *think* it?" he asked me, angrier than I'd ever seen him. "You, of all people! How could you ever think I would kill my own son?"

"I didn't!" I protested, though I knew he was barely listening to me at the moment.

"You might as well have."

I couldn't blame him for being angry. It was a horrible accusation. But I hadn't really been making it so much as considering all the possibilities.

Alex took the dishes from my arms, mouthed the word "Sorry" to me, and then slipped past Bowyn to go upstairs, leaving us to hash this out. Bowyn turned away, as if to follow after her, but I reached out and clamped my hand firmly on his arm.

"Bowyn," I said, forcing myself to keep my voice low. "I know you loved Jay—"

"I *still* love him!"

"I *know* that," I said, "and so does Alex."

"You were just debating if I had a motive for killing him."

"We were going over logical possibilities. That's all. We weren't necessarily taking them seriously."

"What about you? You didn't want me moving away, any more than I wanted to go. So maybe *you* killed him."

I hoped he didn't seriously believe that. But of course, as Alex and I had already concluded, I *did* have that as a possible motive. "I was on that list too. You heard me say so."

Unfortunately Bowyn wasn't interested in listening to anything else I had to say right now. He turned and stalked upstairs without another word. I let him go. Part of me desperately wanted to grab him and pull him back, to make him believe I loved him and would never think anything bad about him. But I knew I would just make him angrier. I just had to hope, when he'd calmed down, he'd understand neither Alex nor I had been making accusations. We'd just been considering every possibility. I knew *I* hadn't done it, and no matter how logical I was being, there was no way I could seriously believe Bowyn had done anything to hurt his child.

Of course, that still left us with Seth. He didn't want either Bowyn or Marianne to leave the Temple. I didn't want Marianne to leave, either, but… well, Bowyn was the one I was in love with. Bowyn was essential to the everyday functioning of the Temple, and Marianne kept the finances in order. Seth would be lost without them. But that was why I thought it unlikely it could be him. He had to have known how dangerous pennyroyal could be. Women sometimes died from taking too much, attempting to bring about abortions. Would he have risked Marianne's life? I doubted it.

Which brought me back to square one. And now Bowyn was pissed at me, on top of that. This day was getting off to a wonderful start.

# Chapter Twenty-Eight

AFTER FAILING to find a secret passageway—though still not convinced there wasn't one there somewhere—I went upstairs and sought Alex out again. Not surprisingly, she was in the kitchen, barking orders at her staff. She didn't bark at me, but I knew better than to get in her way for long.

"I'd like to see Christopher's room," I told her.

I wasn't sure what I was looking for there. Evidence of drugs, perhaps, though what new information that would give me, I wasn't sure. Still, it seemed worth taking a look. Perhaps I could tell if he'd been there since supposedly going to rehab.

"Second floor. There are labels on the doors. He has a roommate, though, so you might not want to just barge in."

I found the room without difficulty—the fifth one down the hall on the left, marked with a paper card that read "Christopher Nillson and Paul Denning." I knocked on the door. There was no answer, so I stood there for a moment debating whether or not to enter. Technically the Brethren were responsible for everything that went on in the Temple, and that gave us the legal right to search a room if we suspected something illegal was inside.

On the other hand, that's what some of us like to call "being a dick." I had no real reason to suspect anything illegal. Well, possibly a drug stash. But frankly, if Christopher still had heroin, I doubted he would have left it in his room while he was gone. And Paul hadn't done anything wrong, to my knowledge, so he deserved to be treated respectfully.

I went downstairs and asked some of the neophytes in the living room if they'd seen Paul around and was eventually directed to one of the yoga classes going on out on the back lawn. This was a spot the ravens hadn't shown any interest in—they were mostly still gathered near the chapel. I recognized the instructor from my early days at the Temple—Maggie Goldstein, an older woman with a terminally cheerful demeanor. I didn't think I'd ever seen her without a smile on her face. She smiled at me now and waved briefly before lowering her head to her knee while I took a seat on the grass nearby. I watched the class until it was over and then called out to her students, "Is one of you Paul Denning?"

A young man looked startled, stopping in his tracks to turn in my direction. "That's me."

Paul Denning was a few years older than Christopher, but he still looked barely out of high school. He had a bland face—a bit on the scrawny side, with curly brown hair that didn't look as if it had been washed in the past twenty-four hours. He also had a touch of acne.

Paul looked disconcerted when I asked to see his room. "Well… it's pretty messy…."

I assured him I wasn't the bed-making police. "I'd just like to see if there's anything of Christopher's that might tell us where he's gone."

"He's still at that rehab program in Berlin," Paul said, and I realized he hadn't been told anything about Christopher failing to arrive at the clinic.

"I'd really like to check the room, if you don't mind."

Paul gave me a suspicious look, but he nodded and led the way back to the house.

To say the room was "messy" was an understatement. At least as far as Paul's side of it was concerned. Not only was the bed unmade, but he'd left dirty robes on the floor—why, when there were laundry hampers in the hall, I couldn't fathom—plates of dried and/or moldy half-eaten food on the bureau and partly under the bed, which would drive Alex into fits if she saw it, and books everywhere. His walls were covered with pictures of half or fully naked women. In short, Paul was a bit of a pig.

Christopher's side of the room was a different matter entirely. His bed was rumpled, but the floors were bare and although his dresser had books on it, they were neatly stacked. I opened his dresser drawers, but it took little time to determine there wasn't much of interest in them. Just some folded street clothes, as tidy as everything else. The only pictures on the wall were prints of nineteenth-century paintings of Vikings and the Norse gods.

Unlike Bowyn's room, this one was small and contained few furnishings, so it didn't take long to establish there wasn't anything hidden anywhere.

"Do you two get along all right?" I asked, unable to contain my curiosity. I would have strangled Paul if we'd been roommates.

He shrugged. "Yeah, sure. He's really private. Doesn't say much. He's naked all the time, and that's not really my thing, but I'm cool with it and he's cool with…."

He petered out, as if he'd realized he was rambling, but I prompted, "He's cool with…?"

Paul looked embarrassed. "Well, I like to… you know… in the morning."

"Masturbate?"

"Yeah. I mean, I never would have done that in front of my roommate in college, but Christopher tells me all kinds of stories about stuff he's done—some really sick shit—and he's always naked, so it just doesn't seem like that big a deal."

I smiled sympathetically. "People often do things at the Temple that they wouldn't dream of doing anywhere else."

"No kidding," Paul said with an embarrassed smile. "He never does, though."

"Never… masturbates in front of you?"

"Never jerks off at all," Paul replied. "He says he hates it. He had wet dreams a couple times, and he was so freaked out he yanked the sheets off his bed and had to shower."

*Poor kid*, I thought. Sex had been completely stolen from him, made into something other people used him for, or a tool he could use to manipulate others. But it wasn't something he could enjoy.

I changed the subject. "You mentioned he was in rehab?"

Paul's eyes went wide. Perhaps he thought he'd betrayed a confidence. "I thought you knew that, Brethren."

"I knew," I assured him. "What I'm wondering is, did you know he was using? Before we found out about it and sent him to rehab, I mean?"

Paul couldn't look me in the eye, and he took a very long time to answer. "He wasn't bothering anybody."

I wasn't really in the mood to lecture him about the dangers of drug addiction. He was loyal to Christopher and that, at least, was admirable. "Listen, Paul. I'm not here to make things worse for Christopher, and I'm not going to punish you for keeping a friend's secret for him. I'm just trying to piece some things together so we can help him."

That didn't sound convincing, even to me. Authority figures always claimed to be your friend just before they slammed down on you. But it was a little late for the subtle approach. "Do you know where Christopher keeps his stash?"

Was "stash" even what they called it these days? I wasn't really up on drug slang.

Paul hesitated and then shook his head. "I don't think he has one."

When I raised my eyebrows in disbelief, he quickly added, "He comes back to the room stoned all the time—or, he did before he went away. Really late at night. But I never saw him shoot up."

"He came *back* to the room stoned?" If it was true he didn't keep it in his room, then Christopher was either hiding the heroin in some other part of the house, or he was visiting someone else's room and getting it there. And that brought us back to the possibility of someone in the Temple being a dealer.

"Yeah."

"How often did that happen?"

Again, Paul looked uncomfortable. "Well, nearly every night."

*Christ.* "And how long was it going on?"

"Ever since he came to the Temple, pretty much. I mean, for the first couple weeks, he was really trying to go straight. It was rough on him. He didn't sleep hardly at all; he was shaking; he always had the shits and even puked a few times. I didn't know what the hell was happening—I thought he was dying from something. But when I begged him to tell… you guys… he told me it was just withdrawal and made me swear not to tell anyone. He thought he could beat it, and he didn't want to get kicked out."

It broke my heart to think anyone in the Temple could be going through something like that and be afraid to tell us. "How long do you think it was before he started using again?"

"Not long," Paul said sadly. "One morning, I woke up and he was lying in his bed, just kind of staring at nothing. I tried to talk to him, but he was… I could tell he was on something. I didn't get much out of him, then, but later he told me a little. He said it was too hard to beat, but it was okay, 'cause someone was taking care of him now."

"Who?"

"I don't know. He used to slip out every night to meet whoever it was, after most people were asleep." Paul nodded to the door to the servants' passage in the corner of the room. "Through there. Then he'd come back about an hour later."

I opened the door and peered inside. It was lighter in there at this time of day, thanks to a tiny bit of light coming through the small windows. It was still shadowy and musty, but I decided now would be a good time to see if I could find anything that wasn't visible in the middle of the night. I thanked Paul for letting me poke around in his room and slipped into the passageway, closing the door behind me. No doubt Paul thought I was… eccentric, to say the least.

One thing was obvious in the light of day—the dust on the floor was still visible off to my right, but it had been nearly swept away off to the left, probably by the hem of a robe. Christopher must have taken that route most often, and few people came from the other direction. It might seem overly convenient for me, but there were only three rooms off to the right. Not everyone was enthralled with the servants' passageways, especially at this time of the year when they were freezing cold.

I followed the least dusty passageway until it came to the stairwell I'd come down during my pursuit of Christopher—I assumed—two nights earlier. If I were to go down, it would take me past the kitchen on the first floor, but I followed the steps upward to the third floor instead. At the top, a narrow corridor hugged the outer wall for the length of Bowyn's room before turning to the right, while the stairs continued up to the attic. They were fairly dusty, but the way to Bowyn's room was swept clear, as I already knew it would be.

After passing the servants' door that led into Bowyn's room, the passageway ended. There was a door that opened up into the third floor hallway. When I walked across the hall and peered into the servants' door there, the floor was covered in dust and obviously hadn't been walked on recently. And that left me exactly nowhere. I'd already known he was sneaking up to the third floor, but there were twelve rooms up there, including Bowyn's, Seth's, Alex's, and Marianne's. Rafe, as far as I knew, was staying in Seth's room, and the other rooms housed several initiates I didn't know. And, of course, he could have snuck up to one of the attic bedrooms.

I RETURNED to the room I was sharing with Bowyn and was disappointed to find it empty. I suppose I'd been hoping we could patch things up after the argument—or whatever it was—that we'd had downstairs. But without Bowyn there, I had no desire to hang out in the room by myself, working on the libretto. No doubt I'd spend more time fretting than anything else.

But the libretto needed to be finished, and I was ridiculously close. So I grabbed the laptop and took it up to the library. At least there, in front of the fake fireplace, I could focus without one ear listening for Bowyn to open the door.

I'd slipped my handwritten notes into the laptop case before going to bed the previous night, and now I withdrew them as the laptop was booting up. It was child's play, really, to complete the translation of the libretto once I'd substituted the English words for the Enochian.

"The thread has broken, but the fiber remains strong. It can be rewoven on a distaff of song. Come! And once more inhabit your mortal flesh!"

Those few lines caused the hair on my forearms to tingle like something in a bad horror film, and yes, I could actually see goose bumps rise up on my skin. I wondered for just a second what possible evolutionary benefit goose bumps might have provided our ancient ancestors before I pushed my chair away from the desk and stood up.

I crossed the room and slid open the drawer that contained the Ficino manuscript, activating the black lights on either side. The cold bluish light flickered on, causing the ancient, faded writing to luminesce, and I sought out the pages with the illustrations. There, in the center of the room, surrounded by the choir platforms and the altar, was the large pit, and in the center of that, the drawing of a man I'd seen earlier.

*Once more inhabit your mortal flesh.*

I'd thought when I'd first looked at it that the man was standing, and Ficino had sketched him full-on because it was easier and clearer than drawing a man as seen from above. But I'd been wrong. The man was, in fact, lying on the floor of the pit.

Because he was dead.

# Chapter Twenty-Nine

I HEARD the door to the airlock open and turned, expecting to see Seth. But it was Bowyn who stepped out into the library, looking a bit sheepish. "I saw your laptop was gone and it's too chilly outside to be working on the lawn, so I figured you'd be up here."

I smiled at him. "Brilliant deduction, Holmes!"

He seemed encouraged by the fact that I didn't seem angry. I wasn't, of course.

"I'm sorry," he said. "I overreacted."

"I was… being insensitive."

I don't think either of us really knew what to say after that, but Bowyn didn't waste any more time on words. He crossed the room and wrapped his strong arms around me, drawing me close. For a minute or two, I breathed in his faint, musky scent and bathed in the heat of his firm body, grateful the storm had passed. More of a brief New England downpour, really. But it had been unpleasant, just the same.

My mouth found Bowyn's and he groaned, allowing me to share his breath, inhale him. We kissed and caressed each other until we both grew painfully erect and the thought of fucking on the carpet in the library started to seem like a good idea. And really, why not? With Seth and Rafe as randy as they both were, I doubted we'd be the first.

We didn't remove our robes—just hoisted them up to our waists so we could lie mouth-to-cock on the soft, plush carpet and suck and nibble and lick each other frantically. There was nothing slow and sensual about our lovemaking this time. We were desperate for release and went about it like animals rutting, until we both spasmed at nearly the same moment and I tasted Bowyn's seed in my mouth as I squirted into his.

We lay there for a long time, allowing our cocks to finish bucking, both of us swallowing again and again, until we were done. I felt exhausted and wonderful and raunchy as hell. Part of me wished Seth or somebody else would walk in at that moment and see us like that, just to complete the sleazy picture. But that didn't happen, and at last we pulled apart. We kissed, tasting ourselves in each other's mouths, before we stood and allowed our robes to fall, making us moderately respectable again.

"That was fun," Bowyn growled, pulling me in for another kiss.

It certainly had been, but after we nuzzled a bit longer, my thoughts couldn't help drifting back to what had been occupying them before Bowyn entered the library. I gave him one last kiss before pulling gently away. "I need you to see something."

I showed him the diagram in the manuscript and explained what the libretto had ultimately translated to.

As I should have suspected, he found this more amusing than frightening. "Raising the dead? Are you serious?"

"Ficino and other Neoplatonists believed that there is a perfect form of the body residing in the spirit world—the *anima mundi*—or if you prefer, in the mind of God. Healing occurs when the physical body is synchronized, so to speak, with the true image of the body. And this is done by balancing the bodily humors to bring the body in alignment with its perfect, fully functioning form."

Bowyn still looked amused. "Sounds very New Age."

"It is, a bit," I admitted. "But we're not talking about peaceful chimes and synthesizer chords to make you feel more relaxed. We're talking about a piece of music that Ficino spent his lifetime perfecting, with every note mathematically calculated to resonate within our bodies. You felt it, didn't you? When Christopher was singing?"

"I felt something, and I admit I was disturbed by it. But you can't seriously believe music can bring a dead body back to life."

I wasn't sure what I believed. It seemed absurd. But part of me had always felt music did have that kind of power, if we could only find a way to tap into it. It was why I'd dedicated my life to its study. "Let me ask you this," I replied. "Do you believe in an eternal soul—some part of us that can survive death?"

Bowyn looked skeptical. The doctrine of the soul, as taught by Christian churches, wasn't really a big part of the teachings of the Temple. Most of us tended to believe in life after death if for no other reason than that we'd been raised to believe in it, but it wasn't considered essential to our doctrine. "I don't know," he said after some thought. "I suppose so."

"And do you believe that some people have died—on the operating table, say, or in accidents—and then been brought back to life? The classic 'near-death experience'?"

"I guess. Unless they weren't really completely dead."

"Proving that has always been difficult," I admitted, "but there have certainly been cases where there has been no brain activity for several hours. In one case, a woman had her body temperature lowered and her heart stopped in order for the doctor to perform an extremely delicate operation on her brain. During that time, she had no brain activity at all, but when they revived her, she reported conversations she'd overheard during the operation and described an instrument the doctor used, even though she'd never seen it before."

Bowyn shrugged. "So, fine. I'll grant that it may be possible for someone to actually die and then be brought back."

"There are also cases in which people claim to have been called back by the voices of their loved ones, calling their name or telling them that they loved them."

"Fine."

"So then you'll concede that, if the body is still intact, and the spirit hasn't moved on to… whatever afterlife it's supposed to go to… then it might be possible to call it back, using the human voice, or—"

"Music?"

"Why not? If the music resonates with the spirit and draws it back to the physical world?"

Bowyn leaned in to examine the diagram in the manuscript carefully. "It's not as if you can just assemble a choir to perform this ritual whenever somebody is on their deathbed. Plus, Seth is claiming it has to be done during the new moon at eleven o'clock. That's pretty specific. It doesn't seem as though conditions would line up correctly very often."

"Perhaps not. But that doesn't make it impossible. Besides," I added, "some people have supposedly been dead for days before coming back. In one case I read about, the body had even begun to decay." Admittedly, that one may have been apocryphal.

Bowyn scrunched up his face as though he smelled something rank and pulled away from the manuscript. "Does Seth know what the ritual is really for?"

"I don't know."

"I think we need to have a talk with him."

AFTER CLOSING up the drawer, I collected the laptop and followed Bowyn downstairs. I wasn't sure where Seth was at the moment. Perhaps in his room. But he didn't answer when we knocked on his door, so we continued down to the main floor, me still carrying the laptop tucked under one arm.

We passed by the door to the dining room as we came down the stairs into the front hall. Normally, this close to lunchtime, I wouldn't have bothered to stop there, since I would just get in the way of Alex and her staff as they went about setting out the large trays of food. But something caught my eye and made me stop.

It was Marianne and Alex hugging. Not simply a let's-patch-things-up type of hug, which I would have been glad enough to see, but something more serious. It looked as if Marianne was crying and Alex was trying to console her, while the kitchen staff did their best to squeeze past without disturbing them, carrying trays of hot food.

Bowyn saw it at the same time I did, but whereas my first response was to stop and evaluate the situation, he immediately brushed by me, intent on fixing whatever was wrong. I went after him. Alex looked up as we approached and whispered into Marianne's ear.

Marianne turned around, tears streaming down her face.

"What is it?" Bowyn asked.

It was Alex who answered. "Somebody left a note in Marianne's room."

Marianne held a crumpled sheet of notepaper out to Bowyn and he took it from her. He read it quickly, his expression darkening. I drew close so I could read it in his hand.

It was handwritten in a very precise, small script, and it was unsigned. *"I'm really sorry I hurt you. But it's better this way. I wish someone had done the same for me, before I was born."*

*Christopher.* That was the first name that came to my mind, and from the way Bowyn looked at me, I suspected he was thinking the same thing. It made sense, in a sick, twisted kind of way, that a boy who'd been as severely abused as Christopher might think forcing a pregnant mother to miscarry was an act of mercy.

Bowyn gestured for us to follow him and then led us out into the front hall, away from the bustling staff. "Does anyone still doubt it was deliberate?"

Nobody answered him, so he turned to me. "I guess you were right about him coming back here and hiding out somewhere."

"It can't be Christopher," Marianne insisted, wiping her eyes with the back of one hand. "He's a good kid."

"Anyone could have written that note," Alex agreed. But she didn't sound convinced. We all knew it was *possible* it was Christopher. We simply didn't know for certain.

"Where did you find this?" Bowyn asked Marianne.

"It was on the mantle of my fireplace."

"So it was put there during the service," Bowyn said, "Or at least after you left your room for breakfast."

Marianne shook her head. "It might have been there earlier. I didn't notice it until I put on my amber necklace, about fifteen minutes ago."

"Could it have been there last night?"

"No," she said adamantly. "I was wearing that necklace yesterday for the funeral, and I took it off just after Resh, before I went to bed."

"What about when the ravens were freaking out last night?" I asked. "Could it have already been on the mantle when that was going on?"

"I suppose. I really didn't look. Things were too chaotic."

"And I assume you don't lock your bedroom door?"

She rolled her eyes at me. "Does anybody around here?"

"So whoever it was," Bowyn summed up, "they could have put it on your mantle any time from a little past midnight up 'til maybe a half hour ago, and they could have entered through your bedroom door or the servants' door."

"Doesn't narrow it down much," Alex observed.

"No, not really," Bowyn agreed. "But I'm putting my money on Christopher sneaking around in the servants' passages."

We all looked at each other for a long moment while neophytes carrying platters of what smelled like apple pie with a heavy dose of cinnamon, and one of the gigantic urns filled with fresh coffee, entered the hall to set up the dessert tables.

At last Alex sighed and said, "I'll call the police again."

# Chapter Thirty

THE POLICE were none too happy to hear from us for the third time in as many days, particularly when they were greeted at the door by a young female neophyte who didn't have enough sense to throw on a robe before opening the door for visitors. Fortunately the officers were well aware that the Temple had a policy of open nudity, and they chose to ignore it—once she was able to convince them she was over eighteen.

The neophyte summoned Bowyn, and he escorted the officers into the sitting room, where the Brethren had gathered after lunch. This was a small room at the front of the house that had probably been used as a parlor to entertain visitors in the Victorian era, and it was easily closed off from the living room and the front hall. Seth and Rafe had been found in the chapel, going over preparations for tonight's ritual, and they'd joined us, though Seth was looking every bit as inconvenienced as the police were.

"You all know this house better than I do," Officer Westcott stated. "If this Christopher is hiding out here, where could he be setting up camp?"

"We don't know," Seth replied.

Bowyn added, "There aren't any rooms currently unoccupied where he could be squatting. Marianne and I went door to door just before you arrived, and nobody admits to letting him hide out in their room or even seeing him."

"Which leads me to wonder if he really wrote this note?"

Seth gave him a sour look. "And if he didn't?"

Westcott tapped the note against his palm, returning Seth's gaze calmly. At last, he said, "Well, then somebody else would have written it."

"And that somebody else appears to be confessing to putting the pennyroyal in Marianne's tea."

"Perhaps." The officer turned to Alex. "Mrs. Harriman, the results of the fingerprint analysis came back this morning. Only a few prints were found, and I'm afraid they're all yours."

Alex's face flushed at the thinly veiled accusation, but it was Marianne who responded vehemently, "*Somebody* contaminated the tea, and it wasn't Alex. The note proves that!"

"It would seem so…," Westcott said.

It was nice to see Marianne sticking up for Alex, but I knew it was possible Alex had written the note herself to redirect suspicion away from her. Did I believe that? No. But it was possible. And clearly Westcott believed it.

I noticed the younger officer was looking uncomfortable and followed his gaze to find Rafe giving him a look that would have made most people blush. It wasn't overt—no tongue flashing or licking of the lips or anything like that—but Rafe had a way of conveying sexual energy with his eyes, and he was beaming that energy directly into this poor young man's heterosexual brain. I don't approve of flirting with straight men just to see how uncomfortable you can make them—a favorite pastime of some gay men I know—but I was beginning to find both these policemen tiresome. They didn't seem to be taking us seriously, as if any crime committed against us was probably deserved.

I found myself wishing Rafe would flash the guy.

Seth stood up, apparently having decided this was all a waste of time. "I'm afraid I have work to get back to. If there's nothing else, gentlemen, I'll thank you for your time."

BOWYN AND I cornered Seth after the police left, dragging him to one side in the sitting room while Alex went to check on the after-lunch cleanup. Rafe had grown bored enough to start plinking on the keys of the old out-of-tune upright piano, and somehow Marianne had roped him into one of those obnoxious, unending duets of "Heart and Soul."

"I've finished the libretto," I told Seth.

"Wonderful!"

"Seth," I went on. "Are you seriously telling me you have no idea what the mass is for?"

He waved a hand in the air dismissively. "I didn't want to put ideas into your head until you'd had a chance to work it out for yourself. The man I bought the manuscript from believed it might be the culmination of Ficino's work on healing the body through music. Perhaps it might even reverse the effects of aging. Of course, I was skeptical about *that* claim…."

"Don't be," I interrupted. "At least, as far as Ficino was concerned, *he* appears to have believed the music had healing properties. In fact, he seemed to think it could heal the *dead*."

The piano stopped abruptly while Seth stared at me, attempting to process what I'd just told him, and I heard Rafe say, "The dead?"

I turned to him. "The dead."

Briefly I explained what I'd learned from the libretto. Marianne and Rafe looked dumbstruck, but Seth merely raised his eyebrow and said, "Interesting."

"Interesting?" Marianne commented. "It's ridiculous! Dead people don't come back to life just because they've heard a good symphony."

I shrugged. "Not generally. But people do claim to have come back from the dead for other reasons if something reminds them to come back. And they often claim to have heard sounds and music while in a noncorporeal state."

"It doesn't sound impossible…," Seth said, looking contemplatively out the window. The courtyard was still shrouded in mist.

Had there been a skeptic in the room, then of course it *would* have sounded impossible to him or her. But we all believed in the supernatural—in spirits and ghosts. We believed in the ability to summon these spirits. The only thing *we* were skeptical about was whether or not it was possible to summon the spirit of a dead man back into his body… and keep it there.

"Let's have a show of hands!" Rafe exclaimed, as if he'd just thought of a wonderful new party game. "Who volunteers to commit suicide before tonight's perform—*Ow!*"

That last was because Marianne had punched him hard in the shoulder. "Not funny."

"You aren't still going to perform the mass tonight, are you?" Bowyn asked Seth.

That seemed to snap Seth out of his thoughts. He looked at Bowyn in surprise. "What? Of course! Why not?"

"Maybe because resurrecting the dead never ends well."

"Haven't you read *Frankenstein*?" Marianne interjected. "'Herbert West: Reanimator'? 'The Monkey's Paw'?"

Seth gave her a look full of pity. "Those are horror stories—not scholarly academic works on the subject. There are, in fact, no scholarly works on the subject that I'm aware of, apart from collections of anecdotal evidence concerning the so-called near-death experiences Jeremy was referring to."

"*Night of the Living Dead*," Marianne added.

Seth ignored her. "This magickal working—the entire thing—hasn't been performed for over five hundred years, Jeremy. For all we know, it was *never* performed. And according to the illustrations and charts included with the mass, all of the astrological correspondences are favorable for a test tonight at eleven. I don't intend to just put that off for several more years because Marianne has watched too many horror films."

"Except that we don't have a corpse," I pointed out.

"We have a pile of raven corpses we haven't yet figured out how to dispose of."

I was about to point out that ravens might not respond to music the same way a person would, but then I remembered how the birds had behaved on the hill when Christopher sang. Certainly the music had seemed to call to them.

"That's another thing," Marianne persisted. "What about the ravens? Don't you think that's some kind of message or warning?"

I could tell Seth's patience was wearing thin, but he stated calmly, "I have no idea why a flock of ravens has decided to camp out on our lawn. Perhaps they're migrating."

"That's more than a flock," I said, "and ravens don't migrate."

"As it may be. But since we haven't yet attempted to resurrect a dead body, I don't see how the ravens could have anything to do with that."

The argument went on like this for several more minutes, with Seth answering all our objections in a reasonable manner. Since I would have to perform the tenor solo in Christopher's absence, I could have dug in my heels and flat-out refused to do it. But the more we discussed it, the harder it became for me to come up with reasonable excuses to counter Seth. And he kept appealing to my not-so-secret desire to be one of the world's leading authorities on Ficino.

"You know it will drive you crazy," Seth pointed out, "if you pass up the chance to find out whether or not his theories were correct. Sooner or later, you'll *have to* see this ritual performed, Jeremy. You know I'm right."

He was, but I was still putting up a token resistance. "It just seems as if we're rushing it...."

"We are," he admitted. "But that can't be helped."

Ultimately I knew I wanted this almost as much as he did. "All right," I said, "I'll sing the part. But I warn you, that final note is a bit high for me."

"I'm sure you'll do magnificently," Seth said, smiling and patting me on the shoulder. He gave me a quick peck on the mouth. "Now, my love, if you'll excuse me, I have to go select a... subject... for our little experiment tonight and finalize the details with Timothy. Please be at the chapel by ten."

He left the room, and Rafe straggled along after him like a faithful puppy.

"Shall I notify your next of kin now?" Bowyn asked me. "Or would you rather they never find out that you were dragged into the Pit of Hell by the gibbering, undead thing you're about to create?"

"I have no backbone."

"Bones just get in the way when you're being devoured alive."

"I see your point. I'd hate to give the poor monster indigestion."

Marianne stood up from the piano and faced us with both hands on her hips and a cross look on her face. "Will you two please stop it? I can't believe you let him talk you into this."

I merely held up my hands in surrender while Bowyn laughed.

"I knew he'd give in," he told her. "Seth's right about him being way too curious to pass this up."

Marianne sighed dramatically and turned, making a gesture with her hand to indicate we should follow her out. "Come along. Both of you."


I KNEW what she was up to. One of the things Marianne was very good at was divination, particularly with the tarot, and she wasn't going to let me go through with this without doing a reading.

"I know you don't believe in divination," she told me as we entered her room on the third floor, "but you'll have to humor me this once."

I hadn't seen her room since I came back. It was different now. Far more "girlish," with a lot more pink than I remembered from eight years ago and posters of cutesy unicorns and winged horses. Perhaps this was just the natural result of Jack no longer sharing the room with her. There were a number of pictures of him on the mantle, and here and there I saw something I associated with him—a book on shamanic journeying, a deerskin drum, a large didgeridoo standing in the corner. But Marianne had claimed the space as her own.

"It's not that I don't believe in it," I said. "I just don't really see the point. Either the prediction comes true, in which case it didn't do me much good to know about it beforehand, or it doesn't, in which case I'll never know if the prediction was accurate to begin with."

"If it doesn't come true," she countered, "that's probably because you did something to alter the course of events."

"Or it was just a bogus prediction. There's no way to tell the difference."

She retrieved her tarot deck from her dresser and took a seat in the large bay window. They were folded up in the familiar blue silk with yellow moons and stars I'd seen at the gazebo, and she gave me a sour look as she unwrapped them. "Don't be so cynical. Have a seat."

I sat on the window seat opposite her, with enough space between us for her to lay the blue cloth down.

Marianne shuffled the deck and said, "Magicians should always do a divination before a major magickal working. That's Magick 101. I don't know why you and Seth don't feel like you need to."

"Arrogance?" I supplied helpfully.

Bowyn laughed, but Marianne didn't seem amused. "Cut the deck," she ordered, holding the cards out to me.

I reached out and lifted about half the cards up off the deck, then handed them back to her. She placed those cards under the remainder of the deck. The point of this little maneuver wasn't really to mix the cards up—they'd already been shuffled. It was to make me touch the deck, so the deck could read my psychic energy and allow Marianne to get a glimpse into my future.

"Full spread?" she asked.

I shook my head. "Let's just do something quick and dirty." I really wasn't in the mood for this, and I wanted to review the tenor solo I was supposed to be singing tonight. It wasn't an easy part, regardless of how much time I'd spent studying it.

She frowned at me but drew the first card off the top of the deck and laid it down on the cloth. "This is what lies behind you—your past."

It was the eight of Cups, which I had to admit seemed appropriate. The card depicted a man turning his back on eight golden cups to fare out into the world, wrapped in his cloak and carrying a walking staff, as if he'd be traveling for a while. The cups represented emotion and abundance, and I was immediately reminded of how I'd turned my back on my relationship with Bowyn, as well as all the other people I'd cared about. The significance of the eight cups wasn't lost on me either. I'd been "traveling" for eight years... and alone that entire time.

Marianne looked intently at the card, then peered up at me. "That one seems pretty obvious, doesn't it?"

"Yes." I glanced at Bowyn and found those clear blue eyes watching me intently.

"Let's move on, then. This next card represents your present situation."

"Does it say I'm in a room having my fortune told?"

Marianne tried to look disapproving, but I caught her concealed smile as she dipped her head. She placed the card on the cloth.

The four of Swords. The image was striking—a knight lying as if dead on top of his crypt. Or perhaps the knight himself was part of the crypt—a stone effigy. His sword lay underneath him along the wall of the crypt, and hanging on the wall above him, looking as if they were about to fall and impale him at any moment, were three more swords.

Marianne looked puzzled. "I'm not really sure what to make of that one. It could mean that you're lying in stasis, waiting for something to happen."

She sounded unsure, and I was skeptical. "It seems to me that I've been doing more this week than I've done in years."

"Maybe it will make more sense in context." Marianne put a third card down. "This is what the future holds."

It was, of course, one of the darkest cards in the tarot. Not Death—everybody's favorite—but the Tower.

"Is that bad?" I asked, causing Marianne's eyebrows to shoot up, giving her a rather comical expression.

"Bad? It's a tower being struck by lightning, falling apart, and sending people tumbling to their deaths. What do *you* think?"

Bowyn and I exchanged a look and then said in unison, "That's bad."

Marianne glared at me. "This is serious, Jeremy. This card warns of catastrophic change—something earth-shattering."

It wasn't exactly that I wasn't taking the divination seriously. Marianne had a fair amount of ability with the cards, and the warning did give me pause. But it wasn't going to change anything. "Look, hon," I said, "I'd be lying if I said I didn't have serious reservations about doing the ritual, but we all know that Seth won't be dissuaded—"

"That doesn't mean you have to help him!"

"And he's right about me. My curiosity about whether or not Ficino was right is overriding my reluctance. I have to know if music has this kind of power. It's been my life's work! Besides, what if this 'earth-shattering change' the card is warning us about is a change in our worldview? What if the change is ultimately good?"

Marianne looked at me, her nose pinched and her lips pressed together in a tight line. I got the impression she thought that was such a stupid idea it hardly warranted comment. She might have been right. Thankfully, Bowyn intervened before she could rip me a new one.

"If you'll excuse us," he told her as he took hold of my elbow, "I need to talk to Doctor Faustus here alone for a while."

Marianne sighed in frustration as she gathered up the cards. "Fine. Maybe you can talk some sense into him."

I HAD expected Bowyn to start lecturing me as soon as we got back to our room, but apparently I'd misjudged his plan. The moment the door closed, he stripped off his robe and drew me in for a long, passionate kiss. His tongue sought out mine, and I gave myself over to the wonderful softness of his lips and the deep probing of his rigid tongue until my body and cock became so aroused by his symbolic fucking I thought I might come right then and there. But Bowyn broke the kiss and commanded me, "On the bed."

I assumed he meant naked, so I stripped off my own robe and climbed on top of the maroon bedspread. Bowyn pulled open the drawer of the nightstand and slipped a condom over his erection. Then he climbed on top of me, a bottle of lube in his hand.

I lifted my legs to give him access, and he prepared both of us. Then he eased in and leaned forward over me so he could brace himself on his elbows and look directly into my eyes. In order to keep him inside, I had to pull my legs up in the air and hook them over his muscular ass—not the most comfortable position in the world, but one we loved, because it allowed us to have intimate conversations with our bodies joined together. In the eight years I'd been away, I'd never allowed another man to fuck me in this position. This was *ours,* even when it had seemed I might never see Bowyn again. We'd shared so many tender moments, joined like this, Bowyn moving slowly within me as we talked.

"You said you still loved me," Bowyn whispered, his blue eyes gazing sleepily into mine. But I knew he was anything but sleepy.

"I *do* love you," I replied. "Absolutely."

"And I love you." He slid a little deeper into me, as if taking possession, causing me to groan with desire.

I didn't want to spoil the moment, but we'd been dancing around the subject since I came back—the real reason I'd left eight years ago. I had to know. "What about Seth?"

"What about him?"

"Do you love him?"

Bowyn blinked at me. "Of course. I thought you did too."

"I did." My heart constricted within my chest, as if an invisible hand were slowly squeezing it. "I guess I still do." I took a deep breath and plowed ahead. "But I never loved him more than I loved you."

Bowyn looked deep into my eyes, his brow furrowed. "Of course not. Did you think… I did? That I loved him more than I loved you?"

I couldn't answer, but he must have seen the truth in my eyes, because he pulled me tight to his chest. "Babe," he whispered into my ear. "Never. You were always at the center of my heart. I do love Seth, but he never took your place."

The vise grip on my heart eased. My voice sounded small when I spoke, muffled by his shoulder. "But you didn't come with me…."

"The Temple needed me. And I needed the Temple. There was nothing for me back in Durham." He pulled back to look at me, and I saw his eyes were glistening. "But I thought I was going to die when you left."

I took a tremulous breath. I couldn't say at that moment whether leaving had been the best choice for me. Maybe it had been. The Temple had been overwhelming to a twenty-seven-year-old. *Seth* had been overwhelming. But I shouldn't have given Bowyn an ultimatum. I should have been willing to talk it out more. All I could say now was "I'm sorry."

"So am I." He kissed me and seemed to remember the position our bodies were in. He moved his cock within me and I couldn't help moaning. "But what happens after tonight?"

I hadn't wanted to think of that. Not yet. But Bowyn was right—we couldn't put it off any longer. I'd have to leave soon. "I don't know," I replied honestly.

"Do you want to stay here?"

I did. More than anything. The thought of leaving Bowyn again was agonizing. But that didn't mean it was a sensible option. "I'm not sure I can turn my back on my career," I said. "It may not seem as if being a music professor is all that glamorous—"

"I never said there was anything wrong with it."

I slid my arms along his naked sides, loving the warmth and smoothness of his skin. "At any rate, it's my career. And it took me a long time to get where I am."

Bowyn's blue eyes looked deep into mine. "What if I went with you?" he asked.

It meant a lot that he would even contemplate it, but we both knew that couldn't work. "You were miserable at the thought of leaving," I pointed out. "Even for Jay's sake."

Bowyn slid partway out of me for a moment while he considered that and then slid back in, in a slow, languid motion that forced a another quiet groan out of me. "I suppose you're right. It's not the sex. Honestly. The older I get, the less casual sex without any commitment really appeals to me. But my entire life is here—all of it except you. With Jay… well, I didn't really feel I had a choice…."

"But with me, you do."

He hesitated, knowing that didn't sound right. But I understood. "I have my life," I said before he could attempt to assuage any imagined hurt feelings, "and you have yours. It isn't fair for either of us to expect the other to give everything up."

"We're only three hours apart," Bowyn insisted.

"It's a long drive, but…." I grew silent, wondering if we could really make a long-distance relationship like that work. I had vacations here and there throughout the school year, of course. A professor never truly gets time off. There are always papers to be graded, lesson plans to work on… but I could do those here as well as in Durham, couldn't I? And Bowyn could come and go more or less as he pleased, as long as he wasn't gone too long at a stretch.

"We've had nothing for eight years," Bowyn said softly into my ear as he moved himself inside me once more. "I can't do that again. Even if I only see you a few times a year, it will be heaven, compared to that."

"Yes," I agreed.

He kissed me and the conversation ceased as we gave ourselves over to our lovemaking. I loved Bowyn and he loved me. I'd been foolish to leave eight years ago. Or at least, if I'd needed to get away for my sake, I'd been foolish to make demands and sever all ties between us when he couldn't meet those demands. Because really what I'd wanted, all those years ago, was to know that he loved me. I'd tested him, and I thought he'd failed the test. But it was the test that had failed. I should never have forced Bowyn to choose between the life he loved—the life where he was needed—and me. It was as selfish as if he'd demanded I give up my education and plans to be a teacher for *him*.

But that was in the past now. We had a second chance. And I knew we would both be miserable if we didn't take it.

# Chapter Thirty-One

THE FOG appeared to have settled in for a while, and by nightfall the Temple grounds resembled Victorian London. Bowyn and I had difficulty finding our way to the chapel, fake gas lamps notwithstanding. The ravens were still squatting all around the building, obscuring the cobblestone path, though they merely sat there, hunched down in the cold, watching us.

Unlike the choir rehearsal a few nights ago, few people attended the ritual. Apart from Seth, Rafe, Bowyn, and me, only the choir was present, conducted by Timothy. Alex had claimed to be too busy, and Marianne had refused to participate after reiterating her dire warnings to me and Bowyn. I couldn't blame her—I still had concerns about the wisdom of proceeding myself.

Timothy, for his part, spent most of the preritual preparation muttering under his breath about an early death and why hadn't he made out a will yet? He kept eyeing the dead raven Seth had carefully laid out on a white cloth on an altar table in the center of the room, clearly unsettled by its presence. The members of the choir seemed just as uneasy.

A large bowl of fruit, of all things, had been placed on one of the tables. There had been no specific mention of such a thing in Ficino's notes concerning the ritual, but there had been a small circle in a specific location that none of us had been able to identify. That, combined with the reference to an unburnt offering of "all fruits" in the fragment of ancient Greek Rafe's uncle had translated, led us to make an educated guess about what that circle meant. We weren't certain about exactly what "all fruits" was supposed to include, but Seth had sent Rafe out that afternoon to scour the local markets for fruit that would have been native to Italy during Ficino's time—olives, oranges, figs, persimmons, pomegranates, lemons, and various nuts.

I think Seth would have preferred to perform the entire ritual without setting up standard wards. Dee and Kelley had never bothered with wards, apparently assuming the angelic spirits would never harm them, and they weren't a part of the standard Enochian ritual. But of course this wasn't really an Enochian ritual—it predated Enochian and combined elements of ancient Greek and medieval magick—and Bowyn and I were almost as on edge as Timothy was. We pressured Seth until he finally agreed to do the LBRP. It couldn't hurt to at least take that mild precaution.

When the LBRP was over, Bowyn went to sit in the pews with Rafe while I took my place with the choir.

Then the ritual began.

STANDING IN the center of the room, Seth presented an imposing figure, if a bizarre one. His ritual robes consisted of one large cloak with a hood, currently thrown back. The cloak was designed to broaden his shoulders a bit, not so much with padding as with something akin to cloth epaulettes that bunched the cloak up on top and gave it a severe cut. Made out of Seth's favorite combination of silver and burgundy, the cloak was his only raiment. It opened in the front to expose his superb nude body, shaven and painted with the symbols of the seven chakras and various other occult symbols. One of the chakra symbols was painted on his forehead in the position of the third eye, giving him an exotic, vaguely Egyptian appearance, and the rest were painted in their positions down the center of his body, ending with the "root" chakra at the base of his substantial endowment. It was a look that risked appearing laughable, but on him it was striking and I found it incredibly erotic.

Though the illustration that showed the ritual space layout in the Ficino manuscript did provide the magician with a few short Latin phrases here and there throughout the ritual, though at what point in the ritual was unclear, the magician had very little to do apart from channel the energy raised by the choir. Well, I say "little to do," but really that takes a lot of effort to do effectively, and if our rehearsal was any indication, the amount of energy raised could be difficult for an inexperienced magician to control. But Seth had been doing magick since I was in preschool.

He stood in the center of the chapel and raised his hands toward the domed ceiling, startling us all by shouting out, so that it reverberated throughout the enclosed space, *"Incipiamus!"*

Let us begin.

Seth fell silent, and after a brief pause, Timothy raised his baton for the choir to begin singing.

From the first note I sang, I could feel the power building within me. I sang in unison with the tenors for the Kyrie and the Gloria. There were in fact three more short sections to the mass after the Credo—the Sanctus, the Benedictus, and the Agnus Dei—but I'd yet to see those performed, due to the tragic ending of the Credo at the last performance. Timothy had assured me the choir knew those sections and fortunately, I knew my part for them as well. My impression was that the Credo was the essential magickal component of the mass, whereas the final sections were simply there to cool things down and round out the mass.

When we came to the Credo, the solo melody carried me off in a way it never had when I'd rehearsed it on my own. I could feel the energy flowing through the choir and being shaped and focused by my voice like water through a funnel. And it was Seth who took that focused energy and directed it, told it where to flow, while the dome of the chapel above us once more became alive with the fluttering of batwings in the darkness.

I don't know exactly when I became aware that something was horribly wrong—that I could sense Seth wasn't directing the energy as he should have been. He wasn't focusing on the poor, pathetic ruin of a bird lying on the table in the center of the room, but on something underneath it, deep in the earth. Why? Did he even *know* what he was directing the energy toward? Seth wasn't the sort of magician to leave even minute details to chance, so I knew, whatever he was doing, there had to be a purpose to it.

But it seemed to be disturbing the atmosphere in the room. The bats that had been fluttering wildly in random patterns underneath the dome had begun to grow more agitated, until they were literally flying in a circle, a great ring of fur and wings that churned the air over our heads.

Seth raised his hands to the heavens, looking immensely powerful and radiant, as if the energy flowing through him were illuminating him from within. Then he intoned the text of the ancient Greek libretto in a voice that echoed off the chamber walls. "From me accept the sacrifice, the unburnt offering of all fruits that complete has been poured forth for you, out of the gods and the sons of Ouranos…."

I had come to the crescendo of the piece, my voice rising and rising in pitch until I summoned up all the energy and control I possessed to sing the climactic note, pure and strong with the power feeding through me.

"Take in hand the scepter of Zeus, and with Hades share the rule of earthly things, send to the light the souls of those below—"

That was when, for the first time in my life, I felt and heard my voice crack, producing an odd, discordant sound like two notes being sung off-key.

Then the stained glass windows high above us shattered.

Perhaps not all of them, but more than one, as the heavy bodies of ravens hurtled through and fell, dead and bloody, to the marble floor. Seth cried out, shielding his face with his hands as fragments of broken glass rained down upon his head and naked body. Hundreds of live ravens flew into the chapel through the broken windows and filled the space with frantic, flapping wings and razor-sharp beaks and talons. They swarmed around us, crazed, knocking the tall candelabras and incense braziers to the floor, snuffing out the flames and plunging us into darkness while the men and women in the choir screamed. There was a resounding *clang* as the metal bowl of fruit offerings tumbled off the table, scattering its contents across the marble floor.

And above all the noise of frantic humans and screeching birds, I could hear Seth's voice rising in an agonized scream.

Somebody more possessed of his senses than I found the light switch, and the artificial electric gaslights blazed on, illuminating a hellish scene. The ravens focused on the center of the room—on Seth, who screamed in pain and terror while Bowyn and others flailed at the birds and attempted to scatter them. Other members of the choir rushed past me, but they appeared to be heading for the door.

I moved to help Seth, but something jerked me to a halt—Rafe, disappearing behind one of the massive outer columns about thirty feet from me. He didn't come out again.

While my conscience was telling me to get my ass into the center of the room and help people fight off the ravens, I knew I wouldn't be able to accomplish much more than the other twenty-odd people there. And another voice in the back of my head was screaming at me to follow Rafe. Unless he was hiding behind the column, he couldn't have just disappeared back there… unless there was a door. And if there was a door, I'd be willing to bet it somehow led into the cellar of the Temple.

With a last glance at the chaos in the center of the chapel, I tossed down my sheet music and flew up the aisle between two rows of pews in pursuit of Rafe. When I came to the column, I circled around it and my suspicions were confirmed. Rafe wasn't hiding there—he'd vanished. And now that I knew what I was looking for, I searched the elaborate

Victorian molding on the wall opposite the column and was easily able to locate a thin crack that might mark the edge of a door. I could see no handle, but it clicked when I pushed on it, and then swung inward.

Curving down to my left, narrow stone steps led into the darkness below the chapel.

I hadn't brought a flashlight, but I could see a light at the bottom of the steps, so I descended. I stepped out into a small stone chamber—a crypt, with walls covered with orderly bronze plaques, gray-green with age, and stone sarcophagi laid out in the center of the room. Rafe was waiting for me down there, and I saw him standing on the other side of one of the sarcophagi. But it was what lay on the sarcophagus that drew my attention more than Rafe did, setting every hair on my body on edge and making me want to scream in horror.

Even in death, Christopher was beautiful, but his skin was waxen and so pale as to seem almost white. He'd been dead at least a couple of days, I felt certain. There was no trace of life left in him, no suggestion that blood had been circulating in those veins recently. He was as lifeless as a porcelain doll. He'd been stripped of his clothes and bathed, his hair combed back from his forehead as though he were fresh out of the shower, and he'd been dressed in a pure white linen robe. He'd then been laid out on the flat sarcophagus with his hands crossed over his chest in the position of Osirus Slain. The smell of cinnamon permeated the still, musty air, and I suspected the body had been anointed with oil of Abramelin.

"You failed!" Rafe snarled at me, yanking my attention back to him. His characteristic cool smugness had vanished, and for the first time I saw how ugly he could be when his features were distorted with anger. "You've all failed! I spent fifteen years translating that manuscript and finding someone who could pull off the ritual."

"Rafe," I interrupted, my voice trembling, "how did Christopher die?"

"That pompous ass thought he could do it with your help. He promised me immortality… forever young…."

"How did Christopher die?" I repeated, raising my voice.

Rafe scoffed, waving his hand in dismissal. "How do you think?" He walked over to where a sleeping bag was laid out on a single-person camping pad, next to some bread, peanut butter, fruit, and a container of orange juice, all stolen from Alex's kitchen, I was sure. There were a couple of books there and a large camping flashlight, which Rafe snatched up in his right hand. "The way he was always going to die.

The way he was *meant* to die. Just a bit more in the dose than he was expecting, and he died the happiest death he could imagine."

"You *killed* him?" I was so shocked that my entire body felt numb. *This kind of shit doesn't happen... not here....*

Rafe moved quickly as he came at me. I jumped back in panic, but he stopped short of attacking, his face so close to mine I could feel his breath against my lips. "So you could save him!" he hissed. "So you could bring him back! I've known for years what the ritual was for! I just needed someone powerful enough to carry it out. But you don't have any real power, do you? Seth doesn't have any real power. None of you do! You're just a bunch of deluded amateurs."

That hurt. Perhaps because it might be true. The study of magick had given me a feeling of power over the years, a sense that I might be able to control the strands of fate and luck that wove throughout my life. But underlying that was always the fear it was all nonsense and I was a fool. A fool like billions of others who put their faith in magick or various faiths and deities, perhaps, so hardly alone in my delusion. But a fool nonetheless.

"I never claimed I could resurrect the dead, Rafe." Thought about it, perhaps. But never claimed it.

"Jeremy!"

It was Bowyn's voice calling from the steps above us. I'd left the door open and he must have seen me disappear, as I'd seen Rafe. I was inexpressibly relieved, but before I could answer him, Rafe gave out an inarticulate shout of rage and struck me on the temple with the flashlight. The plastic light cracked and pieces of it went flying. I went down from the blow, collapsing to my knees in a blinding flash of pain while Rafe threw down the broken flashlight and bolted across the chamber and out through a door on the other side of the room.

"Jeremy!" Bowyn came down the steps and rushed to my side. "Are you hurt?"

Stupid question. Of course I was hurt. But it takes a lot more to knock a man unconscious than television and movies would lead us to believe. My head was throbbing and I felt vaguely nauseated, but I was able to stand with some help from Bowyn. "It's Rafe," I said. "He killed Christopher."

Bowyn had seen the corpse as soon as he helped me to my feet, and he was staring at it in stunned disbelief.

Now that I could see the doorway more clearly, I saw there was a tunnel on the other side of it. And I was pretty certain where the tunnel led.

"He ran down there," I said, urging Bowyn forward with one hand around his wrist. "If he gets to the house, he'll be able to grab a car from the garage and we'll lose him."

WE DIDN'T have a flashlight, but those ubiquitous fake gas lamps were built into wall sconces every twenty feet or so along the tunnel, connected by metal pipes that probably housed electrical wires. They bathed the passageway in a flickering yellow light. The walls of the tunnel were old, most likely made when the house was built. In places they were carved out of the granite that provided the bedrock of northern New Hampshire. In other places layers of stone and mortar had been built up to keep dirt walls from collapsing inward. It was a damp place, with water trickling down the walls, creating pools Bowyn and I had to hop over or skirt around. But it was a fairly straight line to the house and we traversed the distance quickly.

The tunnel exited in the house, in the cellar bathroom near the showers. I hadn't found it because the door was part of the grid of tile on the wall at the far end of the room. There was a handle on the tunnel side, but not on the bathroom side. Like the entrance in the chapel, a person would have to know where to press in order to open it.

The fastest way to get outside was up the stairs by the old root cellar, so that's where Bowyn and I headed. It let out into the kitchen, which was surprisingly empty. But as soon as we ran out into the hall, we found out why—Alex was in the office across the hall, talking on the phone, while her assistants and a couple of the members of the choir huddled near the door.

"I'm not sure what happened," she was telling somebody on the other end of the line. "Some kind of animal attack. I've been told he's seriously injured. Yes, our address is—"

Bowyn and I pushed our way past the gathered neophytes and slammed open the door at the end of the hall. It opened out onto a back stoop with a narrow cobblestone path connecting it to the main path. This branched out, leading to the chapel in one direction and to the garage in the other.

Not that we could actually see much of this. The fog was heavy now, and it was difficult to see anything in the darkness but the lamps along the path. Even those seemed distant and far away. As Bowyn and I turned toward the garage, something brushed my face. I flinched, thinking I was under attack again, but it was just a quick flick of something against my skin and then it was gone.

"Goddamn it!" I heard Rafe shout from somewhere I couldn't quite pinpoint. "Where the fuck is the garage?"

That seemed odd, since even in the fog I could see the lights burning around the garage door. Had he really gotten that turned around?

"The police are already on their way, Rafe," I shouted. "Just turn yourself in."

I didn't really expect him to listen to that. It was a pretty stupid idea, really. His only real chance of not going to prison was to grab a car and book it out of there—head north to Canada before word got out he was on the run. But it was what people always said in the movies.

Now off to my right, I heard him make a rude noise. "You should have fucked him, Jeremy. He would have done it for a little heroin."

"I didn't want to fuck him," I snapped. "I wanted to help him."

"I was a beautiful boy too. Nobody helps beautiful boys unless we're naked with our legs in the air. Christopher knew that. Where the fuck have all the lights gone?" His voice was an odd combination of arrogance and panic now.

This was too much for Bowyn. I'd lost track of him in the fog, but I could hear his voice, hear the emotion threatening what little control he had left. "He was just a *kid*, you stupid motherfucker! How could you do that to a kid?"

"That innocent little kid killed your son, Bowyn."

There was a shocked silence, during which I felt something brush by my body in the darkness again. This time I thought it felt like… feathers.

"What the fuck are you talking about?" Bowyn snarled. But he already knew the answer. We'd all read the note.

"I didn't think he'd do it. I didn't think he had the balls. But I just had to promise it wouldn't kill Marianne. That and tell him he'd get a little extra in his shot that night."

If I'd had a baseball bat and Rafe's head had been within striking distance at that moment, I probably would have used it. Fortunately for him and my conscience, that wasn't the case.

"Fuck me!" I heard Rafe gasp in the darkness. "What *is* that?"

"Why?" Bowyn shouted, his voice cracking. "Why would you make him do that, you worthless, psychotic piece of shit?"

I was gradually becoming aware that the lights *were* disappearing. I could no longer see the gaslights near any of the buildings, and the one nearby appeared to be flickering, as if I were seeing it through the leaves of a tree that was blowing in the wind. But I knew they weren't leaves.

They were ravens. We were in the center of a whirlwind of birds, and I wasn't certain that Bowyn and Rafe were aware of it yet.

Rafe answered Bowyn, his voice defiant, "Because Seth was falling apart! Between Jeremy acting too good for him, and you and Marianne threatening to leave, he was going to pieces. I needed him to focus on the ritual. Which meant you and Marianne had to stay."

"So you made Christopher do your dirty work for you, you fucking coward!" Bowyn sounded enraged.

"He was happy to help," Rafe said. "Until he started feeling guilty about how much it hurt Marianne. He started freaking out on me and talking about begging her to forgive him. We needed a body for the ritual, anyway—I'd already picked him months ago."

I was struck in the shoulder by a large wing and then another brushed my face. "Bowyn! Where are you?"

"*Jeremy!*"

Suddenly they were everywhere, screeching furiously and beating upon my body with their wings. I shielded my face with my hands and arms, but the ravens didn't seem intent upon injuring me. I sustained a few scratches from their talons, but it was Rafe who began to scream as if he were being murdered.

Somehow Bowyn found his way to my side and hunched over me, shielding me with his arms. We knelt down upon the grass and huddled under the onslaught of thousands of birds while Rafe's screams rose in pitch and competed with the screams of the ravens. It sounded as if they were killing him, but there was nothing Bowyn or I could do, surrounded by a maelstrom of wings and beaks and talons. It went on and on, those screams seemingly without end while my entire body trembled in terror.

Even more horrible than Rafe's screams was the moment they changed to choked gurgles, as if his throat had been torn out, and then stopped.

Bowyn and I remained huddled low against the cold, damp grass for a long time after that, until the screeching of the ravens faded away, moving off into the distance. In the quiet that followed, the only sound I could hear was a barely audible sucking and gurgling noise. I dreaded finding out what was making it.

We could no longer feel wings brushing the air around us. After a few minutes, Bowyn raised his head and said quietly, "They're gone."

We stood and looked around. The lamps were visible once again in the fog. Not a single raven could be seen anywhere.

There was a dark patch on the ground about twenty feet away from us. Bowyn walked toward it, leaving me alone for a moment, still quivering and trying to swallow to rid myself of a dry throat. But when I heard him say, under his breath, "Oh my fucking God...." I had to move closer.

The ravens had shredded Rafe's robe, leaving him lying naked on the grass. But blood saturated the grass where the birds had continued to scratch at him with beaks and talons even after the robe had been torn away. His eyes looked up at the moonless night sky without eyelids while perfect teeth glistened in the lamplight, devoid of lips. His entire face— the entire upper half of his body, in fact—had been almost completely stripped of skin, exposing bloody muscle and tissue underneath.

One of Rafe's hands was raised over his chest, still twitching as if to ward off his attackers. But the thing that made me turn away and vomit into the grass was that faint, slow sucking noise, bubbling up from the ruin of his throat. Even though Rafe would be dead in a matter of moments, there were still a few gurgling breaths left in that torn and shredded body.

# Chapter Thirty-Two

WHEN THE ambulance arrived, the police came with them as a matter of routine—the same two who seemed to be assigned permanent Temple duty. Bowyn and I learned Seth was still alive. He'd been scratched up quite a bit and his right eye was severely damaged. I heard the EMTs talking about the likelihood of him losing it. But he was expected to survive. We were unable to get close as he was tended to and carried to the ambulance on a stretcher.

Bowyn took Officer Westcott aside before the ambulance left and told him, "There are a couple more… bodies. It's probably too late to save them, but…."

Westcott told the ambulance to hang back for a few minutes while Bowyn and I led him, his partner, and one of the EMTs across the lawn to where Rafe lay.

"Jesus Christ," Westcott said under his breath when he saw the horror lying in the grass. I admit I took a grim satisfaction in watching his companion lose his supper at the sight of it. Petty, I know. But I hated to think I was the only lightweight present.

The EMT who'd come with us examined the body, declaring Rafe dead.

"Who *was* that?" Westcott asked.

"Rafe."

"That punk who kept staring at my partner?" The officer's dislike of Rafe was obvious.

"That's him," I replied.

"Get Mr. Harriman to the hospital," Westcott commanded the EMT. "We'll have to call the state police in for this one."

After the EMT left, Westcott turned on us. "Would anyone care to explain to me what the *fuck* did that to a grown man?"

"Ravens," Bowyn replied.

"Ravens," Westcott echoed, his voice dripping with contempt. "He was ripped to shreds by birds."

"Very big birds," I amended.

"I've seen maybe three ravens around here in the past year. It would take a hell of a lot more than three to do this to a man."

"I assure you, we've had a lot more than three ravens hanging around the grounds the past few days. There's a pile of dead ones around here somewhere, from when they attacked the house last night."

"Show me," he demanded.

"I think there's something else you'll want to see first."


THE AMBULANCE pulled out of the circular drive as we walked back across the cobblestone path to the chapel. Westcott's partner had been instructed to run back to the police cruiser to get crime scene tape and mark off the area around Rafe's body. "Then set up some lights and wait for the staties," Westcott added.

Then the senior officer followed me and Bowyn into the chapel.

I hadn't seen the ritual space since I snuck out after Rafe, so I was as shocked as Westcott by the scene of violence we found there. There was blood on the floor, although not in great quantity. Perhaps some of it had come from Seth, but the rest had to have come from the birds. There were perhaps twenty or thirty of them, lying in tragic clumps of bloody feathers, scattered around the floor among crushed fruit and sand from overturned incense bowls. The entire room was full of a light pall of smoke from the incense and snuffed candles.

"Jesus H. Christ," Westcott muttered under his breath. "Where the hell did they all come from?"

"Christopher," I said. Both the police officer and Bowyn raised their eyebrows at me, so I added, "He had an affinity for them and he was out there feeding them every day." I didn't actually believe it was that simple. There had been far too many ravens on the grounds of the Temple to be explained away by Christopher tossing a few handfuls of breadcrumbs around. But Westcott nodded, wanting to believe the easy, "logical" answer.

He walked around the edge of the circle, surveying the carnage. "You realize we'll be questioning everybody who was in this building tonight."

"Of course," Bowyn said.

"So are you going to tell me what you were doing with all of these candles and symbols on the floor? Or do I have to waste the next several hours piecing it all together?"

"We were performing a new moon ritual," Bowyn replied, "based upon a choral piece we came across in a manuscript from the fifteenth century."

"What did it have to do with ravens?"

"The ravens weren't invited. They broke in during the ritual and attacked Seth." Technically that was correct. Bowyn was leaving some details out, of course, such as the fact that there had been a dead raven used in the ritual. No doubt Westcott would learn of that interesting little tidbit from Timothy or one of the choir members. But nothing Bowyn had said could be construed as a lie. And he was right to be cautious until we'd consulted with a lawyer. Westcott seemed like the kind of man who might easily jump to the conclusion that we were performing some kind of ritual human sacrifice.

Westcott was clearly skeptical about the idea of ravens deliberately disrupting a religious ceremony to attack the priest. But his night was just getting started.

"This isn't what I wanted to show you," I told the officer. "There's something else downstairs."

I led him and Bowyn to the secret door and down the curved stone steps into the crypt.

"You're fucking kidding me," Westcott said, the moment he saw Christopher's neatly laid out corpse. "Who the hell is this?"

"This," Bowyn said grimly, "is Christopher."

Westcott moved closer and curled his fingers under one of Christopher's wrists, as if feeling for a pulse.

"I'm pretty sure he's been dead for at least twenty-four hours," I said. I couldn't be certain, but I suspected that Christopher's death had corresponded with the raven attack on the house. *Something* had prompted the attack, and a supernatural explanation was as good as any other, as far as I was concerned.

Westcott gave me a sour look before unhooking his flashlight from his belt and shining it into Christopher's eyes one at a time to test for pupil dilation. "How do you know that?"

"Because Rafe told me, before he attacked me and ran into that tunnel there."

I started from the beginning, explaining how I'd followed Rafe through the hidden door in the chapel and found him here. "Apparently he'd been supplying Christopher with heroin and he gave Christopher an overdose."

"On purpose, you mean?"

I'd moved closer to the sleeping bag Christopher had been using. I didn't want to disturb the evidence, but it turned out I didn't have to—the glassine bag with Christopher's "works" in it was lying right beside the sleeping bag in plain sight. There was also a bowl with traces of a greenish herb in it, a few feet away from the sleeping bag in a corner. I leaned over it and could detect the lingering spearmint-like odor of pennyroyal.

"Yes," I answered.

"Why?"

"Rafe promised Christopher heroin in exchange for putting the pennyroyal in Marianne's tea. But when Christopher felt guilty about it and left that note for her, Rafe decided he could no longer be trusted to keep quiet. So he gave Christopher an extra-large dose that night."

Westcott looked confused. "Why the hell would Rafe want to make Miss Truit miscarry?"

"Because if she'd had the baby, she and Bowyn would have left and that would have been devastating to Seth. Rafe was obsessed with Seth." That was fudging the truth a bit. What Rafe had been obsessed with was the eternal youth he thought Seth could give him—youth and immortality.

"I also suspect Rafe had planned on killing Christopher all along," I added.

"Why? What did Christopher do to him?"

I looked at that still, waxen face, eyes now staring blankly up at the ceiling, since Westcott had opened them. "He was beautiful."

WE WENT back up into the chapel so Westcott could find his partner and photograph the scene there and in the crypt. It was Westcott who ordered Bowyn to take me to the hospital when he finally noticed I had a gash in my temple from the flashlight Rafe had conked me with. I was also covered in scratches from the ravens, just as Bowyn was. I doubted there was anything seriously wrong with us, but it wouldn't hurt to be looked at. It would also allow me and Bowyn to escape his questioning for a short time.

As the three of us passed through the chapel once again, Bowyn suddenly stopped and grabbed my shoulder. I stopped walking and turned to him, but he was transfixed by something in the circle, so I followed his gaze with my eyes.

The raven on the altar was watching us.

I don't mean he was lying dead on the altar in such a way as to *appear* that one of his eyes was watching us. The raven was sitting up, blinking his eyes and turning his head to get a better look at us. I suppose it might have been possible the bird had never been truly dead—perhaps he'd just been unconscious all that time—but that was hard for me to believe. It had been well over twenty-four hours since this raven had smashed into some part of the house and fallen into the courtyard.

He was panting, as though he were injured or frightened, but when Bowyn took a tentative step toward him, the raven gave out a squawk and leapt up off the altar. Its large, ebony wings beat violently at the air for a moment, as if it might not be able to stay airborne, but then the raven seemed to find its rhythm, and with a few great downward thrusts it soared across the room and through the open chapel door, disappearing into the darkness beyond.

# Chapter Thirty-Three

SETH WAS in intensive care at Androscoggin Valley Hospital for three days before they moved him to a regular hospital room. The cuts and scratches on his face and body hadn't been bad, but his right eye had been torn from its socket, causing severe trauma to the optic nerve and some internal bleeding. The damage could have made him blind in his left eye as well, but he'd been lucky on that part.

While he was recovering, the police scoured the Temple grounds for evidence in the murder investigation, and all the residents were questioned multiple times. None of us at the Temple had had the faintest idea that there was a crypt underneath the chapel—not even Timothy. The sarcophagi in it dated back to the eighteen hundreds, just after the house was built, and most shared the name of Aldridge, the surname of the family that had lived there for almost a hundred years. Seth must have known about the crypt and the secret passage to the basement, since he'd been in charge of the renovations. He would have had to approve the hidden door in the bathroom. Obviously he'd told Rafe about it, but had he known Rafe was using the crypt to hide Christopher while the young man was supposed to be in rehab? When Westcott interviewed him at the hospital, Seth insisted he hadn't.

Bowyn and I had shown Westcott the enormous pile of dead ravens that had resulted from the attack on the house. He'd found that disturbing, but it corroborated our story about Rafe being attacked by a flock of them, so he was prepared to believe Rafe's death was the result of some freakish case of food poisoning or something in the raven population.

"Maybe there's some kind of disease spreading through the birds in Canada," he speculated. "Something that affects the brain."

"Mad Raven Disease?" Bowyn quipped and managed to elicit one of the only smiles we ever saw from Officer Westcott.

Christopher's death couldn't be explained by psychotic birds, but Westcott was willing to believe us when we told him Rafe had confessed to killing him. It made as much sense to the police officer as anything else he could come up with. He also seemed willing to believe Rafe was motivated by an unhealthy obsession with Seth, since Westcott was already half-convinced Seth was on the road to becoming Charles Manson or Jim Jones.

Thus the official story was that Rafe had been an unstable individual who joined a religious group—Westcott was no doubt using the word "cult" in his reports—and became obsessed with its leader, Seth. When Marianne became pregnant, she and Bowyn threatened to leave, which upset Seth. Rafe decided the pregnancy had to be terminated in order to please Seth, and he took advantage of Christopher's drug addiction to manipulate the young man into doing his dirty work for him. When Christopher was sent away to rehab, Rafe drove to Berlin and convinced Christopher to come back with him. Christopher lived in the crypt during the day, supplied with enough heroin to keep him happy, and snuck out at night to tamper with the spearmint tea and raid the kitchen for food. He was only supposed to be there for a few days, until I left and stopped poking into his business. Then he could "return" from rehab and go back to his life as usual at the Temple.

Except he liked Marianne and felt guilty about causing the miscarriage. So he told Rafe he was going to confess what he'd done. That caused Rafe to panic and give Christopher an overdose, so Christopher couldn't tell anyone about Rafe's part in the mess. The raven attack seemed a bit convenient, and I suspect Westcott thought Bowyn and I might have killed Rafe ourselves in retaliation for Bowyn losing his son. The problem with that theory, though, was the fact that Bowyn and I hadn't been covered in blood when the police arrived, and there really hadn't been time for us to clean up. So… mad ravens it was.

All wrapped up, neat and tidy, as far as the police were concerned.

Except there were still some things bugging *me*.

SETH CAME home on the day of Christopher's funeral. It may seem odd that we buried Christopher in the Temple cemetery after what he'd done to Marianne and Bowyn, and initially we hadn't been sure about it. We'd contacted his father, and the man had been predictably callous about the death of his only son. The moment he realized a funeral service in Berlin might cost him some money, he hung up.

We'd already made the decision to pay for a modest burial for Rafe in the Berlin cemetery. Like Christopher, he had no family. There had been no response from his uncle via e-mail. But unlike Christopher, no one at the Temple had really liked Rafe. He'd been attractive and available to just about anyone who wanted to play, but that hadn't disguised the fact he was an arrogant asshole. I'd heard there were community funds for burials when no family came forward to claim the body, but asshole or not—*murderer* or not—he'd still been one of us. So we paid for his funeral expenses out of Temple funds. But nobody attended services for him. Perhaps Seth might have, had he been out of the hospital, but he wasn't released until two days afterward.

Christopher was another matter. What he'd done for a fix was horrendous, but most people at the temple were unaware Marianne had been pregnant to begin with. Rumors had been going around about a possible miscarriage, but few people were connecting Christopher to it. Of those of us who knew what he'd done, many of us, myself included, pitied him and felt we'd failed him when he came to us for help.

Ultimately I'd found myself huddled around the kitchen table late one night with Alex, Bowyn, and Marianne, discussing the matter. Marianne had said, "Fine. We'll bury him there. But I don't want his grave anywhere near Jay's or Jack's. And if I ever end up there myself, don't put me near him, or I swear I'll come back and haunt you all for the rest of your lives."

Seth presided over the funeral, his new eye patch and graying hair making him resemble a modern-day Odin. Under the circumstances it seemed fitting. Though Marianne refused to attend and Alex had stayed behind with her for solidarity, quite a lot of the initiates and neophytes were there. Paul, his roommate, stood by the graveside crying openly. And though Bowyn was conflicted over the whole mess, he was standing beside me, holding my hand. When the final bells rang out over the Temple grounds, I heard a guttural squawk over our heads and looked up to see a lone raven flying over the cemetery, heading north.

It was the only raven I'd seen at the Temple since the night of the ritual.

"I WISH I'd been out of the hospital for Rafe's funeral," Seth said as he walked alongside me and Bowyn after the service. "I did... care for him, you know. And despite everything he did, I think he cared for me, at least a little."

For some reason I found that oddly comforting—the possibility that, along with all the superficial sex and psychotic delusions Rafe had brought to the Temple, there had been at least a small amount of real affection between him and Seth.

"We would have shipped him back to Greece," Bowyn said, "if his uncle had responded to Marianne's e-mails."

"There was no uncle," I said.

Bowyn raised his eyebrows at me. "How do you know?"

"Because Rafe told me he'd spent fifteen years translating the manuscript. He needed someone who could transcribe the Renaissance musical notation and someone with enough magickal experience to pull off the ritual. But he didn't need a Greek translator."

"Then all that money we sent to his 'uncle's' bank account was just going to drugs?"

"Mostly," I agreed. "I'm sure he was hoarding some of it, in addition to the few hundred thousand he got from the sale of the manuscript."

Seth turned to look at me sharply. He'd been keeping us on his left, so he didn't have to actually stop walking to do it. "The sale of the manuscript?"

I wasn't relishing this confrontation, but it couldn't be put off. "If he'd been translating it for fifteen years—which means he started working on it when he was in his teens—then of course it had to be in his possession. I'm guessing it was his family that bought it at auction after World War II. When his parents passed away, he retained possession of it. So you must have bought it from him. Correct?"

Seth frowned. "Correct. I hadn't thought it necessary to inform everyone of that, but... yes, I met him at an auction for a different manuscript in Munich. He wasn't planning on selling the Ficino at the time. He told me he was there hoping to encounter someone who knew about Ficino's work. We discovered that we were... compatible... and I agreed to help him, in exchange for the purchase of the manuscript, so it could be preserved in our library."

"So you knew there was no 'Uncle Adrian,'" I persisted.

Seth took a long time to answer as the hems of our robes dragged across the grass and made a soft, steady hissing noise. "I knew," he said finally.

"Seth!" Bowyn exclaimed. "What did you think he was using that money for?"

"Just spending money," Seth replied irritably. "I know it was dishonest of us, but he wanted some funds for spending money without having to dip into the savings he had back in Greece. Transferring money from a foreign bank takes time and incurs fees, so we set up a local bank account and told Marianne that Rafe's uncle had access to it. It wasn't that much when you stretch it out over the year. The Temple can take it out of my funds if you're upset about it."

Some companies might still call it "embezzlement," I thought.

But before Bowyn could continue down that path, I said, "Rafe wasn't using that money for food or clothes. He was using it to purchase heroin."

"I thought Christopher told you he was sneaking out to the rest area to get the drugs," Seth said.

"He did. But he was lying."

"Lying?"

"Christopher's roommate said he slipped out into the secret passage late at night and he returned, stoned, about an hour later. There was no way Christopher was walking all the way to that rest area, letting some guy blow him, and then walking back in an hour. It would take him closer to two hours at a minimum. He had to be getting the heroin from somebody here at the Temple—but not Rafe."

Seth was reaching the end of his patience. "I thought you just said it was Rafe who was buying the heroin with the funds he was taking from the Temple!"

"Yes, I did. I should have said that it wasn't *just* Rafe supplying Christopher with drugs."

"Who are you accusing *now*?"

"I should think that would be obvious." I stopped walking so Bowyn and Seth were forced to stop and turn to face me. I looked pointedly at Seth and said, "You."

Seth was slick, but he wasn't slick enough to disguise the brief look of panic that flashed across his face, just before he turned away and began walking again. "You're overthinking things, my love. I admit, I was attracted to Christopher, but—"

"But you couldn't have him," I interrupted, moving to catch up with him. Bowyn straggled behind, looking confused. "He came here thinking he'd finally found a haven, someplace he didn't have to prostitute himself to his father or to other men. But you wanted him and he wanted drugs. He also knew where to *get* drugs, but he didn't have any money. So Rafe came up with a plan…."

Seth was beginning to grow angry now. "You're obsessed with blaming all of this unpleasantness on Rafe."

"Why would Rafe care about getting Seth into bed with Christopher?" Bowyn asked.

Seth nodded. "Exactly."

"Rafe wasn't interested in Christopher himself—at least, not after one or two tumbles. And he could have bought off Christopher for that easily enough. But he knew the ritual needed a body," I persisted. "A human body—not some dead animal. So he set up this fake uncle to get money from the Temple without drawing the attention it would if Seth withdrew the funds directly." I didn't have to explain that part. Both Seth and Bowyn knew Marianne saw all bank transactions, including Seth's. "Then Rafe insisted that Christopher put him in touch with the dealer, so Rafe could remain in control of the supply. In return for a more or less steady supply of heroin, Christopher allowed you to do whatever you wanted to him, as long as he could be stoned while you were doing it."

"I thought you knew me better than this, Jeremy."

Bowyn was looking distressed. "Jeremy, come on. Why would Rafe bother with all of that? If he wanted to give Christopher an overdose, all he had to do was give him some heroin a day or two before the ceremony, just like he confessed to doing. There's no reason for this elaborate plot involving Seth."

Seth smiled, vindicated, but I said, "Seth would never have agreed to keep Christopher's death a secret and use his body in the ritual unless he'd been party to it all along—a party to supplying Christopher with illegal drugs for months—and was there the night Rafe administered the overdose."

Seth's smile faded and Bowyn's eyes widened. It was Bowyn who stopped us then. "During the ritual…. Seth, you weren't directing energy at the altar. It looked like you were sending it down through the floor…."

"Into the crypt," I finished, looking directly at Seth. "Because you knew Christopher's body was there. And you were clinging to the desperate hope the ritual might work—that you'd be able to bring Christopher back and absolve both you and Rafe. You hadn't wanted Christopher to die. I believe that. But when Rafe killed him, you were trapped into going along with his plan."

Had I been alone with Seth, I think he would have continued to deny it. He was a showman, above all else, always ready with a quick comeback, a bit of misdirection, a little sleight of hand. But he couldn't stand up to the two of us united against him. He looked at Bowyn, searching for the faith he'd always depended upon—the faith that had enabled him to endure the skepticism he'd always received from me. Bowyn had always stood by him, even when the rest of us didn't. But for once Seth didn't find the support he needed in Bowyn's eyes, and he looked away, his shoulders slumping.

"He was so beautiful," Seth said after a long moment. "I knew Rafe was jealous, but he joined in anyway. And Christopher seemed okay with it. So… I thought everybody was more or less getting what they wanted. I didn't know where it was going."

I believed him. I knew Seth was capable of deluding himself into thinking that satisfying his own desires would lead to everybody else being happy. He'd always thought like that.

But this time it had ended with two people dead.

# Chapter Thirty-Four

BOWYN AND I both turned Seth in to the Berlin police, and he didn't resist. When Westcott searched his room, he turned up several bags of heroin in the bottom of a drawer. Seth claimed to know nothing about them, which might have even been true. I suspect Rafe may have hidden them there, since he couldn't visit Christopher's dealer every night. Seth claimed not to know who the dealer was, which might also have been true. That man would remain free, since the only two people who could identify him were now dead and buried. But I was fairly certain the dealer didn't reside at the Temple, which was a small blessing. If he had, Christopher would have been able to work out a better deal than he was getting from Rafe.

It would be difficult to link Seth directly to Christopher's death, since Rafe had already confessed to it. I liked to think Seth was just as horrified as anyone with a conscience would have been when he discovered Christopher wasn't going to wake up from that particular dose. But Rafe had implicated him in almost a year's worth of drug dealing and procurement, so his choice was to risk going to prison for a very long time, or hide the body and try to bring Christopher back from the dead. As preposterous as the second option may have seemed to him, it was still preferable to spending the rest of his life in jail.

The trial would go on for a little over a year, but ultimately the jury would convict Seth solely on the drug charges, unable to make up its mind on the depth of his involvement in Christopher's murder. But those charges carried a maximum sentence of twenty years in prison. His lawyer believed she could get that cut down, but it was likely Seth would be going away for at least a decade.

I REMAINED at the Temple for the rest of my sabbatical—about two months—using continued work on the Ficino manuscript as my excuse. But really I just didn't want to go back to Durham. I didn't want to leave

Bowyn and I didn't want to leave the Temple. For all the unhappiness I'd witnessed since I arrived, I'd also discovered the Temple was very much still my home.

Things were different after Seth was arrested, even before we knew the outcome of the trial. Though the Order had technically existed before Bowyn and I met him, Seth had been the heart of it and of the Temple. Without him, it was questionable whether they could even continue. During the two months I remained at the Temple, several initiates packed up and left, including Paul Denning. Despite the fact that the divinity of Seth Harriman had never been part of the Order teachings, thank God, many of the initiates had thought of him that way—if not exactly as a god, then certainly as an enlightened spiritual leader. It was frustrating to see just how many initiates were there because they believed in Seth, rather than in what Seth and the other senior initiates had tried to teach them. But the majority held on, at least for a while, to see how things would be from this point forward.

The Temple itself belonged to the Order. It had originally been Seth's and Alex's property, but they'd long ago transferred ownership to the Order, which was registered as an LLC. Without Seth, the board, which now consisted of Alex, Bowyn, Marianne, and—to my surprise— me, had the authority to elect a new chairman of the board. We elected Bowyn. Alex intended to stay on and Marianne agreed to stay for at least another year while she sorted out what she wanted to do with her future. So the Temple and the Order might possibly continue, unless so many members bailed it was no longer worth running.

ON THE morning Bowyn gave his first sermon, he and I retreated to the gazebo after the service and were joined there by Alex and Marianne for a quick conference. Bowyn was fretting about the fact that his service hadn't had the same impact Seth's always had.

"Give it time," Alex told him. "You just need more practice."

"Seth would have done it ten times better."

She smiled at him and shook her head. "Don't try to imitate Seth. He's an occult P.T. Barnum. You're not. Thank the gods. I think we've all had enough of fire-jugglers and trapeze artists for a while." She said this with the affectionate, long-suffering smile she'd often had when discussing Seth.

"You just need to find your own voice," Marianne agreed. "And you know what? Maybe we don't have to have just one person running the show all the time. Maybe it would be nice to have other senior initiates do a service now and then."

Bowyn looked surprised. It would be a radical change from the way things had been done over the past decade, but I thought she might be onto something. The Temple needed to move away from the cult of adoration Seth had built up around himself and become something more egalitarian, in which senior initiates had more say in what was taught and how it was presented.

Alex had to get back to the lunch prep and Marianne had a class in tarot she was teaching, so they left Bowyn and me alone in the gazebo. Bowyn seemed to be lost in thought, perhaps contemplating what Marianne had said, so I sat on the chilly wooden bench for a while, saying nothing as I watched the initiates walking to their classes across the wide expanse of lawn. The trees had all lost their leaves by now, their bare branches stark against a clear blue sky. I loved the colors of autumn and I loved the first snow, but this drab, brownish time of year in between always saddened me.

At last, Bowyn sighed and sat down beside me, snuggling close so the warmth of his body comforted me. "I don't know if I can do this," he said.

"Do what?"

"Keep this place together," he replied.

I shrugged. "Would you prefer to let it all fall apart?"

"No."

"Will anybody else do it?"

He shook his head. "No. I mean, Alex will keep her part running, just as she always has, and Marianne will keep the books, just as *she* always has. At least, I hope she'll continue on. But I'm the only one who can step in and try to keep the whole system running."

"Bowyn," I said, feeling a bit exasperated. "Do you really think that's what Seth did? Keep everything running smoothly?"

He thought about it for a moment and then smiled. "That doesn't seem likely, does it?"

"Seth could barely keep *himself* together, never mind the Temple," I said. "You've always been the one running things. And that's not going to change." The cold bench was starting to make my ass hurt, so I stood up and straddled Bowyn's lap, facing him. This of course pushed my robe up to crotch level in the front, and he responded by wrapping his cold hands around a particular part of my anatomy.

"Ah fuck!" I gasped, making Bowyn laugh with delight.

"Just warming my hands."

"Jackass." I cringed for a moment while his cold hands adjusted to the temperature under my robe and I could speak again. "What will be different," I continued, still gritting my teeth a little, "is that you'll no longer have a charismatic figurehead representing the Order, and that will be a problem. It's sad, but people are drawn by a strong personality more than by a good philosophy. So if you want the Order to stay strong, you'll have to put yourself out there."

Bowyn thought about that for a moment while his hands began to massage me under my robe. They were warming up, so I was beginning to enjoy it. There were people wandering by the gazebo, but I wasn't above getting a hand job in public. I'd rediscovered my inner exhibitionist since my arrival.

"Am I charismatic?" Bowyn asked me.

I laughed and gazed at him affectionately. "Well, you're beautiful, which won't hurt. And yes, I think you're charismatic. You just need to get used to no longer hiding in Seth's shadow."

"Are you still going back to Durham?"

"At the end of December… yes. But I'll be back. Often."

Some of the people wandering by the gazebo had ceased to wander and were watching us openly now. But when Bowyn whispered "Let's go back to the room" in my ear, I didn't protest. Even at the Temple, there were times when privacy was best.

So we left the gazebo and walked up the cobblestone path to the house, holding hands. The early November air was getting too cold for the lightweight robes we were wearing, and it was probably time to dig out the heavier winter robes. But for now, the warmth of our hands was enough to keep out the chill.

JAMIE FESSENDEN set out to be a writer in junior high school. He published a couple of short pieces in his high school's literary magazine and had another story place in the top 100 in a national contest, but it wasn't until he met his partner, Erich, almost twenty years later, that he began writing again in earnest. With Erich alternately inspiring and goading him, Jamie wrote several screenplays and directed a few of them as micro-budget independent films. He then began writing novels and published his first novella in 2010.

After nine years together, Jamie and Erich have married and purchased a house together in the wilds of Raymond, New Hampshire, where there are no street lights, turkeys and deer wander through their yard, and coyotes serenade them on a nightly basis. Jamie recently left his "day job" as a tech support analyst to be a full-time writer.

Visit Jamie: jamiefessenden.wordpress.com
Facebook: www.facebook.com/pages/Jamie-Fessenden-Author/102004836534286
Twitter: @JamieFessenden1

Also from Dreamspinner Press

# ICARUS ASCENDING

LA PRIVATE DETECTIVES: BOOK ONE

# LEE JAMES

www.dreamspinnerpress.com

Also from Dreamspinner Press

GNOMON

LUCHIA DERTIEN

www.dreamspinnerpress.com

Also from Dreamspinner Press

BENJAMIN DAHLBECK

# MOUNTAIN
## MURDER MYSTERY

Also from Dreamspinner Press

J. I. RADKE

ROOKS AND ROMANTICIDE

www.dreamspinnerpress.com

Also from Dreamspinner Press

Also from Dreamspinner Press

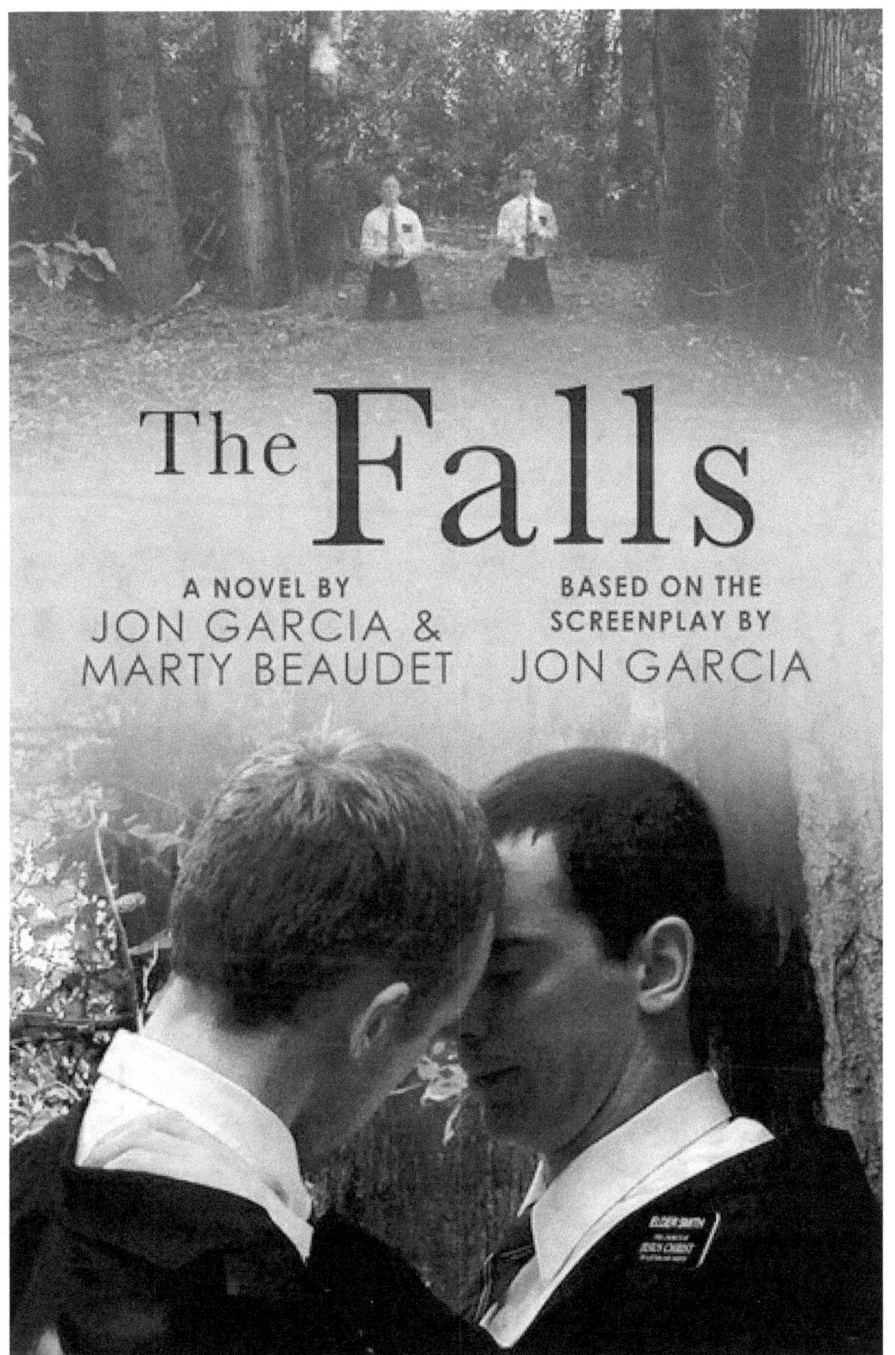

The Falls

A NOVEL BY
JON GARCIA &
MARTY BEAUDET

BASED ON THE
SCREENPLAY BY
JON GARCIA

Also from Dreamspinner Press

'TIL DARKNESS FALLS

Pearl Love

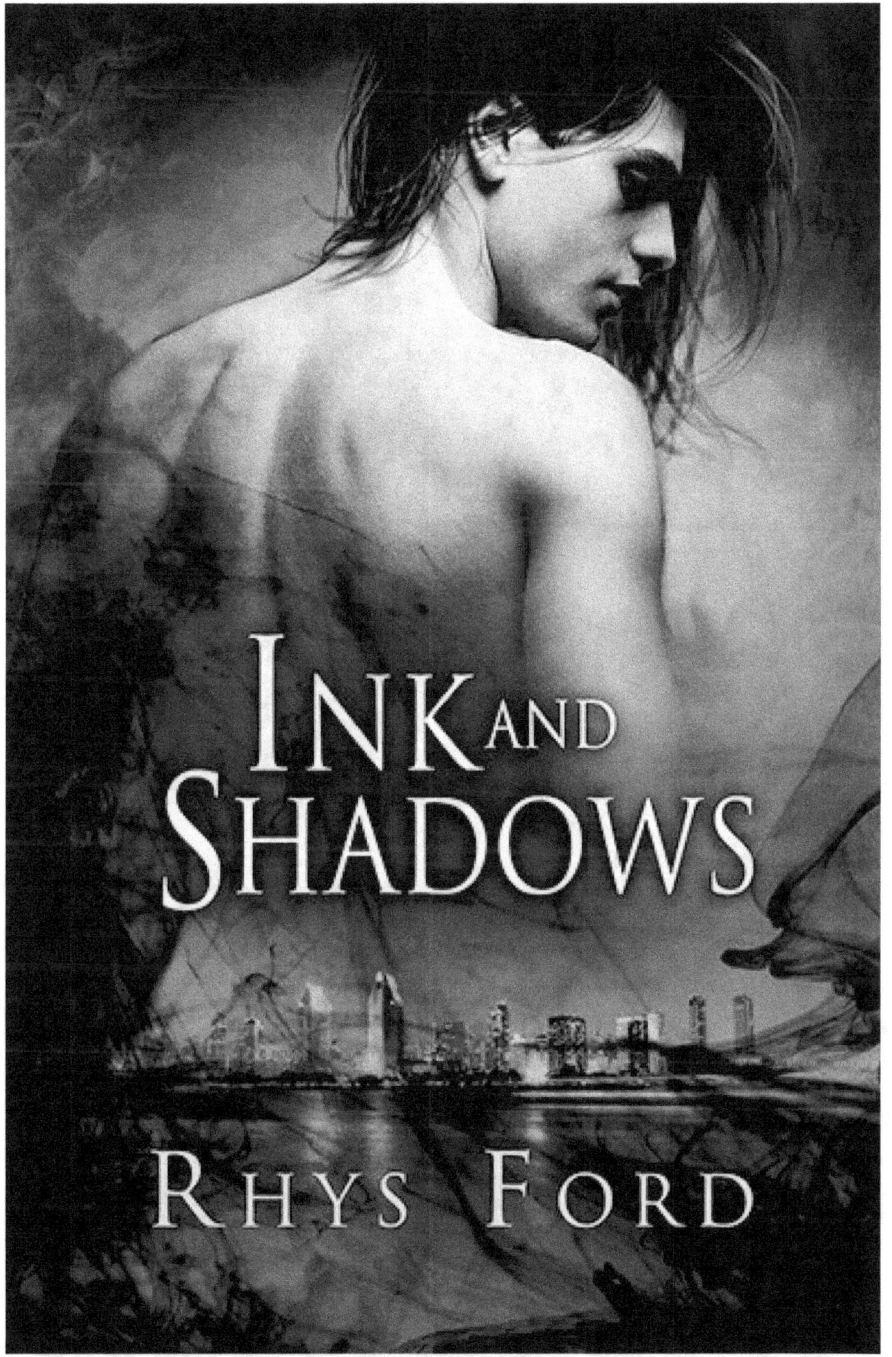

For more
great fiction
from

# DSP PUBLICATIONS

visit us online.
WWW.DSPPUBLICATIONS.COM

www.ingramcontent.com/pod-product-compliance
Lightning Source LLC
Chambersburg PA
CBHW070105260626
47160CB00004B/1333